PROMETHEAN HORRORS

PROMETHEAN HORRORS

HORRORS

Classic Tales of Mad Science

edited by
XAVIER ALDANA REYES

This collection first published in 2019 by
The British Library
96 Euston Road
London NW1 2DB

Introduction and notes © 2019 Xavier Aldana Reyes

'The Secret of the Scaffold' by Auguste Villiers de L'Isle-Adam
translated by Brian Stableford, reproduced from *The Scaffold and
Other Cruel Tales* with the permission of the translator.

Dates attributed to each story relate to first publication.

Cataloguing in Publication Data
A catalogue record for this publication is available from the British Library

ISBN 978 0 7123 5284 0
Limited edition ISBN 978 0 7123 5355 7
e-ISBN 978 0 7123 6705 9

Frontispiece illustration by Enrique Bernardou
Engraving on page 270 by Cornelis Bloemart after Abraham van Diepenbeeck,
from M. des Marolles' *Tableaux du Temple des Muses* (Paris, 1655)

Cover design by Mauricio Villamayor with illustration by Enrique Bernardou

Text design and typesetting by Tetragon, London
Printed in England by CPI Group (UK) Ltd, Croydon, CRO 4YY

CONTENTS

I would like to dedicate this book to my former supervisor and friend Catherine Spooner and to thank her for the many ways in which she has supported me through the years.

'Without passion, we'd be truly dead.'

INTRODUCTION

Alongside the aristocratic tyrant, the evil monk, the seductive vampire and the vengeful revenant, the mad scientist is one of the key figures of the Gothic literary tradition. He—and it is overwhelmingly a 'he'—has a long history of fictional representations that goes back to, at least, Faust. A savant who sells his soul to the Devil in exchange for unlimited knowledge and worldly goods, the German legend is said to have been based on the real alchemist, astrologer and magician Johann Georg Faust (c. 1480–1540). British writer Mary Shelley also did much to solidify the image of the mad scientist in popular culture. In her 1818 novel *Frankenstein*, Victor longs to find the elixir of life, much like the alchemists he admires, and ends up creating life by stitching together human remains into a creature he eventually reanimates. The man's subsequent horror, an indeterminate one connected both to the 'monster' and to the enormity of his actions, is a blueprint for the promethean nightmares promised by scientific breakthroughs. Where other Gothic figures may be born evil, the mad scientist is guilty of being malcontent, of not thinking about the consequences of pushing nature too far. Many writers, such as Herman Melville, Sir Ronald Ross and W. C. Morrow, followed in Shelley's footsteps. In fact, some of the most widely studied Gothic and science fiction novels belong to the mad science subgenre: Robert Louis Stevenson's *Strange Case of Dr Jekyll and Mr Hyde* (1886), Arthur Machen's 'The Great God Pan' (1890), H. G. Wells's *The Island of Doctor Moreau* (1896) and *The Invisible Man* (1897), H. P. Lovecraft's 'Herbert West—Reanimator' (1922) and John W. Campbell's 'Who Goes There?' (1938) are only some examples. It may be argued that the differences between these texts are very significant, but this is because 'science' is a very ample world that can relate to any study of the physical and natural world. Mad scientists may be botanists, as in Nathaniel Hawthorne's 'Rappaccini's Daughter' (1844); they may be mesmerists, as in Edgar Allan Poe's 'The Facts in the Case of M. Valdemar' (1845); they may be anatomists, as in Stevenson's 'The Body Snatcher' (1884); or they may be researchers interested in developing new technologies to record thoughts or transfer matter through space, as in L. T. Meade's 'The Blue Laboratory' (1897) and George Langelaan's 'The Fly' (1957), respectively. The various tales included in this collection are a testament to the versatility, heterogeneity and complexity of these most human of Gothic villains.

At the same time, mad scientists display a series of recurring characteristics that have ensured their entrenchment as archetypes. First of all, mad scientists are consumed and led by their passions and ambitions, which are inextricable from their work. This means they are often ruthless, driven by goals and results rather than by common moral codes or by the need to act with caution and measure. They are also prepared to sacrifice individuals for the sake of knowledge and science—in their view, the stakes are higher than the life of a puny mortal. In this respect, mad scientists can be iconoclasts; they can go against the grain for what they believe is the greater good. This is why they may be more ambivalent than other human 'monsters' like the serial killer and more readily generate feelings of pity and sympathy. The most famous are tragic heroes, eminently flawed geniuses awaiting a hubristic fall. When boiled down to their essentials, mad scientists reflect the human desire to know more about the world and its history, about our place in the universe and about the nature of the phenomenological world. The inquisitive human spirit does not rest easy, so the mad scientist's desire to challenge our material limitations as well as those of our bodies are understandable: who has not, at one point or another, wished they could escape death or be able to fly? Unlike the larger social and scientific communities to which they belong, however, mad scientists work alone. Their scepticism towards widespread beliefs, as well as their unconventional methods and ethically questionable testing, forces them into secrecy. Like their inventions, these men are often prototypes, so they cannot operate socially and become ostracized. One must make an effort to step out of the crowd and into the mind of the mad scientist; this is another aspect that makes them fascinating. Finally, mad scientists, in their worst incarnations, are mean-spirited. Loneliness can build resentment and lead them to seek revenge or show detractors that they are wrong in their lack of support. Mad scientists are therefore likely to use their discoveries to turn the tables on their 'enemies' or for personal gain. They can carry out vendettas against unfaithful lovers or even plot the destruction of the world and its peoples. More often than not, however, they become their own victims. The 'mad' in 'mad scientist', then, does not simply denote evil: it points to the character's radical difference from those we deem 'ordinary'.

Frankenstein and *Strange Case of Dr Jekyll and Mr Hyde* are, together with Bram Stoker's *Dracula* (1897), the most adapted Gothic texts ever. This has undoubtedly helped the mad scientist become a household monster, but it also means his image has been strongly filtered through the lens of cinema. The iconic laboratories in Fritz Lang's *Metropolis* (1927) and James Whale's *Frankenstein* (1931), full of scientific bric-a-brac, bubbling beakers and electric machines, have become as recognizable a Gothic setting as the medieval castle on the cliff, and Colin Clive's hysterical pronouncement that the creature is 'alive!' is perhaps one of horror cinema's most famous lines. Yet, as this collection shows, the mad scientist has consistently returned to the pages of Gothic literature throughout the past two hundred years, and his legacy there is as important as that of his cinematic and televisual counterparts. My selection offers the reader a variety of stories that capture the different compelling aspects of this figure. Here you will find men who create poisonous humans; who experiment with the suspension and perpetuation of life; who are interested in the way consciousness operates after death; who believe our senses can be stimulated into perceiving a hidden reality; who will compromise their integrity in order to find test subjects. What unites them all is an unhealthy obsession with resisting stasis, with wanting to reach beyond their circumstances. These mad scientists are modern incarnations of Prometheus, trying to steal fire from the gods. If blood-sucking or the extraction of life is a key characteristic of the vampire and shape-shifting that of the werewolf, then the mad scientist is marked by his magical capacity to alter the present—at a price.

XAVIER ALDANA REYES

Xavier Aldana Reyes is Reader in English Literature and Film at Manchester Metropolitan University and a member of the Manchester Centre for Gothic Studies. He has edited Horror: A Literary History *for British Library Publishing, along with collections of stories by Algernon Blackwood, William Hope Hodgson and H. P. Lovecraft.*

ACKNOWLEDGEMENTS

I would like to thank Rob Davies and Jonny Davidson at the British Library for their enthusiasm and support. It is incredibly exciting to see the British Library continuing to support weird fiction with a dedicated series. I am very grateful for their help with the acquisition and reproduction of the stories selected for this volume.

I would like to thank Peter Haining, Mike Ashley, Rafael Díaz Santander, Óscar Sacristán and Michael Simms for their respective anthologies of mad science and Frankenstein-influenced stories. Reading them inspired me to propose this book.

Finally, I would like to thank the kind and indispensable Rocío Rødtjer for agreeing to review the introduction from her secret laboratory in the States. May José Fernández Bremón's time come soon!

THE SANDMAN

E. T. A. Hoffmann

One of the key figures of German Romanticism and a huge influence on the development of the fantastic tale in Continental Europe in the nineteenth century, E. T. A. Hoffmann (1776–1822) wrote many stories—and one key novel, *The Devil's Elixirs* (*Die Elixiere des Teufels*, 1815)—that psychologically and imaginatively expanded the parameters of the Gothic fictions he had eagerly consumed as a young man. Some of the best of these appeared in his prose collection in two volumes *Night Pieces* (*Nachtstücke*, 1816–17).

Of the tales in *Night Pieces* the most well known is 'The Sandman' ('Der Sandmann'), whose complex plot includes mesmerism and one of literature's most memorable automata, the lifelike Olympia. 'The Sandman' gained Gothic notoriety through Sigmund Freud's essay 'The Uncanny' ('Das Unheimliche', 1919), where the story is used to illustrate the workings of the uncanny, or the experience of perceiving something as strangely familiar. Aside from being a particularly discombobulating example of horror fiction, 'The Sandman' is interesting for its portrayal of Coppelius/Coppola, an inventor who, in his attempts to create life *ex nihilo*, constitutes an early example of the mad scientist playing God. The following translation by John Oxenford comes from *Tales from the German*, published in 1844.

NATHANIEL TO LOTHAIRE

CERTAINLY YOU MUST ALL BE UNEASY THAT I HAVE NOT WRITten for so long—so very long. My mother, I am sure, is angry, and Clara will believe that I am passing my time in dissipation, entirely forgetful of the fair angel-image that is so deeply imprinted in my heart and mind. Such, however, is not the case. Daily and hourly I think of you all, and in my sweet dreams the kindly form of my lovely Clara passes before me, and smiles upon me with her bright eyes as she was wont when I appeared among you. Alas, how could I write to you in the distracted mood which has hitherto disturbed my every thought! Something horrible has crossed my path of life. Dark forebodings of a cruel, threatening, fate spread themselves over me like dark clouds, which no friendly sunbeam can penetrate. Now will I tell you what has befallen me. I must do so, that I plainly see—but if I only think of it, it will laugh out of me like mad. Ah, my dear Lothaire, how shall I begin it? How shall I make you in any way sensible that that which occurred to me a few days ago could really have such a fatal effect on my life? If you were here you could see for yourself, but now you will certainly take me for a crazy ghost-seer. In a word, the horrible thing which happened to me, and the painful impression of which I in vain endeavour to escape, is nothing more than this; that some days ago, namely on the 30th of October, at twelve o'clock at noon, a barometer-dealer came into my room and offered me his wares. I bought nothing, and threatened to throw him down stairs, upon which he took himself off of his own accord.

You suspect that only relations of the most peculiar kind, and exerting the greatest influence over my life can give any import to this occurrence, nay, that the person of that unlucky dealer must have a hostile effect upon me. So it is, indeed. I collect myself with all my might, that patiently and quietly I may tell you so much of my early youth as will bring all plainly and clearly in bright images before your active mind. As I am about to begin I fancy that I hear you laughing and Clara saying: "Childish stories indeed!" Laugh at me I beseech you, laugh with all your heart. But, heavens, my hair stands on end, and it seems as if I am asking you to laugh at me, in mad despair, as Franz Moor asked Daniel.* But to my story.

Excepting at dinner time I and my brothers and sisters saw my father very little during the day. He was, perhaps, busily engaged at his ordinary occupation. After supper, which, according to the old custom was served up at seven o'clock, we all went with my mother into my father's work-room, and seated ourselves at the round table. My father smoked tobacco and drank a large glass of beer. Often he told us a number of wonderful stories, and grew so warm over them that his pipe continually went out. I had to light it again, with burning paper, which I thought great sport. Often, too, he would give us picture-books, and sit in his armchair silent and thoughtful, puffing out such thick clouds of smoke that we all seemed to be swimming in the clouds. On such evenings as these my mother was very melancholy, and immediately the clock struck nine, she would say: "Now children, to bed—to bed! The Sandman is coming, I can see." And certainly on all these occasions I heard something with a heavy, slow step go bouncing up the stairs. That I thought must be the Sandman. Once that dull noise and footstep were particularly fearful, and I

---

* Two characters in Schiller's play of "Die Räuber."

asked my mother, while she took us away: "Eh, mamma, who is this naughty Sandman, who always drives us away from papa? What does he look like?" "There is no Sandman, dear child," replied my mother. "When I say the Sandman comes, I only mean that you are sleepy and cannot keep your eyes open,—just as if sand had been sprinkled into them." This answer of my mother's did not satisfy me—nay, in my childish mind the thought soon matured itself that she only denied the existence of the Sandman to hinder us from being terrified at him. Certainly I always heard him coming up the stairs. Full of curiosity to hear more of this Sandman, and his particular connection with children, I at last asked the old woman who tended my youngest sister what sort of man he was. "Eh, Natty," said she, "do you not know that yet? He is a wicked man, who comes to children when they will not go to bed, and throws a handful of sand into their eyes, so that they start out bleeding from their heads. These eyes he puts in a bag and carries them to the half-moon to feed his own children, who sit in the nest up yonder, and have crooked beaks like owls with which they may pick up the eyes of the naughty human children."

A most frightful image of the cruel Sandman was horribly depicted in my mind, and when in the evening I heard the noise on the stairs, I trembled with agony and alarm. My mother could get nothing out of me, but the cry of "The Sandman, the Sandman!" which was stuttered forth through my tears. I then ran into the bedroom, where the frightful apparition of the Sandman terrified me during the whole night. I had already grown old enough to perceive that the nurse's tale about the Sandman and the nest of children in the half-moon could not be quite true, but, nevertheless, this Sandman remained a fearful spectre, and I was seized with the utmost horror, when I heard him not only come up the stairs, but violently force open my father's room-door and enter. Sometimes he

staid away for a long period, but oftener his visits were in close succession. This lasted for years, and I could not accustom myself to the
terrible goblin; the image of the dreadful Sandman did not become
more faint. His intercourse with my father began more and more to
occupy my fancy. An unconquerable fear prevented me from asking
my father about it, but if I—I myself could penetrate the mystery,
and behold the wondrous Sandman—that was the wish which grew
upon me with years. The Sandman had brought me into the path
of the marvellous and wonderful, which so readily finds a domicile
in the mind of a child. Nothing was to me more delightful than to
read or hear horrible stories of goblins, witches, pigmies, &c.; but
above them all stood the Sandman, whom, in the oddest and most
frightful shapes, I was always drawing with chalk or charcoal on the
tables, cupboards, and walls. When I was ten years old, my mother
removed me from the children's room into a little chamber, situated
in a corridor near my father's room. Still, as before, we were obliged
speedily to take our departure as soon as, on the stroke of nine, the
unknown was heard in the house. I could hear in my little chamber
how he entered my father's room, and then it soon appeared to me
that a thin vapour of a singular odour diffused itself about the house.
Stronger and stronger with my curiosity grew my resolution to form
in some manner the Sandman's acquaintance. Often I sneaked from
my room to the corridor, when my mother had passed, but never
could I discover any thing, for the Sandman had always gone in at
the door when I reached the place where I might have seen him. At
last, urged by an irresistible impulse, I resolved to hide myself in my
father's room and await the appearance of the Sandman.

By the silence of my father, and the melancholy of my mother,
I perceived one evening that the Sandman was coming. I, therefore,
feigned great weariness, left the room before nine o'clock, and hid

myself in a corner close to the door. The house-door creaked, and the heavy, slow, groaning step went through the passage and towards the stairs. My mother passed me with the rest of the children. Softly— very softly, I opened the door of my father's room. He sat as usually, stiff and silent, with his back turned to the door. He did not perceive me, and I swiftly darted into the room and behind the curtain, drawn before an open press, which stood close to the door, and in which my father's clothes were hanging. The steps sounded nearer and nearer—there was a strange coughing and scraping and murmuring without. My heart trembled with anxiety and expectation. A sharp step close—very close to the door,—a smart stroke on the latch, and the door was open with a rattling noise. Screwing up my courage with all my might, I cautiously peeped out. The Sandman was standing before my father in the middle of the room, the light of the candles shone full upon his face. The Sandman, the fearful Sandman, was the old advocate Coppelius, who had often dined with us.

But the most hideous form could not have inspired me with deeper horror than this very Coppelius. Imagine a large broad-shouldered man, with a head disproportionately big, a face the colour of yellow ochre, a pair of grey bushy eyebrows, from beneath which a pair of green cat's eyes sparkled with the most penetrating lustre, and with a large nose curved over his upper lip. His wry mouth was often twisted into a malicious laugh, when a couple of dark red spots appeared upon his cheeks, and a strange hissing sound was heard through his compressed teeth. Coppelius always appeared in an ashen-grey coat, cut in old-fashioned style, with waistcoat and breeches of the same colour, while his stockings were black, and his shoes adorned with buckles set with precious stones. The little peruke scarcely reached further than the crown of his head, the curls stood high above his large red ears, and a broad hair-bag projected stiffly from his neck, so that the silver buckle which fastened his folded cravat might be plainly seen. The whole figure was hideous and repulsive, but most disgusting to us children were his coarse brown hairy fists; indeed, we did not like to eat what he had touched with them. This he had remarked, and it was his delight, under some pretext or other, to touch a piece of cake, or some nice fruit, that our kind mother might privately have put in our plate, in order that we, with tears in our eyes, might, from disgust and abhorrence, no longer be able to enjoy the treat intended for us. He acted in the same manner on holidays, when my father gave us a little glass of sweet wine. Then would he swiftly draw his fist over it, or perhaps he would even raise the glass to his blue lips, and laugh most devilishly, when we could only express our indignation by soft sobs. He always called us the little beasts, we dared not utter a sound when he was present, and we heartily cursed the ugly, unkind man, who deliberately marred our slightest pleasures. My mother seemed to hate the repulsive Coppelius as much as we did, since as soon as he showed himself her liveliness, her free and cheerful mind was changed into a gloomy solemnity. My father conducted himself towards him, as though he was a superior being, whose bad manners were to be tolerated, and who was to be kept in good humour at any rate. He need only give the slightest hint, and the favourite dishes were cooked, and the choicest wines served.

When I now saw this Coppelius, the frightful and terrific thought took possession of my soul, that indeed no one but he could be the Sandman. But the Sandman was no longer that bugbear of a nurse's tale, who provided the owl's nest in the half-moon with children's eyes,—no, he was a hideous spectral monster, who, wherever he appeared, brought with him grief, want, and destruction—temporal and eternal.

I was rivetted to the spot as if enchanted. At the risk of being discovered, and as I plainly foresaw, of being severely punished, I remained with my head peeping through the curtain. My father received Coppelius with solemnity. "Now to our work!" cried the latter with a harsh, grating voice, as he flung off his coat. My father silently and gloomily drew off his night-gown, and both attired themselves in long black frocks. Whence they took these, I did not see. My father opened the door of what I had always thought to be a cupboard, but I now saw that it was no cupboard, but rather a black hollow, in which there was a little hearth. Coppelius entered, and a blue flame began to crackle up on the hearth. All sorts of strange utensils lay around. Heavens!—As my old father now stooped down to the fire, he looked quite another man. A frightful convulsive pain seemed to have distorted his mild reverend features into a hideous repulsive diabolical countenance. He looked like Coppelius: the latter was brandishing red-hot tongs, and with them taking shining masses busily out of the thick smoke, which he afterwards hammered. It seemed to me, as if I saw human faces around without any eyes—but with deep holes instead. "Eyes here, eyes!" said Coppelius in a dull roaring voice. Overcome by the wildest terror, I shrieked out, and fell from my hiding place upon the floor. Coppelius seized me, and showing his teeth, bleated out, "Ah—little wretch,—little wretch!"—then dragging me up, he flung me on the hearth, where the fire began to singe my hair. "Now we have eyes enough—a pretty pair of child's eyes." Thus whispered Coppelius and taking out of the flame some red-hot grains with his fists, he was about to sprinkle them in my eyes. My father upon this raised his hands in supplication, and cried: "Master, master, leave my Nathaniel his eyes!" Coppelius uttered a yelling laugh, and said: "Well let the lad have his eyes and cry his share in the world, but we will examine the mechanism of his hands and feet." And then he seized me so forcibly that my joints cracked, and screwed off my hands and feet, and then put them on again; one here and the other there. "Every thing is not right here!—As good as it was—the old one has understood it!" So did Coppelius say, in a hissing, lisping tone, but all around me became black and dark, a sudden cramp darted through my bones and nerves—and I lost all feeling. A gentle warm breath passed over my face; I woke as out of a sleep of death. My mother had been stooping over me. "Is the Sandman yet there?" I stammered. "No, no, my dear child, he has gone away long ago,—he will not hurt you!"—So said my mother, and she kissed and embraced her recovered darling.

Why should I weary you, my dear Lothaire! Why should I be so diffuse with details, when I have so much more to tell. Suffice it to say, that I had been discovered while watching, and ill-used by Coppelius. Agony and terror had brought on delirium and fever, of which I lay sick for several weeks. "Is the sandman still there?" That was my first sensible word and the sign of my amendment—my recovery. I can now only tell you, the most frightful moment in my juvenile years. Then you will be convinced that it is no fault of my eyes, that all to me seems colourless, but that a dark fatality has actually suspended over my life a gloomy veil of clouds, which I shall perhaps only tear away in death.

Coppelius was no more to be seen; it was said he had left the town.

About a year might have elapsed, when, according to the old custom, we sat at the round table. My father was very cheerful, and told much that was entertaining, about his travels in his youth; when, as the clock struck nine, we heard the house-door creak on the hinges, and slow steps, heavy as iron, groaned through the passage and up the stairs. "That is Coppelius," said my mother, turning pale. "Yes!—that is Coppelius!" repeated my father, with a faint broken voice. The tears started from my mother's eyes. "But father—father!" she cried, "must it be so?" "He comes to me for the last time, I promise you," was the answer. "Only go now—go with the children—go—go to bed. Good night!"

I felt as if I were pressed into cold, heavy stone,—my breath was stopped. My mother caught me by the arm as I stood immoveable. "Come, come, Nathaniel!" I allowed myself to be led, and entered my chamber! "Be quiet—be quiet—go to bed—go to sleep!" cried my mother after me; but tormented by restlessness, and an inward anguish perfectly indescribable, I could not close my eyes. The hateful, abominable Coppelius stood before me with fiery eyes, and laughed at me maliciously. It was in vain that I endeavoured to get rid of his image. About midnight there was a frightful noise, like the firing of a gun. The whole house resounded. There was a rattling and a rustling by my door, and the house-door was closed with a violent sound. "That is Coppelius!" I cried, and I sprang out of bed in terror. There was then a shriek as if of acute inconsolable grief. I darted into my father's room; the door was open, a suffocating smoke rolled towards me, and the servant girl cried: "Ah, my master, my master!" On the floor of the smoking hearth lay my father dead, with his face burned and blackened, and hideously distorted,—my sisters were shrieking and moaning around him,—and my mother had fainted. "Coppelius!—cursed Satan, thou hast slain my father!" I cried, and lost my senses. When, two days afterwards, my father was laid in his coffin, his features were again as mild and gentle as they had been in his life. My soul was comforted by the thought that his compact with the devilish Coppelius could not have plunged him into eternal perdition.

The explosion had awakened the neighbours, the occurrence had become the common talk, and had reached the ears of the magistracy, who wished to make Coppelius answerable. He had, however, vanished from the spot, without leaving a trace.

If I tell you, my dear friend, that the barometer-dealer was the accursed Coppelius himself, you will not blame me for regarding a phenomenon so unpropitious as boding some heavy calamity. He was dressed differently, but the figure and features of Coppelius are too deeply imprinted in my mind, for an error in this respect to be possible. Besides, Coppelius has not even altered his name. As I hear he gives himself out as a Piedmontese optician, and calls himself Giuseppe Coppola.

I am determined to cope with him, and to avenge my father's death, be the issue what it may.

Tell my mother nothing of the hideous monster's appearance. Remember me to my dear sweet Clara, to whom I will write in a calmer mood.—Farewell.

CLARA TO NATHANIEL

It is true that you have not written to me for a long time, but nevertheless I believe that I am still in your mind and thoughts. For assuredly you were thinking of me most intently, when designing to send your last letter to my brother Lothaire, you directed it to me, instead of him. I joyfully opened the letter, and did not perceive my error till I came to the words: "Ah, my dear Lothaire." Now, by rights I should have read no farther, but should have handed over the letter to my brother. Although you have often in your childish teasing mood, charged me with having such a quiet, womanish, steady disposition, that like the lady, even if the house were about to fall in, I should smooth down a wrong fold in the window curtain before I ran away, I can hardly tell you how your letter shocked me. I could scarcely breathe,—my eyes became dizzy. Ah, my dear Nathaniel, how could such a horrible event have crossed your life? To be parted from you, never to see you again,—the thought darted through my breast like a burning dagger. I read and read. Your description of the repulsive Coppelius is terrific. For the first time I learned how your good old father died a shocking violent death. My brother Lothaire, to whom I gave up the letter as his property, sought to calm me, but in vain. The fatal barometer-maker, Giuseppe Coppola followed me at every step, and I am almost ashamed to confess that he disturbed my healthy and generally peaceful sleep with all sorts of horrible visions. Yet soon,—even the next day, I was quite changed again. Do not be offended, dearest one, if Lothaire tells you, that in spite of your strange misgiving, that Coppelius will in some manner injure you, I am in the same cheerful unembarrassed frame of mind as ever.

I will honestly confess to you that, according to my opinion, all the terrible things of which you speak, merely occurred in your own mind, and that the actual external world had little to do with them. Old Coppelius may have been repulsive enough, but his hatred of children was what really caused the abhorrence of your children towards him.

In your childish mind the frightful sandman in the nurse's tale was naturally associated with old Coppelius, who, even if you had not believed in the sandman, would still have been a spectral monster, especially dangerous to children. The awful nightly occupation with your father, was no more than this, that both secretly made alchemical experiments, and with these your mother was constantly dissatisfied, since besides a great deal of money being uselessly wasted, your father's mind being filled with a fallacious desire after higher wisdom was alienated from his family—as they say, is always the case with such experimentalists. Your father no doubt, by some act of careless-ness, occasioned his own death, of which Coppelius was completely guiltless. Would you believe it, that I yesterday asked our neighbour, the clever apothecary, whether such a sudden and fatal explosion was possible in such chemical experiments? "Certainly," he replied, and in his way told me at great length and very circumstantially how such an event might take place, uttering a number of strange-sounding names, which I am unable to recollect. Now, I know you will be angry with your Clara; you will say that her cold disposition is impenetrable to every ray of the mysterious, which often embraces man with invisible arms, that she only sees the variegated surface of the world, and has the delight of a silly child, at some gold-glittering fruit, which contains within it a deadly poison.

Ah! my dear Nathaniel! Do you not then believe that even in free, cheerful, careless minds, here may dwell the suspicion of some dread power, which endeavours to destroy us in our own selves? Forgive me, if I, a silly girl, presume in any manner to indicate, what I really think of such an internal struggle; I shall not find out the right words after all, and you will laugh at me, not because my thoughts are foolish, but because I set about so clumsily to express them.

If there is a dark power, which with such enmity and treachery lays a thread within us, by which it holds us fast, and draws us along a path of peril and destruction, which we should not otherwise have trod; if, I say, there is such a power, it must form itself within us, or from ourselves; indeed, become identical with ourselves, for it is only in this condition that we can believe in it, and grant it the room which it requires, to accomplish its secret work. Now, if we have a mind, which is sufficiently firm, sufficiently strengthened by cheerful life, always to recognize this strange hostile operation as such, and calmly to follow the path which belongs to our inclination and calling, then will the dark power fail in its attempt to gain a power, that shall be a reflection of ourselves. Lothaire adds that it is certain, that the dark physical power, if of our own accord, we have yielded ourselves up to it, often draws within us some strange form, which the external world has thrown in our way, so that we ourselves kindle the spirit, which, as we in our strange delusion believe, speaks to us in that form. It is the phantom of our own selves, the close relationship with which, and its deep operation on our mind casts us into hell, or transports us into heaven. You see, dear Nathaniel, that I and my brother Lothaire have freely given our opinion on the subject of dark powers, which subject, now I find I have not been able to write down the chief part without trouble, appears to me somewhat deep. Lothaire's last words I do not quite comprehend. I can only suspect what he means, and yet I feel as if it were all very true. I beg of you, get the ugly advocate, Coppelius, and the barometer-seller, Giuseppe Coppola, quite out of your head. Be convinced that these strange fears have no power over you, and that it is only a belief in their hostile influence that can make them hostile in reality. If the great excitement of your mind did not speak from every line of your letter, if your situation did not give me the deepest pain, I could joke about the Sandman-Advocate, and the barometer-seller, Coppelius. Be cheerful, I have determined to appear before you as your guardian-spirit, and if the ugly Coppelius takes it in his head to annoy you in your dreams, to scare him away with loud peals of laughter. I am not a bit afraid of him nor of his disgusting hands; he shall neither spoil my sweetmeats as an advocate, nor my eyes as a sandman. Ever yours, my dear Nathaniel.

NATHANIEL TO LOTHAIRE

I am very sorry that in consequence of the error occasioned by my wandering state of mind, Clara broke open the letter intended for you, and read it. She has written me a very profound philosophical epistle, in which she proves, at great length, that Coppelius and Coppola only exist in my own mind, and are phantoms of myself, which will be dissipated directly I recognize them as such. Indeed, one could not believe that the mind which often peers out of those bright, smiling, childish eyes, like a sweet charming dream, could define with such intelligence, in such a professor-like manner. She appeals to you—you, it seems have been talking about me. I suppose you read her logical lectures, that she may learn to divide and sift every thing acutely. Pray leave it off. Besides it is quite certain that the barometer-dealer, Giuseppe Coppola, is not the advocate Coppelius. I attend the lectures of the professor of physics, who has lately arrived. His name is the same as that of the famous natural philosopher, Spalanzani, and he is of Italian origin. He has known Coppola for years, and moreover it is clear from his accent that he is really a Piedmontese. Coppelius was a German, but I think no honest one. Calmed I am not, and though you and Clara may consider me a gloomy visionary, I cannot get rid of the impression, which the accursed face of Coppelius makes upon me. I am glad that Coppola has left the town, as Spalanzani says. This professor is a strange fellow—a little round man, with high cheek bones, a sharp nose, pouting lips, and little piercing eyes. Yet you will get a better notion of him than by this description, if you look at the portrait of Cagliostro, designed by Chodowiecki, in one of the Berlin annuals, Spalanzani looks like that exactly. I lately went up stairs, and perceived that the curtain, which was generally drawn completely over a glass door, left a little opening on one side. I know not what curiosity impelled me to look through, a tall and very slender lady most symmetrically formed, and most splendidly attired, sat in the room by a little table on which she had laid her arms, her hands being folded together. She sat opposite to the door, so that I could completely see her angelic countenance. She did not appear to see me, and indeed there was something fixed about her eyes as if, I might almost say, she had no power of sight. It seemed to me that she was sleeping with her eyes open. I felt very uncomfortable, and therefore I slunk away into the auditorium, which was close at hand. Afterwards I learned that the form I had seen was that of Spalanzani's daughter Olympia, whom he kept confined in a very strange and improper manner, so that no one could approach her. After all, there may be something the matter with her; she is silly perhaps, or something of the kind. But why should I write you all this? I could have conveyed it better and more circumstantially by word of mouth. Know that I shall see you in a fortnight. I must again behold my dear, sweet, angelic Clara. The ill-humour will then be dispersed, which, I must confess, has endeavoured to get the mastery over me, since that fatal, sensible letter. Therefore I do not write to her today. A thousand greetings, &c.

———

Nothing more strange and chimerical can be imagined than that which occurred to my poor friend, the young student Nathaniel, and which I, gracious reader, have undertaken to tell you. Have you, kind reader, ever known a something that has completely filled your heart, thoughts, and senses, so as to exclude every thing else? There was in you a fermentation and a boiling, and your blood inflamed to the hottest glow bounded through your veins, and gave a higher colour to your cheeks. Your glance was so strange, as if you wished to perceive, in empty space, forms which to no other eyes are visible, and your speech flowed away into dark sighs. Then your friends asked you: "What is it, revered one?" "What is the matter, dear one." And now you wished to express the internal picture with all its glowing tints, with all its light and shade, and laboured hard to find words only to begin. You thought that in the very first word you ought to crowd together all the wonderful, noble, horrible, comical, frightful, that had happened, so that it might strike all the hearers at once like an electric shock. But every word, every thing that is in the form of speech, appeared to you colourless, cold and dead. You hunt and hunt, and stutter and stammer, and the sober questions of your friends dart like icy breezes upon your internal fire until it is ready to go out; whereas if, like a bold painter, you had first with a few daring strokes drawn an outline of the internal picture, you might with small trouble have laid on the colours brighter and brighter, and the living throng of various forms would have carried your friends along with it, and they, like you, would have seen themselves in the picture that had proceeded from your mind. Now I must confess to you, kind reader, that no one has really asked me for the history of the young Nathaniel, but you know well enough that I belong to the queer race of authors, who, if they have any thing in their mind, such as I have just described, feel as if every one who comes near them, and indeed perhaps the whole world besides, is asking them: "What is it then—tell it, my dear friend?" Thus was I forcibly compelled to tell you of the momentous life of Nathaniel. The singularity and marvellousness of the story filled my entire soul, but for that very reason and because, my reader, I had to make you equally inclined to endure oddity, which is no small matter, I tormented myself to begin the history of Nathaniel in a manner as inspiring, original and striking as possible. "Once upon a time," the beautiful beginning of every tale, was too tame. "In the little provincial town of S— lived"—was somewhat better, as it at least prepared for the climax. Or should I dart at once *medias in res*, with "Go to the devil, cried the student Nathaniel with rage and horror in his wild looks, when the barometer-seller, Giuseppe Coppola?"—I had indeed already written this down, when I fancied that in the wild looks of the student Nathaniel, I could detect something ludicrous, whereas the story is not comical at all. No form of language suggested itself to my mind, which even in the slightest degree seemed to reflect the colouring of the internal picture. I resolved that I would not begin it at all. So take, gentle reader, the three letters, which friend Lothaire was good enough to give me, as the sketch of the picture which I shall endeavour to colour more and more as I proceed in my narrative. Perhaps, like a good portrait-painter, I may succeed in catching many a form in such a manner, that you will find it is a likeness without having the original, and feel as if you had often seen the person with your own corporeal eyes. Perchance, dear reader, you will then believe that nothing is stranger and madder than actual life, and that this is all that the poet can conceive, as it were in the dull reflection of a dimly polished mirror.

In order that that which it is necessary in the first place to know, may be made clearer, we must add to these letters the circumstance, that shortly after the death of Nathaniel's father, Clara and Lothaire, the children of a distant relative, who had likewise died, and left them orphans, were taken by Nathaniel's mother to her own home. Clara and Nathaniel formed a strong attachment for each other, and no one in the world having any objection to make, they were betrothed, when Nathaniel left the place to pursue his studies in G—. He is, according to the date of his last letter, hearing the lectures of the celebrated professor of physics, Spalanzani.

Now I could proceed in my story with confidence, but at this moment Clara's image stands so plainly before me, that I cannot look another way, as indeed was always the case when she gazed at me, with one of her lively smiles. Clara could not by any means be reckoned beautiful; that was the opinion of all who are competent judges of beauty, by their calling. Nevertheless, the architects praised the exact symmetry of her frame, and the painters considered her neck, shoulders, and bosom almost too chastely formed, but then they all fell in love with her wondrous Magdalen-hair, and above every thing prated about *battonisch* colouring. One of them, a most fantastical fellow, singularly compared Clara's eyes to a lake by Ruysdael, in which the pure azure of a cloudless sky, the wood and flowery field, the whole cheerful life of the rich landscape are reflected. Poets and composers went still further. "What is a lake—what is a mirror!" said they, "can we look upon the girl without wondrous, heavenly songs and tunes flashing towards us from her glances, and penetrating our inmost soul, so that all there is awakened and stirred. If even then we sing nothing that is really sensible, there is not much in us, and that we can feelingly read in the delicate smile which plays on Clara's lips, when we presume to tinkle something before her, which is to pass for a song, although it is only a confused jumble of tones." So it was. Clara had the vivid fancy of a cheerful, unembarrassed child, a deep, tender, feminine disposition, an acute, clever understanding. The misty dreams had but a bad chance with her, since, though she did not talk,—as indeed talking would have been altogether repugnant to her tacit nature, her bright glance and her firm ironical smile would say to them: "Good friends, how can you imagine that I shall take your fleeting shadowy images for real forms with life and motion?" On this account Clara was censured by many as cold, unfeeling and prosaic; while others, who conceived life in its clear depth, greatly loved the feeling, acute, childlike girl, but none so much as Nathaniel, whose perception in art and science was clear and strong. Clara was attached to her lover with all her soul, and when he parted from her, the first cloud passed over her life. With what transport did she rush into his arms when, as he had promised in his last letter to Lothaire, he had actually returned to his native town and entered his mother's room. Nathaniel's expectations were completely fulfilled; for directly he saw Clara he thought neither of the Advocate Coppelius, nor of her "sensible" letter. All gloomy forebodings had gone.

However, Nathaniel was quite right, when he wrote to his friend Lothaire that the form of the repulsive barometer-seller, Coppola, had had a most hostile effect on his life. All felt, even in the first days, that Nathaniel had undergone a thorough change in his whole temperament. He sank into a gloomy reverie, and conducted himself in a strange manner, that had never been known in him before. Every thing, his whole life, had become to him a dream and a foreboding, and he was always saying that every man, although he might think himself free, only served for the cruel sport of dark powers. These he said it was vain to resist, and man must patiently resign himself to his fate. He went even so far as to say, that it is foolish to think that we do any thing in art and science according to our own self-acting will, for the inspiration which alone enables us to produce any thing, does not proceed from within ourselves, but is the effect of a higher principle without.

To the clear-headed Clara this mysticism was in the highest degree repugnant, but contradiction appeared to be useless. Only when Nathaniel proved that Coppelius was the evil principle, which had seized him at the moment when he was listening behind the curtain, and that this repugnant principle would in some horrible manner disturb the happiness of their life, Clara grew very serious, and said: "Yes, Nathaniel, you are right. Coppelius is an evil, hostile principle; he can produce terrible effects, like a diabolical power that has come invisibly into life; but only then, when you will not banish him from your mind and thoughts. So long as you believe in him he really exists, and exerts his influence; only your belief is his power."

Nathaniel, quite indignant that Clara established the demon's existence only in his own mind, would then come out with all the mystical doctrine of devils and fearful powers. But Clara would break off peevishly, by introducing some indifferent matter, to the no small annoyance of Nathaniel. He thought that such deep secrets were closed to cold, unsusceptible minds, without being clearly aware that he reckoned Clara among these subordinate natures, and therefore he constantly endeavoured to initiate her into the mysteries. In the morning, when Clara was getting breakfast ready, he stood by her, and read out of all sorts of mystical books, till she cried: "But, dear Nathaniel, suppose I blame you as the evil principle, that has a hostile effect upon my coffee? For if to please you, I leave every thing standing still, and look in your eyes, while you read, my coffee will run into the fire, and none of you will get any breakfast."

Nathaniel closed the book at once, and hurried indignantly to his chamber. Once he had a remarkable *forte* for graceful, lively tales, which he wrote down, and to which Clara listened with the greatest delight; now, his creations were gloomy, incomprehensible, formless, so that although Clara, out of compassion, did not say so, he plainly felt how little she was interested. Nothing was more insupportable to Clara than tediousness; in her looks and in her words a mental drowsiness, not to be conquered, was expressed. Nathaniel's productions were, indeed, very tedious. His indignation at Clara's cold, prosaic disposition, constantly increased, and Clara could not overcome her dislike of Nathaniel's dark, gloomy, tedious mysticism, so that they became more and more estranged from each other in mind, without perceiving it. The form of the ugly Coppelius, as Nathaniel himself was forced to confess, grew more dim in his fancy, and it often cost him trouble to colour with sufficient liveliness in his pictures, when he appeared as a ghastly bugbear of fate. At last it struck him that he would make the gloomy foreboding, that Coppelius would destroy his happiness in love, the subject of a poem. He represented himself and Clara as united by true love; but occasionally it seemed as though a black hand darted into their life, and tore away some newly-springing joy. At last, while they were standing at the altar, the hideous Coppelius appeared, and touched Clara's lively eyes. They flashed into Nathaniel's heart, like bleeding sparks, scorching and burning, when Coppelius caught him, and flung him into a flaming, fiery circle, which flew round with the swiftness of the stream, and carried him along with it, amid its roaring. The roar is like that of the hurricane, when it fiercely lashes the foaming waves, which, like black giants with white heads, rise up for the furious combat. But through the wild tumult he hears Clara's voice: "Can you not, then, see me? Coppelius has deceived you. Those, indeed, were not my eyes, which so burned in your breast—they were glowing drops of your own heart's blood. I have my eyes still—only look at them!" Nathaniel reflects: "That is Clara, and I am hers for ever!" Then it seems to him as though thought forcibly entered the fiery circle, which stands still, while the noise dully ceases in the dark abyss. Nathaniel looks into Clara's eyes, but it is only death that, with Clara's eyes, kindly looks on him.

While Nathaniel composed this poem he was very calm and collected; he polished and improved every line, and having subjected himself to the fetters of metre, he did not rest till all was correct and melodious. When at last he had finished and read the poem aloud to himself, a wild horror seized him, and he cried out: "Whose horrible voice is that?" Soon, however, the whole appeared to him a very successful work, and he felt that it must inflame Clara's cold temperament, although he did not clearly consider for what Clara was to be excited, nor what purpose it would answer to torment her with the frightful images which threatened a horrible destiny, destructive to their love. Both of them—that is to say Nathaniel and Clara—were sitting in their mother's little garden, Clara very cheerful, because Nathaniel, during the three days in which he had been writing his poem, had not teased her with his dreams and his forebodings. Even Nathaniel spoke livelily and joyfully about pleasant matters, as he used to do formerly, so that Clara said: "Now for the first time I have you again! Do you not see that we have driven away the ugly Coppelius?" Then it first struck Nathaniel that he had in his pocket the poem, which he had intended to read. He at once drew the sheets out and began, while Clara, expecting something tedious as usual, resigned herself and began quietly to knit. But as the dark cloud rose ever blacker and blacker, she let the stocking fall and looked full into his face. He was carried along unceasingly by his poem, an internal fire deeply reddened his cheeks, tears flowed from his eyes. At last when he had concluded, he groaned in a state of utter exhaustion, and catching Clara's hand, sighed forth, as if melted into the most inconsolable grief: "Oh Clara!—Clara!" Clara pressed him gently to her bosom, and said softly, but very solemnly and sincerely: "Nathaniel, dearest Nathaniel, do throw that mad, senseless, insane stuff into the fire!" Upon this Nathaniel sprang up enraged, and thrusting Clara from him, cried: "Thou inanimate, accursed automaton!" He ran off; Clara, deeply offended, shed bitter tears, and sobbed aloud: "Ah, he has never loved me, for he does not understand me." Lothaire entered the arbour; Clara was obliged to tell him all that had occurred. He loved his sister with all his soul, and every word of her complaint fell like a spark of fire into his heart, so that the indignation which he had long harboured against the visionary Nathaniel, now broke out into the wildest rage. He ran to Nathaniel and reproached him for his senseless conduct towards his beloved sister in hard words, which the infuriated Nathaniel retorted in the same style. The appellation of "fantastical, mad fool," was answered by that of "miserable commonplace fellow." A duel was inevitable. They agreed on the following morning, according to the academical custom of the place, to fight with sharp rapiers behind the garden. Silently and gloomily they slunk about. Clara had overheard the violent dispute, and seeing the fencing-master bring the rapiers at dawn, guessed what was to occur. Having reached the place of combat, Lothaire and Nathaniel had in gloomy silence flung off their coats, and with the fierce desire of fighting in their flaming eyes, were about to fall upon one another, when Clara rushed through the garden door. Sobbing, she cried aloud, "Ye wild cruel men! Strike me down before you attack each other, for how shall I live longer in the world if my lover murders my brother, or my brother murders my lover." Lothaire lowered his weapon, and looked in silence on the ground; but in Nathaniel's heart, amid the most poignant sorrow, revived all the love for the beautiful Clara, which he had felt in the best days of his happy youth. The weapon fell from his hand, he threw himself at Clara's feet. "Can you ever forgive me, my only—my beloved Clara? Can you forgive me, my dear brother, Lothaire?"

Lothaire was touched by the deep contrition of his friend; all three embraced in reconciliation amid a thousand tears, and vowed eternal love and fidelity.

Nathaniel felt as though a heavy burden, which pressed him to the ground, had been rolled away, as though by resisting the dark power, which held him fast, he had saved his whole being, which had been threatened with annihilation. Three happy days he passed with his dear friends, and then went to G—, where he intended to stay a year, and then to return to his native town for ever.

All that referred to Coppelius was kept a secret from the mother, for it was well known that she could not think of him without terror, as she, as well as Nathaniel, accused him of causing her husband's death.

————

How surprised was Nathaniel, when proceeding to his lodging, he saw that the whole house was burned down, and that only the bare walls stood up amid the ashes. However, notwithstanding the fire had broken out in the laboratory of the apothecary who lived on the ground-floor, and had therefore consumed the house from bottom to top, some bold active friends had succeeded in entering Nathaniel's room in the upper storey, in time to save the books, manuscripts, and instruments. They carried all safe and sound into another house, where they took a room, which Nathaniel entered at once. He did not think it at all remarkable that he lodged opposite to Professor Spalanzani; neither did it appear singular when he perceived that his window looked straight into the room where Olympia often sat alone, so that he could plainly recognize her figure, although the features of her face were indistinct and confused. At last it struck him, that Olympia often remained for hours in this attitude, in which he had once seen her through the glass-door, sitting at a little table without any occupation, and that she plainly enough looked over at him with an unvarying glance. He was forced to confess that he had never seen a more lovely form, but with Clara in his heart, the stiff Olympia was perfectly indifferent to him. Occasionally, to be sure, he gave a transient look over his compendium, at the beautiful statue, but that was all. He was just writing to Clara, when he heard a light tap at the door; it paused at his words, and the repulsive face of Coppola peeped in. Nathaniel's heart trembled within him, but remembering what Spalanzani had told him about the countryman, Coppola, and also the sacred promises he had made to Clara with respect to the Sandman Coppelius, he felt ashamed of his childish fear, and collecting himself with all his might, said as softly and civilly as possible: "I do not want a barometer, my good friend; pray, go." Upon this, Coppola advanced a good way into the room, and said in a hoarse voice, while his wide mouth distorted itself into a hideous laugh, and his little eyes under their long grey lashes sparkled forth piercingly: "Eh, eh—no barometer—no barometer? I have besides pretty eyes— pretty eyes!"—"Madman!" cried Nathaniel with horror, "how can you have eyes?—Eyes?" But Coppola had already put his barometer aside, and plunged his hand into his wide coat-pocket, whence he drew lunettes and spectacles, which he placed upon the table. "There— there—spectacles on the nose, those are my eyes—pretty eyes!" And so saying he drew out more and more spectacles so that the whole table began to glisten and sparkle in the most extraordinary manner. A thousand eyes glanced, and quivered convulsively, and stared at Nathaniel; yet he could not look away from the table, and Coppola kept still laying down more and more spectacles, while flaming glances were intermingled more and more wildly, and shot their blood-red rays into Nathaniel's breast. Overcome with horror, he shrieked out: "Hold, hold, frightful man!" He seized fast by the arm Coppola, who was searching his pockets to bring out still more spectacles, although the whole table was already covered. Coppola had greatly extricated himself with a hoarse repulsive laugh, and with the words: "Ah, nothing for you—but here are pretty glasses;" he had collected all the spectacles, put them up, and from the breast-pocket of his coat had drawn forth a number of telescopes large and small. As soon as the spectacles were removed Nathaniel felt quite easy, and thinking of Clara, perceived that the hideous phantom was but the creature of his own mind, and that Coppola was an honest optician, and could by no means be the accursed double of Coppelius. Moreover, in all the glasses which Coppola now placed on the table, there was nothing remarkable, or at least nothing so ghost-like as the spectacles, and to make matters right Nathaniel resolved to buy something of Coppola. He took up a little and very neatly worked pocket-telescope, and looked through the window to try it. Never in his life had he met a glass which brought the objects so sharply, plainly, and clearly before his eyes. Involuntarily he looked into Spalanzani's room; Olympia was sitting as usual before the little table, with her arms laid upon it, and her hands folded. For the first time could he see the wondrous beauty in the form of her face;—only the eyes seemed to him singularly stiff and dead. Nevertheless, as he looked more sharply through the glass, it seemed to him as if moist morn-beams were rising in the eyes of Olympia. It was as if the power of seeing was kindled for the first time; the glances flashed with constantly increasing liveliness. As if spell-bound, Nathaniel reclined against the window, meditating on the charming Olympia. A hemming and scraping aroused him as if from a dream. Coppola was standing behind him: "*Tre zecchini*—three ducats!" Nathaniel, who had quite forgotten the optician, quickly paid him what he asked. "Is it not so? A pretty glass—a pretty glass?" asked Coppola, in his hoarse, repulsive voice, and with his malicious smile. "Yes—yes," replied Nathaniel, peevishly; "good bye, friend." Coppola left the room, not without casting many strange glances at Nathaniel. He heard him laugh loudly on the stairs. "Ah," thought Nathaniel, "he is laughing at me because no doubt, I have paid him too much for this little glass." While he softly uttered these words, it seemed as if a deep deadly sigh was sounding fearfully through the room, and his breath was stopped by inward anguish. He perceived, however, that it was himself that had sighed. "Clara," he said to himself, "is right in taking me for a senseless dreamer, but it is pure madness—nay, more than madness, that the stupid thought, that I have paid Coppola too much for the glass, pains me even so strangely. I cannot see the cause."

He now sat down to finish his letter to Clara; but a glance through the window convinced him that Olympia was still sitting there, and he instantly sprang out, as if impelled by an irresistible power, seized Coppola's glass, and could not tear himself from the seductive view of Olympia, till his friend and brother Sigismund, called him to go to Professor Spalanzani's lecture. The curtain was drawn close before the fatal room, and he could neither perceive Olympia now nor during the two following days, although he scarcely ever left the window, and constantly looked through Coppola's glass. On the third day the windows were completely covered. Quite in despair, and impelled by a burning wish, he ran out of the town-gate. Olympia's form floated before him in the air, stepped forth from the bushes, and peeped at him with large beaming eyes from the clear brook. Clara's image had completely vanished from his mind; he thought of nothing but Olympia, and complained aloud and in a murmuring tone: "Ah, thou noble, sublime star of my love, hast thou only risen upon me, to vanish immediately, and leave me in dark hopeless night?"

When he was retiring to his lodging, he perceived that there was a great bustle in Spalanzani's house. The doors were wide open, all sorts of utensils were being carried in, the windows of the first floor were being taken out, maid servants were going about sweeping and dusting with great hair-brooms, and carpenters and upholsterers were knocking and hammering within. Nathaniel remained standing in the street in a state of perfect wonder, when Sigismund came up to him, laughing, and said: "Now, what do you say to our old Spalanzani?" Nathaniel assured him that he could say nothing because he knew nothing about the professor, but on the contrary perceived with astonishment the mad proceedings in a house otherwise so quiet and gloomy. He then learnt from Sigismund that Spalanzani intended to give a grand festival on the following day,—a concert and ball—and that half the university was invited. It was generally reported that Spalanzani, who had so long kept his daughter most painfully from every human eye, would now let her appear for the first time.

Nathaniel found a card of invitation, and with heart beating highly went at the appointed hour to the professor's, where the coaches were already rolling, and the lights were shining in the decorated saloons. The company was numerous and brilliant. Olympia appeared dressed with great richness and taste. Her beautifully turned face, her figure called for admiration. The somewhat strange bend of her back inwards, the wasp-like thinness of her waist, seemed to be produced by too tight lacing. In her step and deportment there was something measured and stiff, which struck many as unpleas-ant, but it was ascribed to the constraint produced by the company. The concert began. Olympia played the piano with great dexterity, and executed a bravura, with a voice, like the sound of a glass bell, clear, and almost cutting. Nathaniel was quite enraptured; he stood in the hindermost row, and could not perfectly recognize Olympia's features in the dazzling light. He, therefore, quite unperceived, took out Coppola's glass, and looked towards the fair Olympia. Ah! then he saw, with what a longing glance she looked towards him, how every tone first resolved itself plainly in the glance of love, which penetrated, in its glowing career, his inmost soul. The artistical *roulades* seemed to Nathaniel the exultation of a mind illuminated with love, and when, at last, after the cadence, the long trill sounded shrilly through the saloon, he felt as if grasped by glowing arms; he could no longer restrain himself, but with mingled pain and rapture shouted out, "Olympia!" All looked at him, and many laughed. The organist of the cathedral made a more gloomy face than usual, and simply said: "Well, well." The concert had finished, the ball began. "To dance with her—with her!" That was the aim of all Nathaniel's wishes, of all his efforts; but how to gain courage to ask her, the queen of the festival? Nevertheless—he himself did not know how it happened—no sooner had the dancing begun, than he was standing close to Olympia, who had not yet been asked to dance, and, scarcely able to stammer out a few words, had seized her hand. The hand of Olympia was as cold as ice; he felt a horrible deadly frost thrilling through him. He looked into her eye—that was beaming full of love and desire, and at the same time it seemed as though the pulse began to beat, and the stream of life to glow in the cold hand. And in the soul of Nathaniel the joy of love rose still higher; he clasped the beautiful Olympia, and with her flew through the dance. He thought that his dancing was usually correct as to time, but the peculiar rhythmical steadiness with which Olympia moved, and which often put him completely out, soon showed him, that his time was very defective. However, he would dance with no other lady, and would have liked to murder any one who approached Olympia for the purpose of asking her. But this only happened twice, and to his astonishment Olympia remained seated after every dance, when he lost no time in making her rise again. Had he been able to see any other object besides the fair Olympia, all sorts of unfortunate quarrels would have been inevitable, for the half-soft, scarcely-suppressed laughter, which arose among the young people in every corner, was manifestly directed to Olympia, whom they pursued with very curious glances—one could not tell why. Heated by the dance, and by the wine, of which he had freely partaken, Nathaniel had laid aside all his ordinary reserve. He sat by Olympia, with her hand in his, and, highly inflamed and inspired, told his passion, in words which no one understood—neither himself nor Olympia. Yet, perhaps, *she* did; for she looked immoveably in his face, and sighed several times, "Ah, ah!" Upon this, Nathaniel said, "Oh, thou splendid, heavenly lady! Thou ray from the promised land of love—thou deep soul, in which all my being is reflected!" with much more stuff of the like kind; but Olympia merely went on sighing, "Ah—ah!" Professor Spalanzani occasionally passed the happy pair, and smiled on them, with a look of singular satisfaction. To Nathaniel, although he felt in quite another region, it seemed all at once as though Professor Spalanzani was growing considerably darker; he looked around, and, to his no small horror, perceived that the two last candles in the empty saloon had burned down to their sockets, and were just going out. Music and dancing had ceased long ago. "Separation—separation!" he cried, wildly, and in despair; he kissed Olympia's hand, he bent towards her mouth, when his glowing lips were met by lips cold as ice! Just as when he touched Olympia's cold hand, he felt himself overcome by horror; the legend of the dead bride darted suddenly through his mind, but Olympia pressed him fast, and her lips seemed to recover to life at his kiss. Professor Spalanzani strode through the empty hall, his steps caused a hollow echo, and his figure, round which a flickering shadow played, had a fearful, spectral appearance. "Dost thou love me, dost thou love me, Olympia? Only this word!—Dost thou love me?" So whispered Nathaniel; but Olympia, as she rose, only sighed, "Ah—ah!" "Yes, my gracious, my beautiful star of love," said Nathaniel, "thou hast risen upon me, and thou wilt shine, ever illuminating my inmost soul." "Ah—ah!" replied Olympia, going. Nathaniel followed her; they both stood before the professor.

"You have had a very animated conversation with my daughter," said he, smiling; "so, dear Herr Nathaniel, if you have any taste for talking with a silly girl, your visits shall be welcome."

Nathaniel departed, with a whole heaven beaming in his bosom. The next day Spalanzani's festival was the subject of conversation. Notwithstanding the professor had done every thing to appear splendid, the wags had all sorts of incongruities and oddities to talk about, and were particularly hard upon the dumb, stiff Olympia, to whom, in spite of her beautiful exterior, they ascribed absolute stupidity, and were pleased to find therein the cause why Spalanzani kept her so long concealed. Nathaniel did not hear this without increased rage; but, nevertheless, he held his peace, for, thought he, "Is it worth while to convince these fellows that it is their own stupidity that prevents them from recognizing Olympia's deep, noble mind?"

One day Sigismund said to him: "Be kind enough, brother, to tell me how it was possible for a sensible fellow like you to fall in love with that wax face, that wooden doll up there?"

Nathaniel was about to fly out in a passion, but he quickly recollected himself, and retorted: "Tell me, Sigismund, how it is that Olympia's heavenly charms could escape your glance, which generally perceives every thing so clearly—your active senses? But, for that very reason, Heaven be thanked, I have not you for my rival; otherwise, one of us must have fallen a bleeding corpse!"

Sigismund plainly perceived his friend's condition, so he skilfully gave the conversation a turn, and added, after observing that in love-affairs there was no disputing about the object: "Nevertheless it is strange, that many of us think much the same about Olympia. To us—pray do not take it ill, brother,—she appears singularly stiff and soulless. Her shape is symmetrical—so is her face—that is true! She might pass for beautiful, if her glance were not so utterly without a ray of life—without the power of seeing. Her pace is strangely measured, every movement seems to depend on some wound-up clockwork. Her playing—her singing has the unpleasantly correct and spiritless measure of a singing machine, and the same may be said of her dancing. To us, this Olympia has been quite unpleasant; we wished to have nothing to do with her; it seems as if she acts like a living being, and yet has some strange peculiarity of her own." Nathaniel did not completely yield to the bitter feeling, which was coming over him at these words of Sigismund; he mastered his indignation, and merely said, with great earnestness, "Well may Olympia appear awful to you, cold prosaic man. Only to the poetical mind does the similarly organized develop itself. To me alone was her glance of love revealed, beaming through mind and thought; only in the love of Olympia do I find myself again. It may not suit you, that she does not indulge in idle chitchat like other shallow minds. She utters few words, it is true, but these few words appear as genuine hieroglyphics of the inner world, full of love and deep knowledge of the spiritual life in contemplation of the eternal *yonder*. But you have no sense for all this, and my words are wasted on you." "God preserve you, brother," said Sigismund very mildly, almost sorrowfully; "but it seems to me, that you are in an evil way. You may depend upon me, if all—no, no, I will not say any thing further." All of a sudden it seemed to Nathaniel as if the cold prosaic Sigismund meant very well towards him, and, therefore, he shook the proffered hand very heartily.

Nathaniel had totally forgotten, that there was in the world a Clara, whom he had once loved;—his mother—Lothaire—all had vanished from his memory; he lived only for Olympia, with whom he sat for hours every day, uttering strange fantastical stuff about his love, about the sympathy that glowed to life, about the affinity of souls, to all of which Olympia listened with great devotion. From the very bottom of his desk, he drew out all that he had ever written. Poems, fantasies, visions, romances, tales—this stock was daily increased with all sorts of extravagant sonnets, stanzas, and *canzone*, and he read

all to Olympia for hours in succession without fatigue. Never had
he known such an admirable listener. She neither embroidered nor
knitted, she never looked out of window, she fed no favourite bird,
she played neither with lap-dog nor pet cat, she did not twist a slip of
paper nor any thing else in her hand, she was not obliged to suppress
a yawn by a gentle forced cough. In short, she sat for hours, looking
straight into her lover's eyes, without stirring, and her glance became
more and more lively and animated. Only when Nathaniel rose at last,
and kissed her hand and also her lips, she said "Ah, ah!" adding "good
night, dearest!" "Oh deep, noble mind!" cried Nathaniel in his own
room, "by thee, by thee, dear one, am I fully comprehended." He
trembled with inward transport, when he considered the wonderful
accordance that was revealed more and more every day in his own
mind, and that of Olympia, for it seemed to him as if Olympia had
spoken concerning him and his poetical talent out of the depths of
his own mind;—as if the voice had actually sounded from within
himself. That must indeed have been the case, for Olympia never
uttered any words whatever beyond those which have been already
mentioned. Even when Nathaniel, in clear and sober moments, as
for instance, when he had just woke in the morning, remembered
Olympia's utter passivity, and her paucity and scarcity of words, he
said: "Words, words! The glance of her heavenly eye speaks more
than any language here below. Can a child of heaven adapt herself
to the narrow circle which a miserable earthly necessity has drawn?"
Professor Spalanzani appeared highly delighted at the intimacy of his
daughter with Nathaniel. To the latter he gave the most unequivocal
signs of approbation, and when Nathaniel ventured at last to hint at
an union with Olympia, he smiled with his white face, and thought
"he would leave his daughter a free choice in the matter." Encouraged
by these words, and with burning passion in his heart, Nathaniel

resolved to implore Olympia on the very next day, that she would say directly, in plain words, that which her kind glance had told him long ago; namely, that she loved him. He sought the ring which his mother had given him at parting, that he might give it to Olympia as a symbol of his devotion, of his life which budded forth and bloomed with her alone. Clara's letters and Lothaire's came into his hands during the search; but he flung them aside indifferently, found the ring, put it up and hastened over to Olympia. Already on the steps, in the hall he heard a strange noise, which seemed to proceed from Spalanzani's room. There was a stamping, a clattering, a pushing, a hurling against the door, intermingled with curses and imprecations. "Let go, let go, rascal!—scoundrel! Body and soul ventured in it? Ha, ha, ha! that I never will consent to—I, I made the eyes, I the clockwork—stupid blockhead with your clockwork—accursed dog of a bungling watch-maker—off with you—Satan—stop, pipe-maker—infernal beast—hold—begone—let go!" These words were uttered by the voices of Spalanzani, and the hideous Coppelius, who was thus raging and clamouring. Nathaniel rushed in, overcome by the most inexpressible anguish. The professor held a female figure fast by the shoulders, the Italian Coppola grasped it by the feet, and thus they were tugging and pulling, this way and that, contending for the possession of it, with the unmost fury. Nathaniel started back with horror, when in the figure he recognized Olympia. Boiling with the wildest indignation, he was about to rescue his beloved from these infuriated men, but at that moment, Coppola, turning himself with the force of a giant, wrenched the figure from the professor's hand, and then with the figure itself gave him a tremendous blow, which made him reel and fall backwards over the table, where vials, retorts, bottles, and glass cylinders were standing. All these were dashed to a thousand shivers. Now Coppola flung the figure across his shoulders, and, with frightful, yelling laughter, dashed down the stairs, so that the feet of the figure, which dangled in the ugliest manner, rattled with a wooden sound on every step. Nathaniel stood paralysed; he had seen but too plainly that Olympia's waxen, deadly pale countenance had no eyes, but black holes instead—she was, indeed, a lifeless doll. Spalanzani was writhing on the floor; the pieces of glass had cut his head, heart, and arms, and the blood was spirting up, as from so many fountains. But he soon collected all his strength. "After him—after him—why do you pause? Coppelius, Coppelius, has robbed me of my best automaton—a work of twenty years—body and soul set upon it—the clockwork—the speech—the walk, mine; the eyes stolen from you. The infernal rascal—after him; fetch Olympia—there you have the eyes!"

And now Nathaniel saw how a pair of eyes, which lay upon the ground, were staring at him; these Spalanzani caught up, with the unwounded hand, and flung against his heart. At this, madness seized him with its burning claws, and clutched into his soul, tearing to pieces all his thoughts and senses. "Ho—ho—ho—a circle of fire! of fire!—turn thyself round, circle! merrily, merrily, ho, thou wooden doll—turn thyself, pretty doll!" With these words he flew at the professor and pressed in his throat. He would have strangled him, had not the noise attracted many people, who rushed in, forced open Nathaniel's grasp, and thus saved the professor, whose wounds were bound immediately. Sigismund, strong as he was, was not able to master the mad Nathaniel, who with frightful voice kept crying out: "Turn thyself, wooden doll!" and struck around him with clenched fists. At last the combined force of many succeeded in overcoming him, in flinging him to the ground, and binding him. His words were merged into a hideous roar, like that of a brute, and raging in this insane condition he was taken to the mad-house.

Before, gentle reader, I proceed to tell thee what more befell the unfortunate Nathaniel, I can tell thee, in case thou takest an interest in the skilful optician and automaton-maker, Spalanzani, that he was completely healed of his wounds. He was, however, obliged to leave the university; because Nathaniel's story had created a sensation, and it was universally deemed an unpardonable imposition to smuggle wooden dolls instead of living persons into respectable tea-parties—for such Olympia had visited with success. The lawyers called it a most subtle deception, and the more culpable, inasmuch as he had planned it so artfully against the public, that not a single soul—a few cunning students excepted—had detected it, although all now wished to play the acute, and referred to various facts, which appeared to them suspicious. Nothing very clever was revealed in this way. For instance, could it strike any one as so very suspicious, that Olympia, according to the expression of an elegant tea-ite, had, contrary to all usage, sneezed oftener than she had yawned? "The *former*," remarked this elegant person, "was the self-winding-up of the concealed clockwork, which had, moreover, creaked audibly"—and so on. The professor of poetry and eloquence took a pinch of snuff, clapped first the lid of his box, cleared his throat, and said, solemnly, "Ladies and gentlemen, do you not perceive how the whole affair lies? It is all an allegory—a continued metaphor—you understand me—*Sapienti sat.*" But many were not satisfied with this; the story of the automaton had struck deep root into their souls, and, in fact, an abominable mistrust against human figures in general, began to creep in. Many lovers, to be quite convinced at they were not enamoured of wooden dolls, would request their mistress to sing and dance a little out of time, to embroider and knit, and play with their lap-dogs, while listening to reading, &c.; and, above all, not to listen merely, but also sometimes to talk, in such a manner as presupposed actual thought and feeling. With many did the bond of love become firmer, and more chaining, while others, on the contrary, slipped gently out of the noose. "One cannot really answer for this," said some. At tea-parties, yawning prevailed to an incredible extent, and there was no sneezing at all, that all suspicion might be avoided. Spalanzani, as already stated, was obliged to decamp, to escape the criminal prosecution for fraudulently introducing an automaton into human society. Coppola had vanished also.

Nathaniel awakened as from a heavy, frightful dream; he opened his eyes, and felt an indescribable sensation of pleasure streaming through him, with soft heavenly warmth. He was in bed in his own room, in his father's house, Clara was stooping over him, and Lothaire and his mother were standing near. "At last, at last, oh beloved Nathaniel, hast thou recovered from thy serious illness—now thou art again mine!" So spoke Clara, from the very depth of her soul, and clasped Nathaniel in her arms. But with mingled sorrow and delight did the brightly glowing tears fall from his eyes, and he deeply groaned forth: "My own—my own Clara!" Sigismund, who had faithfully remained with his friend in the hour of trouble, now entered. Nathaniel stretched out his hand to him. "And thou, faithful brother, hast not deserted me?" Every trace of Nathaniel's madness had vanished, and he soon gained strength amid the care of his mother, his beloved, and his friends. Good fortune also had visited the house, for an old penurious uncle, of whom nothing had been expected, had died, and had left the mother, besides considerable property, an estate in a pleasant spot near the town. Thither Nathaniel, with his Clara, whom he now thought of marrying, his mother, and Lothaire, desired to go. Nathaniel had now grown milder and more docile than he had ever been, and he now understood, for the first time, the heavenly purity and the greatness of Clara's mind. No one, by the slightest hint, reminded him of the past. Only, when Sigismund took leave of him, Nathaniel said: "Heavens, brother, I was in an evil way, but a good angel led me betimes to the path of light! Ah, that was Clara!" Sigismund did not let him carry the discourse further for fear that deeply wounding recollections might burst forth bright and flaming. It was about this time that the four happy persons thought of going to the estate. They were crossing, at noon, the streets of the city, where they had made several purchases, and the high steeple of the town-house already cast its gigantic shadow over the market-place. "Oh," said Clara, "let us ascend it once more, and look at the distant mountains!" No sooner said than done. Nathaniel and Clara both ascended the steps, the mother returned home with the servant, and Lothaire, not inclined to clamber up so many steps, chose to remain below. The two lovers stood arm in arm in the highest gallery of the tower, and looked down upon the misty forests, behind which the blue mountains were rising like a gigantic city.

"Look there at that curious little grey bush, which actually seems as if it were striding towards us," said Clara. Nathaniel mechanically put his hand into his breast pocket—he found Coppola's telescope, and he looked on one side. Clara was before the glass. There was a convulsive movement in his pulse and veins,—pale as death, he stared at Clara, but soon streams of fire flashed and glared from his rolling eyes, and he roared frightfully, like a hunted beast. Then he sprang high into the air, and, in the intervals of a horrible laughter, shrieked out, in a piercing tone, "Wooden doll—turn thyself!" Seizing Clara with immense force he wished to hurl her down, but with the energy of a desperate death-struggle she clutched the railings. Lothaire heard the raging of the madman—he heard Clara's shriek of agony—fearful forebodings darted through his mind, he ran up, the door of the second flight was fastened, and the shrieks of Clara became louder and louder. Frantic with rage and anxiety, he dashed against the door, which, at last, burst open. Clara's voice became fainter and fainter. "Help—help—save me!"—with these words the voice seemed to die in the air. "She is gone—murdered by the madman!" cried Lothaire. The door of the gallery was also closed, but despair gave him a giant's strength, and he burst it from the hinges. Heavens—Clara, grasped by the mad Nathaniel, was hanging in the air over the gallery,—only with one hand she still held one of the iron railings. Quick as lightning Lothaire caught his sister, drew her in, and, at the same moment, struck the madman in the face with his clenched fist, so that he reeled and let go his prey.

Lothaire ran down with his fainting sister in his arms. She was saved. Nathaniel went raging about the gallery and bounded high in the air, crying, "Fire-circle turn thyself—turn thyself!" The people collected at the sound of the wild shriek, and among them, prominent by his gigantic stature, was the advocate Coppelius, who had just come to the town, and was proceeding straight to the market-place. Some wished to ascend and secure the madman, but Coppelius laughed, saying, "Ha, ha,—only wait—he will soon come down of his own accord," and looked up like the rest. Nathaniel suddenly stood still as if petrified; he stooped down, perceived Coppelius, and yelling out, "Ah, pretty eyes—pretty eyes!"—he sprang over the railing.

When Nathaniel lay on the stone pavement, with his head shattered, Coppelius had disappeared in the crowd.

Many years afterwards it is said that Clara was seen in a remote spot, sitting hand in hand with a kind-looking man before the door of a country house, while two lively boys played before her. From this it may be inferred that she at last found that quiet domestic happiness which suited her serene and cheerful mind, and which the morbid Nathaniel would never have given her.

THE MORTAL IMMORTAL: A TALE

Mary Shelley

Mary Shelley (1797–1851) is one of the most celebrated writers of all time thanks to her *Frankenstein; or, the Modern Prometheus* (1818), which popularized the figure of the mad scientist and the reanimated man. This classic novel was not, however, Shelley's only text to explore themes of resuscitation and immortality. In 'Valerius: The Reanimated Roman' (c. 1819?), a man who dies during the fall of the Roman Empire is brought back centuries later by means unspecified, only to experience isolation and extreme grief as a result. Similarly, in the playful 'The Reanimated Man' (1826), Shelley wrote about the widely reported case, later proven a hoax, of Englishman Roger Dodsworth, allegedly recovered from a glacier and successfully defrosted back to life.

The tale selected for this collection, 'The Mortal Immortal: A Tale' (1833), tells of a man who ends up working for the real-life German physician Cornelius Agrippa (1486–1535). Winzy accidentally imbibes his master's 'Elixir of Immortality', mistaking it for a love potion, and must endure the horror of watching his beloved age while he remains untouched by time. This moralistic tale about the dangers of altering the natural course of life shows how science (and, before it, alchemy) have traditionally been connected to magic and the supernatural.

J ULY 16, 1833.—THIS IS A MEMORABLE ANNIVERSARY FOR ME; on it I complete my three hundred and twenty-third year!

The Wandering Jew?—certainly not. More than eighteen centuries have passed over his head. In comparison with him, I am a very young Immortal.

Am I, then, immortal? This is a question which I have asked myself, by day and night, for now three hundred and three years, and yet cannot answer it. I detected a grey hair amidst my brown locks this very day—that surely signifies decay. Yet it may have remained concealed there for three hundred years—for some persons have become entirely white-headed before twenty years of age.

I will tell my story, and my reader shall judge for me. I will tell my story, and so contrive to pass some few hours of a long eternity, become so wearisome to me. For ever! Can it be? to live for ever! I have heard of enchantments, in which the victims were plunged into a deep sleep, to wake, after a hundred years, as fresh as ever: I have heard of the Seven Sleepers—thus to be immortal would not be so burthensome: but, oh! the weight of never-ending time—the tedious passage of the still-succeeding hours! How happy was the fabled Nourjahad!—But to my task.

All the world has heard of Cornelius Agrippa. His memory is as immortal as his arts have made me. All the world has also heard of his scholar, who, unawares, raised the foul fiend during his master's absence, and was destroyed by him. The report, true or false, of this accident, was attended with many inconveniences to the renowned philosopher. All his scholars at once deserted him—his servants disappeared. He had no one near him to put coals on his ever-burning fires while he slept, or to attend to the changeful colours of his medicines while he studied. Experiment after experiment failed, because one pair of hands was insufficient to complete them: the dark spirits laughed at him for not being able to retain a single mortal in his service.

I was then very young—very poor—and very much in love. I had been for about a year the pupil of Cornelius, though I was absent when this accident took place. On my return, my friends implored me not to return to the alchymist's abode. I trembled as I listened to the dire tale they told; I required no second warning; and when Cornelius came and offered me a purse of gold if I would remain under his roof, I felt as if Satan himself tempted me. My teeth chattered—my hair stood on end:—I ran off as fast as my trembling knees would permit.

My failing steps were directed whither for two years they had every evening been attracted,—a gently bubbling spring of pure living waters, beside which lingered a dark-haired girl, whose beaming eyes were fixed on the path I was accustomed each night to tread. I cannot remember the hour when I did not love Bertha; we had been neighbours and playmates from infancy—her parents, like mine, were of humble life, yet respectable—our attachment had been a source of pleasure to them. In an evil hour, a malignant fever carried off both her father and mother, and Bertha became an orphan. She would have found a home beneath my paternal roof, but, unfortunately, the old lady of the near castle, rich, childless, and solitary, declared her intention to adopt her. Henceforth Bertha was clad in silk—inhabited a marble palace—and was looked on as being highly favoured by fortune. But in her new situation among her new associates, Bertha remained true to the friend of her humbler days; she often visited the cottage of my father, and when forbidden to go thither, she would stray towards the neighbouring wood, and meet me beside its shady fountain.

She often declared that she owed no duty to her new protectress equal in sanctity to that which bound us. Yet still I was too poor to marry, and she grew weary of being tormented on my account. She had a haughty but an impatient spirit, and grew angry at the obstacles that prevented our union. We met now after an absence, and she had been sorely beset while I was away; she complained bitterly, and almost reproached me for being poor. I replied hastily,—

"I am honest, if I am poor!—were I not, I might soon become rich!"

This exclamation produced a thousand questions. I feared to shock her by owning the truth, but she drew it from me; and then, casting a look of disdain on me, she said—

"You pretend to love, and you fear to face the Devil for my sake!"

I protested that I had only dreaded to offend her;—while she dwelt on the magnitude of the reward that I should receive. Thus encouraged—shamed by her—led on by love and hope, laughing at my late fears, with quick steps and a light heart, I returned to accept the offers of the alchymist, and was instantly installed in my office.

A year passed away. I became possessed of no insignificant sum of money. Custom had banished my fears. In spite of the most painful vigilance, I had never detected the trace of a cloven foot; nor was the studious silence of our abode ever disturbed by demoniac howls. I still continued my stolen interviews with Bertha, and Hope dawned on me—Hope—but not perfect joy; for Bertha fancied that love and security were enemies, and her pleasure was to divide them in my bosom. Though true of heart, she was somewhat of a coquette in manner; and I was jealous as a Turk. She slighted me in a thousand ways, yet would never acknowledge herself to be in the wrong. She would drive me mad with anger, and then force me to beg her pardon. Sometimes she fancied that I was not sufficiently submissive, and then she had some story of a rival, favoured by her protectress. She was surrounded by silk-clad youths—the rich and gay—What chance had the sad-robed scholar of Cornelius compared with these?

On one occasion, the philosopher made such large demands upon my time, that I was unable to meet her as I was wont. He was engaged in some mighty work, and I was forced to remain, day and night, feeding his furnaces and watching his chemical preparations. Bertha waited for me in vain at the fountain. Her haughty spirit fired at this neglect; and when at last I stole out during the few short minutes allotted to me for slumber, and hoped to be consoled by her, she received me with disdain, dismissed me in scorn, and vowed that any man should possess her hand rather than he who could not be in two places at once for her sake. She would be revenged!—And truly she was. In my dingy retreat I heard that she had been hunting, attended by Albert Hoffer. Albert Hoffer was favoured by her protectress, and the three passed in cavalcade before my smoky window. Methought that they mentioned my name—it was followed by a laugh of derision, as her dark eyes glanced contemptuously towards my abode.

Jealousy, with all its venom, and all its misery, entered my breast. Now I shed a torrent of tears, to think that I should never call her mine; and, anon, I imprecated a thousand curses on her inconstancy. Yet, still I must stir the fires of the alchymist, still attend on the changes of his unintelligible medicines.

Cornelius had watched for three days and nights, nor closed his eyes. The progress of his alembics was slower than he expected: in spite of his anxiety, sleep weighed upon his eyelids. Again and again he threw off drowsiness with more than human energy; again and again it stole away his senses. He eyed his crucibles wistfully. "Not ready yet," he murmured; "will another night pass before the work is accomplished? Winzy, you are vigilant—you are faithful—you have slept, my boy—you slept last night. Look at that glass vessel. The liquid it contains is of a soft rose-colour: the moment it begins to change its hue, awaken me—till then I may close my eyes. First, it will turn white, and then emit golden flashes; but wait not till then; when the rose-colour fades, rouse me." I scarcely heard the last words, muttered, as they were, in sleep. Even then he did not quite yield to nature. "Winzy, my boy," he again said, "do not touch the vessel—do not put it to your lips; it is a philter—a philter to cure love; you would not cease to love your Bertha—beware to drink!"

And he slept. His venerable head sunk on his breast, and I scarce heard his regular breathing. For a few minutes I watched the vessel— the rosy hue of the liquid remained unchanged. Then my thoughts wandered—they visited the fountain, and dwelt on a thousand charming scenes never to be renewed—never! Serpents and adders were in my heart as the word "Never!" half formed itself on my lips. False girl!—false and cruel! Never more would she smile on me as that evening she smiled on Albert. Worthless, detested woman! I would not remain unrevenged—she should see Albert expire at her feet— she should die beneath my vengeance. She had smiled in disdain and triumph—she knew my wretchedness and her power. Yet what power had she?—the power of exciting my hate—my utter scorn—my—oh, all but indifference! Could I attain that—could I regard her with careless eyes, transferring my rejected love to one fairer and more true, that were indeed a victory!

A bright flash darted before my eyes. I had forgotten the medicine of the adept; I gazed on it with wonder: flashes of admirable beauty, more bright than those which the diamond emits when the sun's rays are on it, glanced from the surface of the liquid; an odour the most fragrant and grateful stole over my sense; the vessel seemed one globe of living radiance, lovely to the eye, and most inviting to the taste. The first thought, instinctively inspired by the grosser sense, was, I will—I must drink. I raised the vessel to my lips. "It will cure me of love—of torture!" Already I had quaffed half of the most delicious liquor ever tasted by the palate of man, when the philosopher stirred. I started—I dropped the glass—the fluid flamed and glanced along the floor, while I felt Cornelius's gripe at my throat, as he shrieked aloud, "Wretch! you have destroyed the labour of my life!"

The philosopher was totally unaware that I had drunk any portion of his drug. His idea was, and I gave a tacit assent to it, that I had raised the vessel from curiosity, and that, frighted at its brightness, and the flashes of intense light it gave forth, I had let it fall. I never undeceived him. The fire of the medicine was quenched—the fragrance died away—he grew calm, as a philosopher should under the heaviest trials, and dismissed me to rest.

I will not attempt to describe the sleep of glory and bliss which bathed my soul in paradise during the remaining hours of that memorable night. Words would be faint and shallow types of my enjoyment, or of the gladness that possessed my bosom when I woke. I trod air—my thoughts were in heaven. Earth appeared heaven, and my inheritance upon it was to be one trance of delight. "This it is to be cured of love," I thought; "I will see Bertha this day, and she will find her lover cold and regardless; too happy to be disdainful, yet how utterly indifferent to her!"

The hours danced away. The philosopher, secure that he had once succeeded, and believing that he might again, began to concoct the same medicine once more. He was shut up with his books and drugs, and I had a holiday. I dressed myself with care; I looked in an old but polished shield, which served me for a mirror; methought my good looks had wonderfully improved. I hurried beyond the precincts of the town, joy in my soul, the beauty of heaven and earth around me. I turned my steps towards the castle—I could look on its lofty turrets with lightness of heart, for I was cured of love. My Bertha saw me afar off, as I came up the avenue. I know not what sudden impulse animated her bosom, but at the sight, she sprung with a light fawn-like bound down the marble steps, and was hastening towards me. But I had been perceived by another person. The old high-born hag, who called herself her protectress, and was her tyrant, had seen me, also; she hobbled, panting, up the terrace; a page, as ugly as herself, held up her train, and fanned her as she hurried along, and stopped my fair girl with a "How, now, my bold mistress? whither so fast? Back to your cage—hawks are abroad!"

Bertha clasped her hands—her eyes were still bent on my approaching figure. I saw the contest. How I abhorred the old crone who checked the kind impulses of my Bertha's softening heart. Hitherto, respect for her rank had caused me to avoid the lady of the castle; now I disdained such trivial considerations. I was cured of love, and lifted above all human fears; I hastened forwards, and soon reached the terrace. How lovely Bertha looked! her eyes flashing fire, her cheeks glowing with impatience and anger, she was a thousand times more graceful and charming than ever—I no longer loved—Oh! no, I adored—worshipped—idolized her!

She had that morning been persecuted, with more than usual vehemence, to consent to an immediate marriage with my rival. She was reproached with the encouragement that she had shown him— she was threatened with being turned out of doors with disgrace and shame. Her proud spirit rose in arms at the threat; but when she remembered the scorn that she had heaped upon me, and how, perhaps, she had thus lost one whom she now regarded as her only friend, she wept with remorse and rage. At that moment I appeared. "O, Winzy!" she exclaimed, "take me to your mother's cot; swiftly let me leave the detested luxuries and wretchedness of this noble dwelling—take me to poverty and happiness."

I clasped her in my arms with transport. The old lady was speechless with fury, and broke forth into invective only when we were far on our road to my natal cottage. My mother received the fair fugitive, escaped from a gilt cage to nature and liberty, with tenderness and joy; my father, who loved her, welcomed her heartily; it was a day of rejoicing, which did not need the addition of the celestial potion of the alchymist to steep me in delight.

Soon after this eventful day, I became the husband of Bertha. I ceased to be the scholar of Cornelius, but I continued his friend. I always felt grateful to him for having, unawares, procured me that delicious draught of a divine elixir, which, instead of curing me of love (sad cure! solitary and joyless remedy for evils which seem blessings to the memory), had inspired me with courage and resolution, thus winning for me an inestimable treasure in my Bertha.

I often called to mind that period of trance-like inebriation with wonder. The drink of Cornelius had not fulfilled the task for which he affirmed that it had been prepared, but its effects were more potent and blissful than words can express. They had faded by degrees, yet they lingered long—and painted life in hues of splendour. Bertha often wondered at my lightness of heart and unaccustomed gaiety; for, before, I had been rather serious, or even sad, in my disposition. She loved me the better for my cheerful temper, and our days were winged by joy.

Five years afterwards I was suddenly summoned to the bedside of the dying Cornelius. He had sent for me in haste, conjuring my instant presence. I found him stretched on his pallet, enfeebled even to death; all of life that yet remained animated his piercing eyes, and they were fixed on a glass vessel, full of a roseate liquid.

"Behold," he said, in a broken and inward voice, "the vanity of human wishes! a second time my hopes are about to be crowned, a second time they are destroyed. Look at that liquor—you remember five years ago I had prepared the same, with the same success;—then, as now, my thirsting lips expected to taste the immortal elixir—you dashed it from me! and at present it is too late."

He spoke with difficulty, and fell back on his pillow. I could not help saying,—

"How, revered master, can a cure for love restore you to life?"

A faint smile gleamed across his face as I listened earnestly to his scarcely intelligible answer.

"A cure for love and for all things—the Elixir of Immortality. Ah! if now I might drink, I should live for ever!"

As he spoke, a golden flash gleamed from the fluid; a well-remembered fragrance stole over the air; he raised himself, all weak as he was—strength seemed miraculously to re-enter his frame—he stretched forth his hand—a loud explosion startled me—a ray of fire shot up from the elixir, and the glass vessel which contained it was shivered to atoms! I turned my eyes towards the philosopher; he had fallen back—his eyes were glassy—his features rigid—he was dead!

But I lived, and was to live for ever! So said the unfortunate alchymist, and for a few days I believed his words. I remembered the glorious drunkenness that had followed my stolen draught. I reflected on the change I had felt in my frame—in my soul. The bounding elasticity of the one—the buoyant lightness of the other. I surveyed myself in a mirror, and could perceive no change in my features during the space of the five years which had elapsed. I remembered the radiant hues and grateful scent of that delicious beverage—worthy the gift it was capable of bestowing—I was, then, IMMORTAL!

A few days after I laughed at my credulity. The old proverb, that "a prophet is least regarded in his own country," was true with respect to me and my defunct master. I loved him as a man—I respected him as a sage—but I derided the notion that he could command the powers of darkness, and laughed at the superstitious fears with which he was regarded by the vulgar. He was a wise philosopher, but had no acquaintance with any spirits but those clad in flesh and blood. His science was simply human; and human science, I soon persuaded myself, could never conquer nature's laws so far as to imprison the soul for ever within its carnal habitation. Cornelius had brewed a soul-refreshing drink—more inebriating than wine—sweeter and more fragrant than any fruit: it possessed probably strong medicinal powers, imparting gladness to the heart and vigour to the limbs; but its effects would wear out; already were they diminished in my frame. I was a lucky fellow to have quaffed health and joyous spirits, and perhaps long life, at my master's hands; but my good fortune ended there: longevity was far different from immortality.

I continued to entertain this belief for many years. Sometimes a thought stole across me—Was the alchymist indeed deceived? But my habitual credence was, that I should meet the fate of all the children of Adam at my appointed time—a little late, but still at a natural age. Yet it was certain that I retained a wonderfully youthful look. I was laughed at for my vanity in consulting the mirror so often, but I con- sulted it in vain—my brow was untrenched—my cheeks—my eyes— my whole person continued as untarnished as in my twentieth year.

I was troubled. I looked at the faded beauty of Bertha—I seemed more like her son. By degrees our neighbours began to make similar observations, and I found at last that I went by the name of the

Scholar bewitched. Bertha herself grew uneasy. She became jealous and peevish, and at length she began to question me. We had no children; we were all in all to each other; and though, as she grew older, her vivacious spirit became a little allied to ill-temper, and her beauty sadly diminished, I cherished her in my heart as the mistress I had idolized, the wife I had sought and won with such perfect love.

At last our situation became intolerable: Bertha was fifty—I twenty years of age. I had, in very shame, in some measure adopted the habits of a more advanced age; I no longer mingled in the dance among the young and gay, but my heart bounded along with them while I restrained my feet; and a sorry figure I cut among the Nestors of our village. But before the time I mention, things were altered—we were universally shunned; we were—at least, I was—reported to have kept up an iniquitous acquaintance with some of my former master's supposed friends. Poor Bertha was pitied, but deserted. I was regarded with horror and detestation.

What was to be done? we sat by our winter fire—poverty had made itself felt, for none would buy the produce of my farm; and often I had been forced to journey twenty miles, to some place where I was not known, to dispose of our property. It is true we had saved something for an evil day—that day was come.

We sat by our lone fireside—the old-hearted youth and his antiquated wife. Again Bertha insisted on knowing the truth; she recapitulated all she had ever heard said about me, and added her own observations. She conjured me to cast off the spell; she described how much more comely grey hairs were than my chestnut locks; she descanted on the reverence and respect due to age—how preferable to the slight regard paid to mere children: could I imagine that the despicable gifts of youth and good looks outweighed disgrace, hatred, and scorn? Nay, in the end I should be burnt as a dealer in the black art, while she, to whom I had not deigned to communicate any portion of my good fortune, might be stoned as my accomplice. At length she insinuated that I must share my secret with her, and bestow on her like benefits to those I myself enjoyed, or she would denounce me—and then she burst into tears.

Thus beset, methought it was the best way to tell the truth. I revealed it as tenderly as I could, and spoke only of a *very long life*, not of immortality—which representation, indeed, coincided best with my own ideas. When I ended, I rose and said,

"And now, my Bertha, will you denounce the lover of your youth?—You will not, I know. But it is too hard, my poor wife, that you should suffer from my ill-luck and the accursed arts of Cornelius. I will leave you—you have wealth enough, and friends will return in my absence. I will go; young as I seem, and strong as I am, I can work and gain my bread among strangers, unsuspected and unknown. I loved you in youth; God is my witness that I would not desert you in age, but that your safety and happiness require it."

I took my cap and moved towards the door; in a moment Bertha's arms were round my neck, and her lips were pressed to mine. "No, my husband, my Winzy," she said, "you shall not go alone—take me with you; we will remove from this place, and, as you say, among strangers we shall be unsuspected and safe. I am not so very old as quite to shame you, my Winzy; and I dare say the charm will soon wear off, and, with the blessing of God, you will become more elderly-looking, as is fitting; you shall not leave me."

I returned the good soul's embrace heartily. "I will not, my Bertha; but for your sake I had not thought of such a thing. I will be your true, faithful husband while you are spared to me, and do my duty by you to the last."

The next day we prepared secretly for our emigration. We were obliged to make great pecuniary sacrifices—it could not be helped. We realized a sum sufficient, at least, to maintain us while Bertha lived; and, without saying adieu to any one, quitted our native country to take refuge in a remote part of western France.

It was a cruel thing to transport poor Bertha from her native village, and the friends of her youth, to a new country, new language, new customs. The strange secret of my destiny rendered this removal immaterial to me; but I compassionated her deeply, and was glad to perceive that she found compensation for her misfortunes in a variety of little ridiculous circumstances. Away from all tell-tale chroniclers, she sought to decrease the apparent disparity of our ages by a thousand feminine arts—rouge, youthful dress, and assumed juvenility of manner. I could not be angry—Did not I myself wear a mask? Why quarrel with hers, because it was less successful? I grieved deeply when I remembered that this was my Bertha, whom I had loved so fondly, and won with such transport—the dark-eyed, dark-haired girl, with smiles of enchanting archness and a step like a fawn—this mincing, simpering, jealous old woman. I should have revered her grey locks and withered cheeks; but thus!—It was my work, I knew; but I did not the less deplore this type of human weakness.

Her jealousy never slept. Her chief occupation was to discover that, in spite of outward appearances, I was myself growing old. I verily believe that the poor soul loved me truly in her heart, but never had woman so tormenting a mode of displaying fondness. She would discern wrinkles in my face and decrepitude in my walk, while I bounded along in youthful vigour, the youngest looking of twenty youths. I never dared address another woman: on one occasion, fancying that the belle of the village regarded me with favouring eyes, she bought me a grey wig. Her constant discourse among her acquaintances was, that though I looked so young, there was ruin at work within my frame; and she affirmed that the worst symptom about me was my apparent health. My youth was a disease, she said, and I ought at all times to prepare, if not for a sudden and awful death, at least to awake some morning white-headed, and bowed down with all the marks of advanced years. I let her talk—I often joined in her conjectures. Her warnings chimed in with my never-ceasing specu- lations concerning my state, and I took an earnest, though painful, interest in listening to all that her quick wit and excited imagination could say on the subject.

Why dwell on these minute circumstances? We lived on for many long years. Bertha became bed-rid and paralytic: I nursed her as a mother might a child. She grew peevish, and still harped upon one string—of how long I should survive her. It has ever been a source of consolation to me, that I performed my duty scrupulously towards her. She had been mine in youth, she was mine in age, and at last, when I heaped the sod over her corpse, I wept to feel that I had lost all that really bound me to humanity.

Since then how many have been my cares and woes, how few and empty my enjoyments! I pause here in my history—I will pursue it no further. A sailor without rudder or compass, tossed on a stormy sea—a traveller lost on a widespread heath, without landmark or star to guide him—such have I been: more lost, more hopeless than either. A nearing ship, a gleam from some far cot, may save them; but I have no beacon except the hope of death.

Death! mysterious, ill-visaged friend of weak humanity! Why alone of all mortals have you cast me from your sheltering fold? O, for the peace of the grave! the deep silence of the iron-bound tomb! that thought would cease to work in my brain, and my heart beat no more with emotions varied only by new forms of sadness!

Am I immortal? I return to my first question. In the first place, is it not more probable that the beverage of the alchymist was fraught rather with longevity than eternal life? Such is my hope. And then be it remembered, that I only drank *half* of the potion prepared by him. Was not the whole necessary to complete the charm? To have drained half the Elixir of Immortality is but to be half immortal—my Forever is thus truncated and null.

But again, who shall number the years of the half of eternity? I often try to imagine by what rule the infinite may be divided. Sometimes I fancy age advancing upon me. One grey hair I have found. Fool! do I lament? Yes, the fear of age and death often creeps coldly into my heart; and the more I live, the more I dread death, even while I abhor life. Such an enigma is man—born to perish—when he wars, as I do, against the established laws of his nature.

But for this anomaly of feeling surely I might die: the medicine of the alchymist would not be proof against fire—sword—and the strangling waters. I have gazed upon the blue depths of many a placid lake, and the tumultuous rushing of many a mighty river, and have said, peace inhabits those waters; yet I have turned my steps away, to live yet another day. I have asked myself, whether suicide would be a crime in one to whom thus only the portals of the other world could be opened. I have done all, except presenting myself as a soldier or duellist, an object of destruction to my—no, *not* my fellow-mortals, and therefore I have shrunk away. They are not my fellows. The inextinguishable power of life in my frame, and their ephemeral existence, place us wide as the poles asunder. I could not raise a hand against the meanest or the most powerful among them.

Thus I have lived on for many a year—alone, and weary of myself—desirous of death, yet never dying—a mortal immortal. Neither ambition nor avarice can enter my mind, and the ardent love that gnaws at my heart, never to be returned—never to find an equal on which to expend itself—lives there only to torment me.

This very day I conceived a design by which I may end all—without self-slaughter, without making another man a Cain—an expedition, which mortal frame can never survive, even endued with the youth and strength that inhabits mine. Thus I shall put my immortality to the test, and rest for ever—or return, the wonder and benefactor of the human species.

Before I go, a miserable vanity has caused me to pen these pages. I would not die, and leave no name behind. Three centuries have passed since I quaffed the fatal beverage: another year shall not elapse before, encountering gigantic dangers—warring with the powers of frost in their home—beset by famine, toil, and tempest—I yield this body, too tenacious a cage for a soul which thirsts for freedom, to the destructive elements of air and water—or, if I survive, my name shall be recorded as one of the most famous among the sons of men; and, my task achieved, I shall adopt more resolute means, and, by scattering and annihilating the atoms that compose my frame, set at liberty the life imprisoned within, and so cruelly prevented from soaring from this dim earth to a sphere more congenial to its immortal essence.

RAPPACCINI'S DAUGHTER

Nathaniel Hawthorne

Nathaniel Hawthorne (1804–1864) is a key name in the history of the American Gothic. He is the author of the novel *The House of the Seven Gables* (1851) and the collection of short stories in two volumes *Twice-Told Tales* (1837, 1842), which included reprints of such Gothic gems as 'The Minister's Black Veil' (1832) and 'Dr. Heidegger's Experiment' (1837). The latter story featured one of Hawthorne's handful of scientists, a doctor who claims to have received water from the Fountain of Youth. His collection *Mosses from an Old Manse* (1846) collected a few other classics, most notably 'Young Goodman Brown' (1835), 'The Birth-Mark' (1843)—the story of a scientist unhealthily obsessed with a small red birthmark on his wife's cheek—and 'Rappaccini's Daughter' (1844).

'Rappaccini's Daughter', about a woman raised to be poisonous, lends itself to multiple readings: it is simultaneously a warning to zealous parental guardianship, a critique of the corruption of innocence and a study of the femme fatale. But the figure of Beatrice's father, Rappaccini, the botanist who 'cares infinitely more for science than for mankind' and whose 'patients are interesting to him only as subjects for some new experiment', is what grants the story inclusion in this collection.

A YOUNG MAN, NAMED GIOVANNI GUASCONTI, CAME, VERY LONG ago, from the more southern region of Italy, to pursue his studies at the University of Padua. Giovanni, who had but a scanty supply of gold ducats in his pocket, took lodgings in a high and gloomy chamber of an old edifice, which looked not unworthy to have been the palace of a Paduan noble, and which, in fact, exhibited over its entrance the armorial bearings of a family long since extinct. The young stranger, who was not unstudied in the great poem of his country, recollected that one of the ancestors of this family, and perhaps an occupant of this very mansion, had been pictured by Dante as a partaker of the immortal agonies of his Inferno. These reminiscences and associations, together with the tendency to heart-break natural to a young man for the first time out of his native sphere, caused Giovanni to sigh heavily, as he looked around the desolate and ill-furnished apartment.

"Holy Virgin, signor," cried old dame Lisabetta, who, won by the youth's remarkable beauty of person, was kindly endeavouring to give the chamber a habitable air, "what a sigh was that to come out of a young man's heart! Do you find this old mansion gloomy? For the love of heaven, then, put your head out of the window, and you will see as bright sunshine as you have left in Naples."

Guasconti mechanically did as the old woman advised, but could not quite agree with her that the Lombard sunshine was as cheerful as that of southern Italy. Such as it was, however, it fell upon a garden beneath the window, and expended its fostering influences on a variety of plants, which seemed to have been cultivated with exceeding care.

"Does this garden belong to the house?" asked Giovanni.

"Heaven forbid, signor!—unless it were fruitful of better potherbs than any that grow there now," answered old Lisabetta. "No: that garden is cultivated by the own hands of Signor Giacomo Rappaccini, the famous Doctor, who, I warrant him, has been heard of as far as Naples. It is said that he distils these plants into medicines that are as potent as a charm. Oftentimes you may see the signor Doctor at work, and perchance the signora his daughter, too, gathering the strange flowers that grow in the garden."

The old woman had now done what she could for the aspect of the chamber, and, commending the young man to the protection of the saints, took her departure.

Giovanni still found no better occupation than to look down into the garden beneath his window. From its appearance, he judged it to be one of those botanic gardens, which were of earlier date in Padua than elsewhere in Italy, or in the world. Or, not improbably, it might once have been the pleasure-place of an opulent family; for there was the ruin of a marble fountain in the centre, sculptured with rare art, but so wofully shattered that it was impossible to trace the original design from the chaos of remaining fragments. The water, however, continued to gush and sparkle into the sunbeams as cheerfully as ever. A little gurgling sound ascended to the young man's window, and made him feel as if a fountain were an immortal spirit, that sung its song unceasingly, and without heeding the vicissitudes around it; while one century embodied it in marble, and another scattered the perishable garniture on the soil. All about the pool into which the water subsided grew various plants, that seemed to require a plentiful supply of moisture for the nourishment of gigantic leaves, and, in some instances, flowers gorgeously magnificent. There was one shrub in particular, set in a marble vase in the midst of the pool, that bore a profusion of purple blossoms, each of which had the lustre and richness of a gem; and the whole together made a show so resplendent that it seemed enough to illuminate the garden, even had there been no sunshine. Every portion of the soil was peopled with plants and herbs, which, if less beautiful, still bore tokens of assiduous care; as if all had their individual virtues, known to the scientific mind that fostered them. Some were placed in urns, rich with old carving, and others in common garden-pots; some crept serpent-like along the ground, or climbed on high, using whatever means of ascent was offered them. One plant had wreathed itself round a statue of Vertumnus, which was thus quite veiled and shrouded in a drapery of hanging foliage, so happily arranged that it might have served a sculptor for a study.

While Giovanni stood at the window, he heard a rustling behind a screen of leaves, and became aware that a person was at work in the garden. His figure soon emerged into view, and showed itself to be that of no common labourer, but a tall, emaciated, sallow, and sickly-looking man, dressed in a scholar's garb of black. He was beyond the middle term of life, with grey hair, a thin grey beard, and a face singularly marked with intellect and cultivation, but which could never, even in his more youthful days, have expressed much warmth of heart.

Nothing could exceed the intentness with which this scientific gardener examined every shrub which grew in his path; it seemed as if he was looking into their inmost nature, making observations in regard to their creative essence, and discovering why one leaf grew in this shape, and another in that, and wherefore such and such flowers differed among themselves in hue and perfume. Nevertheless, in spite of the deep intelligence on his part, there was no approach to intimacy between himself and these vegetable existences. On the contrary, he avoided their actual touch, or the direct inhaling of their odours, with a caution that impressed Giovanni most disagreeably; for the man's demeanour was that of one walking among malignant influences, such as savage beasts, or deadly snakes, or evil spirits, which, should he allow them one moment of licence, would wreak upon him some terrible fatality. It was strangely frightful to the young man's imagination, to see this air of insecurity in a person cultivating a garden, that most simple and innocent of human toils, and which had been alike the joy and labour of the unfallen parents of the race. Was this garden, then, the Eden of the present world?—and this man, with such a perception of harm in what his own hands caused to grow, was he the Adam?

The distrustful gardener, while plucking away the dead leaves, or pruning the too luxuriant growth of the shrubs, defended his hands with a pair of thick gloves. Nor were these his only armour. When, in his walk through the garden, he came to the magnificent plant that hung its purple gems beside the marble fountain, he placed a kind of mask over his mouth and nostrils, as if all this beauty did but conceal a deadlier malice. But finding his task still too dangerous, he drew back, removed the mask, and called loudly, but in the infirm voice of a person affected with inward disease:

"Beatrice!—Beatrice!"

"Here am I, my father! What would you?" cried a rich and youthful voice from the window of the opposite house; a voice as rich as a tropical sunset, and which made Giovanni, though he knew not why, think of deep hues of purple or crimson, and of perfumes heavily delectable—"Are you in the garden?"

"Yes, Beatrice," answered the gardener, "and I need your help."

Soon there emerged from under a sculptured portal the figure of a young girl, arrayed with as much richness of taste as the most splendid of the flowers, beautiful as the day, and with a bloom so deep and vivid, that one shade more would have been too much. She looked redundant with life, health, and energy; all of which attributes were bound down and compressed, as it were, and girdled tensely, in their luxuriance, by her virgin zone. Yet Giovanni's fancy must have grown morbid, while he looked down into the garden; for the impression which the fair stranger made upon him was as if here were another flower, the human sister of those vegetable ones, as beautiful as they—more beautiful than the richest of them, but still to be touched only with a glove, nor to be approached without a mask. As Beatrice came down the garden-path, it was observable that she handled and inhaled the odour of several of the plants, which her father had most sedulously avoided.

"Here, Beatrice!" said the latter,—"see how many needful offices require to be done to our chief treasure. Yet, shattered as I am, my life might pay the penalty of approaching it so closely as circumstances demand. Henceforth, I fear, this plant must be consigned to your sole charge."

"And gladly will I undertake it," cried again the rich tones of the young lady, as she bent towards the magnificent plant, and opened her arms as if to embrace it. "Yes, my sister, my splendour, it shall be Beatrice's task to nurse and serve thee; and thou shalt reward her with thy kisses and perfume-breath, which to her is as the breath of life!"

Then, with all the tenderness in her manner that was so strikingly expressed in her words, she busied herself with such attentions as the plant seemed to require; and Giovanni, at his lofty window, rubbed his eyes, and almost doubted whether it were a girl tending her favourite flower, or one sister performing the duties of affection to another. The scene soon terminated. Whether Doctor Rappaccini had finished his labours in the garden, or that his watchful eye had caught the stranger's face, he now took his daughter's arm and retired. Night was already closing in; oppressive exhalations seemed to proceed from the plants, and steal upward past the open window; and Giovanni, closing the lattice, went to his couch, and dreamed of a rich flower and beautiful girl. Flower and maiden were different and yet the same, and fraught with some strange peril in either shape.

But there is an influence in the light of morning that tends to rectify whatever errors of fancy, or even of judgment, we may have incurred during the sun's decline, or among the shadows of the night, or in the less wholesome glow of moonshine. Giovanni's first movement on starting from sleep, was to throw open the window, and gaze down into the garden which his dreams had made so fertile of mysteries. He was surprised, and a little ashamed to find how real and matter-of-fact an affair it proved to be, in the first rays of the sun, which gilded the dew-drops that hung upon leaf and blossom, and while giving a brighter beauty to each rare flower, brought everything within the limits of ordinary experience. The young man rejoiced, that, in the heart of the barren city, he had the privilege of overlooking this spot of lovely and luxuriant vegetation. It would serve, he said to himself, as a symbolic language, to keep him in communion with nature. Neither the sickly and thought-worn Doctor Giacomo Rappaccini, it is true, nor his brilliant daughter, were now visible; so that Giovanni could not determine how much of the singularity which he attributed to both, was due to their own qualities, and how much to his wonder-working fancy. But he was inclined to take a most rational view of the whole matter.

In the course of the day, he paid his respects to Signor Pietro Baglioni, professor of medicine in the University, a physician of eminent repute, to whom Giovanni had brought a letter of introduction.

The Professor was an elderly personage, apparently of genial nature, and habits that might almost be called jovial; he kept the young man to dinner, and made himself very agreeable by the freedom and liveliness of his conversation, especially when warmed by a flask or two of Tuscan wine. Giovanni, conceiving that men of science, inhabitants of the same city, must needs be on familiar terms with one another, took an opportunity to mention the name of Dr. Rappaccini. But the Professor did not respond with so much cordiality as he had anticipated.

"Ill would it become a teacher of the divine art of medicine," said Professor Pietro Baglioni, in answer to a question of Giovanni, "to withhold due and well-considered praise of a physician so eminently skilled as Rappaccini. But, on the other hand, I should answer it but scantily to my conscience, were I to permit a worthy youth like yourself, Signor Giovanni, the son of an ancient friend, to imbibe erroneous ideas respecting a man who might hereafter chance to hold your life and death in his hands. The truth is, our worshipful Doctor Rappaccini has as much science as any member of the faculty—with perhaps one single exception—in Padua, or all Italy. But there are certain grave objections to his professional character."

"And what are they?" asked the young man.

"Has my friend Giovanni any disease of body or heart, that he is so inquisitive about physicians?" said the Professor, with a smile. "But as for Rappaccini, it is said of him—and I, who know the man well, can answer for its truth—that he cares infinitely more for science than for mankind. His patients are interesting to him only as subjects for some new experiment. He would sacrifice human life, his own among the rest, or whatever else was dearest to him, for the sake of adding so much as a grain of mustard-seed to the great heap of his accumulated knowledge."

"Methinks he is an awful man, indeed," remarked Guasconti, mentally recalling the cold and purely intellectual aspect of Rappaccini. "And yet, worshipful Professor, is it not a noble spirit? Are there many men capable of so spiritual a love of science?"

"God forbid," answered the Professor, somewhat testily—"at least, unless they take sounder views of the healing art than those adopted by Rappaccini. It is his theory, that all medicinal virtues are comprised within those substances which we term vegetable poisons. These he cultivates with his own hands, and is said even to have produced new varieties of poison, more horribly deleterious than Nature, without the assistance of this learned person, would ever have plagued the world with. That the Signor Doctor does less mischief than might be expected, with such dangerous substances, is undeniable. Now and then, it must be owned, he has effected—or seemed to effect—a marvellous cure. But, to tell you my private mind, Signor Giovanni, he should receive little credit for such instances of success—they being probably the work of chance—but should be held strictly accountable for his failures, which may justly be considered his own work."

The youth might have taken Baglioni's opinions with many grains of allowance, had he known that there was a professional warfare of long continuance between him and Doctor Rappaccini, in which the latter was generally thought to have gained the advantage. If the reader be inclined to judge for himself, we refer him to certain black-letter tracts on both sides, preserved in the medical department of the University of Padua.

"I know not, most learned Professor," returned Giovanni, after musing on what had been said of Rappaccini's exclusive zeal for science—"I know not how dearly this physician may love his art; but surely there is one object more dear to him. He has a daughter."

"Aha!" cried the Professor, with a laugh. "So, now our friend Giovanni's secret is out. You have heard of this daughter, whom all the young men in Padua are wild about, though not half a dozen have ever had the good hap to see her face. I know little of the Signora Beatrice, save that Rappaccini is said to have instructed her deeply in his science, and that, young and beautiful as fame reports her, she is already qualified to fill a professor's chair. Perchance her father destines her for mine! Other absurd rumours there be, not worth talking about, or listening to. So now, Signor Giovanni, drink off your glass of Lacryma."

Guasconti returned to his lodgings somewhat heated with the wine he had quaffed, and which caused his brain to swim with strange fantasies in reference to Doctor Rappaccini and the beautiful Beatrice. On his way, happening to pass by a florist's, he bought a fresh bouquet of flowers.

Ascending to his chamber, he seated himself near the window, but within the shadow thrown by the depth of the wall, so that he could look down into the garden with little risk of being discovered. All beneath his eye was a solitude. The strange plants were basking in the sunshine, and now and then nodding gently to one another, as if in acknowledgement of sympathy and kindred. In the midst, by the shattered fountain, grew the magnificent shrub, with its purple gems clustering all over it; they glowed in the air, and gleamed back again out of the depths of the pool, which thus seemed to overflow with coloured radiance from the rich reflection that was steeped in it. At first, as we have said, the garden was a solitude. Soon, however,—as Giovanni had half-hoped, half-feared, would be the case,—a figure appeared beneath the antique sculptured portal, and came down between the rows of plants, inhaling their various perfumes, as if she were one of those beings of old classic fable, that lived upon sweet

odours. On again beholding Beatrice, the young man was even startled
to perceive how much her beauty exceeded his recollection of it; so
brilliant, so vivid in its character, that she glowed amid the sunlight,
and, as Giovanni whispered to himself, positively illuminated the
more shadowy intervals of the garden path. Her face being now more
revealed than on the former occasion, he was struck by its expression
of simplicity and sweetness; qualities that had not entered into his
idea of her character, and which made him ask anew, what manner
of mortal she might be. Nor did he fail again to observe, or imagine,
an analogy between the beautiful girl and the gorgeous shrub that
hung its gem-like flowers over the fountain; a resemblance which
Beatrice seemed to have indulged a fantastic humour in heightening,
both by the arrangement of her dress and the selection of its hues.

Approaching the shrub, she threw open her arms, as with a passionate ardour, and drew its branches into an intimate embrace; so
intimate, that her features were hidden in its leafy bosom, and her
glistening ringlets all intermingled with the flowers.

"Give me thy breath, my sister," exclaimed Beatrice; "for I am
faint with common air! And give me this flower of thine, which I
separate with gentlest fingers from the stem, and place it close beside
my heart."

With these words, the beautiful daughter of Rappaccini plucked
one of the richest blossoms of the shrub, and was about to fasten it in
her bosom. But now, unless Giovanni's draughts of wine had bewildered his senses, a singular incident occurred. A small orange-coloured
reptile, of the lizard or chameleon species, chanced to be creeping
along the path, just at the feet of Beatrice. It appeared to Giovanni—
but, at the distance from which he gazed, he could scarcely have seen
anything so minute—it appeared to him, however, that a drop or two
of moisture from the broken stem of the flower descended upon the

lizard's head. For an instant, the reptile contorted itself violently, and then lay motionless in the sunshine. Beatrice observed this remarkable phenomenon, and crossed herself, sadly, but without surprise; nor did she therefore hesitate to arrange the fatal flower in her bosom. There it blushed, and almost glimmered with the dazzling effect of a precious stone, adding to her dress and aspect the one appropriate charm, which nothing else in the world could have supplied. But Giovanni, out of the shadow of his window, bent forward and shrank back, and murmured and trembled.

"Am I awake? Have I my senses?" said he to himself. "What is this being?—beautiful, shall I call her?—or inexpressibly terrible?"

Beatrice now strayed carelessly through the garden, approaching closer beneath Giovanni's window, so that he was compelled to thrust his head quite out of its concealment, in order to gratify the intense and painful curiosity which she excited. At this moment, there came a beautiful insect over the garden wall; it had perhaps wandered through the city and found no flowers nor verdure among those antique haunts of men, until the heavy perfumes of Doctor Rappaccini's shrubs had lured it from afar. Without alighting on the flowers, this winged brightness seemed to be attracted by Beatrice, and lingered in the air and fluttered about her head. Now here it could not be but that Giovanni Guasconti's eyes deceived him. Be that as it might, he fancied that while Beatrice was gazing at the insect with childish delight, it grew faint and fell at her feet!—its bright wings shivered! it was dead!—from no cause that he could discern, unless it were the atmosphere of her breath. Again Beatrice crossed herself and sighed heavily, as she bent over the dead insect.

An impulsive movement of Giovanni drew her eyes to the window. There she beheld the beautiful head of the young man—rather a Grecian than an Italian head, with fair, regular features, and a glistening of gold among his ringlets—gazing down upon her like a being that hovered in mid-air. Scarcely knowing what he did, Giovanni threw down the bouquet which he had hitherto held in his hand.

"Signora," said he, "there are pure and healthful flowers. Wear them for the sake of Giovanni Guasconti!"

"Thanks, Signor," replied Beatrice, with her rich voice, that came forth as if it were like a gush of music; and with a mirthful expression half childish and half woman-like. "I accept your gift, and would fain recompense it with this precious purple flower; but if I toss it into the air, it will not reach you. So Signor Guasconti must even content himself with my thanks."

She lifted the bouquet from the ground, and then as if inwardly ashamed at having stepped aside from her maidenly reserve to respond to a stranger's greeting, passed swiftly homeward through the garden. But, few as the moments were, it seemed to Giovanni when she was on the point of vanishing beneath the sculptured portal, that his beautiful bouquet was already beginning to wither in her grasp. It was an idle thought; there could be no possibility of distinguishing a faded flower from a fresh one, at so great a distance.

For many days after this incident, the young man avoided the window that looked into Doctor Rappaccini's garden, as if something ugly and monstrous would have blasted his eye-sight, had he been betrayed into a glance. He felt conscious of having put himself, to a certain extent, within the influence of an unintelligible power, by the communication which he had opened with Beatrice. The wisest course would have been, if his heart were in any real danger, to quit his lodgings and Padua itself, at once; the next wiser, to have accustomed himself, as far as possible, to the familiar and daylight view of Beatrice; thus bringing her rigidly and systematically within the limits of ordinary experience. Least of all, while avoiding her sight, should

Giovanni have remained so near this extraordinary being, that the proximity and possibility even of intercourse, should give a kind of substance and reality to the wild vagaries which his imagination ran riot continually in producing. Guasconti had not a deep heart—or at all events, its depths were not sounded now—but he had a quick fancy, and an ardent southern temperament, which rose every instant to a higher fever-pitch. Whether or no Beatrice possessed those terrible attributes—that fatal breath—the affinity with those so beautiful and deadly flowers—which were indicated by what Giovanni had witnessed, she had at least instilled a fierce and subtle poison into his system. It was not love, although her rich beauty was a madness to him; nor horror, even while he fancied her spirit to be imbued with the same baneful essence that seemed to pervade her physical frame; but a wild offspring of both love and horror that had each parent in it, and burned like one and shivered like the other. Giovanni knew not what to dread; still less did he know what to hope; yet hope and dread kept a continual warfare in his breast, alternately vanquishing one another and starting up afresh to renew the contest. Blessed are all simple emotions, be they dark or bright! It is the lurid intermixture of the two that produces the illuminating blaze of the infernal regions.

Sometimes he endeavoured to assuage the fever of his spirit by a rapid walk through the streets of Padua, or beyond its gates; his footsteps kept time with the throbbings of his brain, so that the walk was apt to accelerate itself to a race. One day, he found himself arrested; his arm was seized by a portly personage who had turned back on recognizing the young man, and expended much breath in overtaking him.

"Signor Giovanni!—stay, my young friend!" cried he. "Have you forgotten me? That might well be the case, if I were as much altered as yourself."

It was Baglioni, whom Giovanni had avoided, ever since their first meeting, from a doubt that the Professor's sagacity would look too deeply into his secrets. Endeavouring to recover himself, he stared forth wildly from his inner world into the outer one, and spoke like a man in a dream.

"Yes; I am Giovanni Guasconti. You are Professor Pietro Baglioni. Now let me pass!"

"Not yet—not yet, Signor Giovanni Guasconti," said the Professor, smiling, but at the same time scrutinizing the youth with an earnest glance. "What, did I grow up side by side with your father, and shall his son pass me like a stranger, in these old streets of Padua? Stand still, Signor Giovanni; for we must have a word or two before we part."

"Speedily, then, most worshipful Professor—speedily!" said Giovanni, with feverish impatience. "Does not your worship see that I am in haste?"

Now, while he was speaking, there came a man in black along the street, stooping and moving feebly, like a person in inferior health. His face was all overspread with a most sickly and sallow hue, but yet so pervaded with an expression of piercing and active intellect, that an observer might easily have overlooked the merely physical attributes, and have seen only this wonderful energy. As he passed, this person exchanged a cold and distant salutation with Baglioni, but fixed his eyes upon Giovanni with an intentness that seemed to bring out whatever was within him worthy of notice. Nevertheless, there was a peculiar quietness in the look, as if taking merely a speculative, not a human interest, in the young man.

"It is Doctor Rappaccini!" whispered the Professor, when the stranger had passed. "Has he ever seen your face before?"

"Not that I know," answered Giovanni, starting at the name.

"He *has* seen you!—he must have seen you!" said Baglioni, hastily. "For some purpose or other, this man of science is making a study of you. I know that look of his! It is the same that coldly illuminates his face, as he bends over a bird, a mouse, or a butterfly, which, in pursuance of some experiment, he has killed by the perfume of a flower;—a look as deep as nature itself, but without nature's warmth of love. Signor Giovanni, I will stake my life upon it, you are the subject of one of Rappaccini's experiments!"

"Will you make a fool of me?" cried Giovanni, passionately. "*That*, Signor Professor, were an untoward experiment."

"Patience, patience!" replied the imperturbable Professor. "I tell thee, my poor Giovanni, that Rappaccini has a scientific interest in thee. Thou hast fallen into fearful hands! And the Signora Beatrice? What part does she act in this mystery?"

But Guasconti, finding Baglioni's pertinacity intolerable, here broke away, and was gone before the Professor could again seize his arm. He looked after the young man intently, and shook his head.

"This must not be," said Baglioni to himself. "The youth is the son of my old friend, and shall not come to any harm from which the arcana of medical science can preserve him. Besides, it is too insufferable an impertinence in Rappaccini thus to snatch the lad out of my own hands, as I may say, and make use of him for his infernal experiments. This daughter of his! It shall be looked to. Perchance, most learned Rappaccini, I may foil you where you little dream of it!"

Meanwhile, Giovanni had pursued a circuitous route, and at length found himself at the door of his lodgings. As he crossed the threshold, he was met by old Lisabetta, who smirked and smiled, and was evidently desirous to attract his attention; vainly, however, as the ebullition of his feelings had momentarily subsided into a cold and dull vacuity. He turned his eyes full upon the withered face that was puckering itself into a smile, but seemed to behold it not. The old dame, therefore, laid her grasp upon his cloak.

"Signor!—Signor!" whispered she, still with a smile over the whole breadth of her visage, so that it looked not unlike a grotesque carving in wood, darkened by centuries—"Listen, Signor! There is a private entrance into the garden!"

"What do you say?" exclaimed Giovanni, turning quickly about, as if an inanimate thing should start into feverish life. "A private entrance into Doctor Rappaccini's garden!"

"Hush! hush!—not so loud!" whispered Lisabetta, putting her hand over his mouth. "Yes; into the worshipful Doctor's garden, where you may see all his fine shrubbery. Many a young man in Padua would give gold to be admitted among those flowers."

Giovanni put a piece of gold into her hand.

"Show me the way," said he.

A surmise, probably excited by his conversation with Baglioni, crossed his mind, that this interposition of old Lisabetta might perchance be connected with the intrigue, whatever were its nature, in which the Professor seemed to suppose that Doctor Rappaccini was involving him. But such a suspicion, though it disturbed Giovanni, was inadequate to restrain him. The instant he was aware of the possibility of approaching Beatrice, it seemed an absolute necessity of his existence to do so. It mattered not whether she were angel or demon; he was irrevocably within her sphere, and must obey the law that whirled him onward, in ever lessening circles, towards a result which he did not attempt to foreshadow. And yet, strange to say, there came across him a sudden doubt, whether this intense interest on his part were not delusory—whether it were really of so deep and positive a nature as to justify him in now thrusting himself into an incalculable position—whether it were not merely the fantasy of a young man's brain, only slightly, or not at all, connected with his heart!

He paused—hesitated—turned half about—but again went on. His withered guide led him along several obscure passages, and finally undid a door, through which, as it was opened, there came the sight and sound of rustling leaves, with the broken sunshine glimmering among them. Giovanni stepped forth, and forcing himself through the entanglement of a shrub that wreathed its tendrils over the hidden entrance, he stood beneath his own window, in the open area of Doctor Rappaccini's garden.

How often is it the case, that, when impossibilities have come to pass, and dreams have condensed their misty substance into tangible realities, we find ourselves calm, and even coldly self-possessed, amid circumstances which it would have been a delirium of joy or agony to anticipate! Fate delights to thwart us thus. Passion will choose his own time to rush upon the scene, and lingers sluggishly behind, when an appropriate adjustment of events would seem to summon his appearance. So was it now with Giovanni. Day after day, his pulses had throbbed with feverish blood, at the improbable idea of an interview with Beatrice, and of standing with her, face to face, in this very garden, basking in the oriental sunshine of her beauty, and snatching from her full gaze the mystery which he deemed the riddle of his own existence. But now there was a singular and untimely equanimity within his breast. He threw a glance around the garden to discover if Beatrice or her father were present, and perceiving that he was alone, began a critical observation of the plants.

The aspect of one and all of them dissatisfied him; their gorgeousness seemed fierce, passionate, and even unnatural. There was hardly an individual shrub which a wanderer, straying by himself through a forest, would not have been startled to find growing wild, as if an unearthly face had glared at him out of the thicket. Several, also, would have shocked a delicate instinct by an appearance of artificialness, indicating that there had been such commixture, and, as it were, adultery of various vegetable species, that the production was no longer of God's making, but the monstrous offspring of man's depraved fancy, glowing with only an evil mockery of beauty. They were probably the result of experiment, which, in one or two cases, had succeeded in mingling plants individually lovely into a compound possessing the questionable and ominous character that distinguished the whole growth of the garden. In fine, Giovanni recognized but two or three plants in the collection, and those of a kind that he well knew to be poisonous. While busy with these contemplations, he heard the rustling of a silken garment, and turning, beheld Beatrice emerging from beneath the sculptured portal.

Giovanni had not considered with himself what should be his deportment; whether he should apologize for his intrusion into the garden, or assume that he was there with the privity, at least, if not by the desire, of Doctor Rappaccini or his daughter. But Beatrice's manner placed him at his ease, though leaving him still in doubt by what agency he had gained admittance. She came lightly along the path, and met him near the broken fountain. There was surprise in her face, but brightened by a simple and kind expression of pleasure.

"You are a connoisseur in flowers, Signor," said Beatrice with a smile, alluding to the bouquet which he had flung her from the window. "It is no marvel, therefore, if the sight of my father's rare collection has tempted you to take a nearer view. If he were here, he could tell you many strange and interesting facts as to the nature and habits of these shrubs, for he has spent a life-time in such studies, and this garden is his world."

"And yourself, lady"—observed Giovanni—"if fame says true, you, likewise, are deeply skilled in the virtues indicated by these rich blossoms, and these spicy perfumes. Would you deign to be my instructress, I should prove an apter scholar than under Signor Rappaccini himself."

"Are there such idle rumours?" asked Beatrice, with the music of a pleasant laugh. "Do people say that I am skilled in my father's science of plants? What a jest is there! No; though I have grown up among these flowers, I know no more of them than their hues and perfume; and sometimes, methinks I would fain rid myself of even that small knowledge. There are many flowers here, and those not the least brilliant, that shock and offend me, when they meet my eye. But, pray, Signor, do not believe these stories about my science. Believe nothing of me save what you see with your own eyes."

"And must I believe all that I have seen with my own eyes?" asked Giovanni pointedly, while the recollection of former scenes made him shrink. "No, Signora, you demand too little of me. Bid me believe nothing, save what comes from your own lips."

It would appear that Beatrice understood him. There came a deep flush to her cheek; but she looked full into Giovanni's eyes, and responded to his gaze of uneasy suspicion with a queen-like haughtiness.

"I do so bid you, Signor!" she replied. "Forget whatever you may have fancied in regard to me. If true to the outward senses, still it may be false in its essence. But the words of Beatrice Rappaccini's lips are true from the heart outward. Those you may believe!"

A fervour glowed in her whole aspect, and beamed upon Giovanni's consciousness like the light of truth itself. But while she spoke, there was a fragrance in the atmosphere around her rich and delightful, though evanescent, yet which the young man, from an indefinable reluctance, scarcely dared to draw into his lungs. It might be the odour of the flowers. Could it be Beatrice's breath, which thus embalmed her words with a strange richness, as if by steeping them in her heart? A faintness passed like a shadow over Giovanni, and flitted away; he seemed to gaze through the beautiful girl's eyes into her transparent soul, and felt no more doubt or fear.

The tinge of passion that had coloured Beatrice's manner vanished; she became gay, and appeared to derive a pure delight from her communion with the youth, not unlike what the maiden of a lonely island might have felt, conversing with a voyager from the civilized world. Evidently her experience of life had been confined within the limits of that garden. She talked now about matters as simple as the daylight or summer clouds, and now asked questions in reference to the city, or Giovanni's distant home, his friends, his mother, and his sisters; questions indicating such seclusion, and such lack of familiarity with modes and forms, that Giovanni responded as if to an infant. Her spirit gushed out before him like a fresh rill, that was just catching its first glimpse of the sunlight, and wondering, at the reflections of earth and sky which were flung into its bosom. There came thoughts, too, from a deep source, and fantasies of a gem-like brilliancy, as if diamonds and rubies sparkled upward among the bubbles of the fountain. Ever and anon, there gleamed across the young man's mind a sense of wonder, that he should be walking side by side with the being who had so wrought upon his imagination—whom he had idealized in such hues of terror—in whom he had positively witnessed such manifestations of dreadful attributes—that he should be conversing with Beatrice like a brother, and should find her so human and so maiden-like. But such reflections were only momentary; the effect of her character was too real, not to make itself familiar at once.

In this free intercourse, they had strayed through the garden, and now, after many turns among its avenues, were come to the shattered fountain, beside which grew the magnificent shrub with its treasury of glowing blossoms. A fragrance was diffused from it, which Giovanni recognized as identical with that which he had attributed to Beatrice's breath, but incomparably more powerful. As her eyes fell upon it, Giovanni beheld her press her hand to her bosom, as if her heart were throbbing suddenly and painfully.

"For the first time in my life," murmured she, addressing the shrub, "I had forgotten thee!"

"I remember, signora," said Giovanni, "that you once promised to reward me with one of these living gems for the bouquet, which I had the happy boldness to fling to your feet. Permit me now to pluck it as a memorial of this interview."

He made a step towards the shrub, with extended hand. But Beatrice darted forward, uttering a shriek that went through his heart like a dagger. She caught his hand, and drew it back with the whole force of her slender figure. Giovanni felt her touch thrilling through his fibres.

"Touch it not!" exclaimed she, in a voice of agony. "Not for thy life! It is fatal!"

Then, hiding her face, she fled from him, and vanished beneath the sculptured portal. As Giovanni followed her with his eyes, he beheld the emaciated figure and pale intelligence of Doctor Rappaccini, who had been watching the scene, he knew not how long, within the shadow of the entrance.

No sooner was Guasconti alone in his chamber, than the image of Beatrice came back to his passionate musings, invested with all the witchery that had been gathering around it ever since his first glimpse of her, and now likewise imbued with a tender warmth of girlish womanhood. She was human: her nature was endowed with all gentle and feminine qualities; she was worthiest to be worshipped; she was capable, surely, on her part, of the height and heroism of love. Those tokens, which he had hitherto considered as proofs of a frightful peculiarity in her physical and moral system, were now either forgotten, or, by the subtle sophistry of passion, transmuted into a golden crown of enchantment, rendering Beatrice the more admirable, by so much as she was the more unique. Whatever had looked ugly, was now beautiful; or, if incapable of such a change, it stole away and hid itself among those shapeless half-ideas, which throng the dim region beyond the daylight of our perfect conscious-ness. Thus did Giovanni spend the night, nor fell asleep, until the dawn had begun to awake the slumbering flowers in Doctor Rappaccini's garden, whither his dreams doubtless led him. Up rose the sun in his due season, and flinging his beams upon the young man's eyelids, awoke him to a sense of pain. When thoroughly aroused, he became sensible of a burning and tingling agony in his hand—in his right hand—the very hand which Beatrice had grasped in her own, when he was on the point of plucking one of the gem-like flowers. On the back of that hand there was now a purple print, like that of four small fingers, and the likeness of a slender thumb upon his wrist.

Oh, how stubbornly does love—or even that cunning semblance of love which flourishes in the imagination, but strikes no depth of root into the heart—how stubbornly does it hold its faith, until the moment come, when it is doomed to vanish into thin mist! Giovanni wrapt a handkerchief about his hand, and wondered what evil thing had stung him, and soon forgot his pain in a reverie of Beatrice.

After the first interview, a second was in the inevitable course of what we call fate. A third; a fourth; and a meeting with Beatrice in the garden was no longer an incident in Giovanni's daily life, but the whole space in which he might be said to live; for the anticipation and memory of that ecstatic hour made up the remainder. Nor was it otherwise with the daughter of Rappaccini. She watched for the youth's appearance, and flew to his side with confidence as unreserved as if they had been playmates from early infancy—as if they were such playmates still. If, by any unwonted chance, he failed to come at the appointed moment, she stood beneath the window, and sent up the rich sweetness of her tones to float around him in his chamber, and echo and reverberate throughout his heart—"Giovanni! Giovanni! Why tarriest thou? Come down!" And down he hastened into that Eden of poisonous flowers.

But, with all this intimate familiarity, there was still a reserve in Beatrice's demeanour, so rigidly and invariably sustained, that the idea of infringing it scarcely occurred to his imagination. By all appreciable signs, they loved; they had looked love, with eyes that conveyed the holy secret from the depths of one soul into the depths of the other, as if it were too sacred to be whispered by the way; they had even spoken love, in those gushes of passion when their spirits darted forth in articulated breath, like tongues of long-hidden flame; and yet there had been no seal of lips, no clasp of hands, nor any slightest caress, such as love claims and hallows. He had never touched one of the gleaming ringlets of her hair; her garment—so marked was the physical barrier between them—had never been waved against him by a breeze. On the few occasions when Giovanni had seemed tempted to overstep the limit, Beatrice grew so sad, so stern, and withal wore such a look of desolate separation, shuddering at itself, that not a spoken word was requisite to repel him. At such times, he was startled at the horrible suspicions that rose, monster-like, out of the caverns of his heart, and stared him in the face; his love grew thin and faint as the morning-mist; his doubts alone had substance. But when Beatrice's face brightened again, after the momentary shadow, she was transformed at once from the mysterious, questionable being, whom he had watched with so much awe and horror; she was now the beautiful and unsophisticated girl, whom he felt that his spirit knew with a certainty beyond all other knowledge.

A considerable time had now passed since Giovanni's last meeting with Baglioni. One morning, however, he was disagreeably surprised by a visit from the Professor, whom he had scarcely thought of for whole weeks, and would willingly have forgotten still longer. Given up, as he had long been, to a pervading excitement, he could tolerate no companions, except upon condition of their perfect sympathy with his present state of feeling. Such sympathy was not to be expected from Professor Baglioni.

The visitor chatted carelessly, for a few moments, about the gossip of the city and the University, and then took up another topic.

"I have been reading an old classic author lately," said he, "and met with a story that strangely interested me. Possibly you may remember it. It is of an Indian prince, who sent a beautiful woman as a present to Alexander the Great. She was as lovely as the dawn, and gorgeous as the sunset; but what especially distinguished her was a certain rich perfume in her breath—richer than a garden of Persian roses. Alexander, as was natural to a youthful conqueror, fell in love at first sight with this magnificent stranger. But a certain sage physician, happening to be present, discovered a terrible secret in regard to her."

"And what was that?" asked Giovanni, turning his eyes downward to avoid those of the Professor.

"That this lovely woman," continued Baglioni, with emphasis, "had been nourished with poisons from her birth upward, until her whole nature was so imbued with them, that she herself had become the deadliest poison in existence. Poison was her element of life. With that rich perfume of her breath, she blasted the very air. Her love would have been poison!—her embrace death! Is not this a marvellous tale?"

"A childish fable," answered Giovanni, nervously starting from his chair. "I marvel how your worship finds time to read such nonsense, among your graver studies."

"By the bye," said the Professor, looking uneasily about him, "what singular fragrance is this in your apartment? Is it the perfume of your gloves? It is faint, but delicious, and yet, after all, by no means agreeable. Were I to breathe it long, methinks it would make me ill. It is like the breath of a flower—but I see no flowers in the chamber."

"Nor are there any," replied Giovanni, who had turned pale as the Professor spoke; "nor, I think, is there any fragrance, except in your worship's imagination. Odours, being a sort of element combined of the sensual and the spiritual, are apt to deceive us in this manner. The recollection of a perfume—the bare idea of it—may easily be mistaken for a present reality."

"Ay; but my sober imagination does not often play such tricks," said Baglioni; "and were I to fancy any kind of odour, it would be that of some vile apothecary drug, wherewith my fingers are likely enough to be imbued. Our worshipful friend Rappaccini, as I have heard, tinctures his medicaments with odours richer than those of Araby. Doubtless, likewise, the fair and learned Signora Beatrice would minister to her patients with draughts as sweet as a maiden's breath. But woe to him that sips them!"

Giovanni's face evinced many contending emotions. The tone in which the Professor alluded to the pure and lovely daughter of Rappaccini was a torture to his soul; and yet, the intimation of a view of her character, opposite to his own, gave instantaneous distinctness to a thousand dim suspicions, which now grinned at him like so many demons. But he strove hard to quell them, and to respond to Baglioni with a true lover's perfect faith.

"Signor Professor," said he, "you were my father's friend—perchance, too, it is your purpose to act a friendly part towards his son. I would fain feel nothing towards you save respect and deference. But I pray you to observe, Signor, that there is one subject on which we must not speak. You know not the Signora Beatrice. You cannot, therefore, estimate the wrong—the blasphemy, I may even say—that is offered to her character by a light or injurious word."

"Giovanni!—my poor Giovanni!" answered the Professor, with a calm expression of pity, "I know this wretched girl far better than yourself. You shall hear the truth in respect to the poisoner Rappaccini, and his poisonous daughter. Yes; poisonous as she is beautiful! Listen! for even should you do violence to my grey hairs, it shall not silence me. That old fable of the Indian woman has become a truth, by the deep and deadly science of Rappaccini, and in the person of the lovely Beatrice!"

Giovanni groaned, and hid his face.

"Her father," continued Baglioni, "was not restrained by natural affection from offering up his child, in this horrible manner, as the victim of his insane zeal for science. For—let us do him justice—he is as true a man of science as ever distilled his own heart in an alembic. What, then, will be your fate? Beyond a doubt, you are selected as the material of some new experiment. Perhaps the result is to be death—perhaps a fate more awful still! Rappaccini, with what he calls the interest of science before his eyes, will hesitate at nothing."

"It is a dream!" muttered Giovanni to himself; "surely, it is a dream!"

"But," resumed the Professor, "be of good cheer, son of my friend! It is not yet too late for the rescue. Possibly, we may even succeed in bringing back this miserable child within the limits of ordinary nature, from which her father's madness has estranged her. Behold this little silver vase! It was wrought by the hands of the renowned Benvenuto Cellini, and is well worthy to be a love-gift to the fairest dame in Italy. But its contents are invaluable. One little sip of this antidote would have rendered the most virulent poisons of the Borgias innocuous. Doubt not that it will be as efficacious against those of Rappaccini. Bestow the vase, and the precious liquid within it, on your Beatrice, and hopefully await the result."

Baglioni laid a small, exquisitely-wrought silver phial on the table, and withdrew, leaving what he had said to produce its effect upon the young man's mind.

"We will thwart Rappaccini yet!" thought he, chuckling to himself, as he descended the stairs. "But, let us confess the truth of him, he is a wonderful man!—a wonderful man, indeed! A vile empiric, however, in his practice, and therefore not to be tolerated by those who respect the good old rules of the medical profession!"

Throughout Giovanni's whole acquaintance with Beatrice, he had occasionally, as we have said, been haunted by dark surmises as to her character. Yet, so thoroughly had she made herself felt by him as a simple, natural, most affectionate and guileless creature, that the image now held up by Professor Baglioni, looked as strange and incredible, as if it were not in accordance with his own original conception. True, there were ugly recollections connected with his first glimpses of the beautiful girl; he could not quite forget the bouquet that withered in her grasp, and the insect that perished amid the sunny air, by no ostensible agency save the fragrance of her breath. These incidents, however, dissolving in the pure light of her character, had no longer the efficacy of facts, but were acknowledged as mistaken fantasies, by whatever testimony of the senses they might appear to be substantiated. There is something truer and more real, than what we can see with the eyes, and touch with the finger. On such better evidence, had Giovanni founded his confidence in Beatrice, though rather by the necessary force of her high attributes, than by any deep and generous faith on his part. But, now, his spirit was incapable of sustaining itself at the height to which the early enthusiasm of passion had exalted it; he fell down, grovelling among earthly doubts, and defiled therewith the pure whiteness of Beatrice's image. Not that he gave her up; he did but distrust. He resolved to institute some decisive test that should satisfy him, once for all, whether there were those dreadful peculiarities in her physical nature, which could not be supposed to exist without some corresponding monstrosity of soul. His eyes, gazing down afar, might have deceived him as to the lizard, the insect, and the flowers. But if he could witness, at the distance of a few paces, the sudden blight of one fresh and healthful flower in Beatrice's hand, there would be room for no further question. With this idea, he hastened to the florist's, and purchased a bouquet that was still gemmed with the morning dew-drops.

It was now the customary hour of his daily interview with Beatrice. Before descending into the garden, Giovanni failed not to look at his figure in the mirror; a vanity to be expected in a beautiful young man, yet, as displaying itself at that troubled and feverish moment, the token of a certain shallowness of feeling and insincerity of character. He did gaze, however, and said to himself, that his features had never before possessed so rich a grace, nor his eyes such vivacity, nor his cheeks so warm a hue of superabundant life.

"At least," thought he, "her poison has not yet insinuated itself into my system. I am no flower to perish in her grasp!"

With that thought, he turned his eyes on the bouquet, which he had never once laid aside from his hand. A thrill of indefinable horror shot through his frame, on perceiving that those dewy flowers were already beginning to droop; they wore the aspect of things that had been fresh and lovely, yesterday. Giovanni grew white as marble, and stood motionless before the mirror, staring at his own reflection there, as at the likeness of something frightful. He remembered Baglioni's remark about the fragrance that seemed to pervade the chamber. It must have been the poison in his breath! Then he shuddered—shuddered at himself! Recovering from his stupor, he began to watch, with curious eye, a spider that was busily at work, hanging its web from the antique cornice of the apartment, crossing and re-crossing the artful system of interwoven lines, as vigorous and active a spider as ever dangled from an old ceiling. Giovanni bent towards the insect, and emitted a deep, long breath. The spider suddenly ceased its toil; the web vibrated with a tremor originating in the body of the small artisan. Again Giovanni sent forth a breath, deeper, longer, and imbued with a venomous feeling out of his heart; he knew not whether he were wicked, or only desperate. The spider made a convulsive gripe with his limbs, and hung dead across the window.

"Accursed! accursed!" muttered Giovanni, addressing himself. "Hast thou grown so poisonous, that this deadly insect perishes by thy breath?"

At that moment, a rich, sweet voice came floating up from the garden:—

"Giovanni! Giovanni! It is past the hour! Why tarriest thou? Come down!"

"Yes," muttered Giovanni again—"she is the only being whom my breath may not slay! Would that it might!"

He rushed down, and, in an instant, was standing before the bright and loving eyes of Beatrice. A moment ago, his wrath and despair had been so fierce that he could have desired nothing so much as to wither her by a glance. But, with her actual presence, there came

influences which had too real an existence to be at once shaken off;
recollections of the delicate and benign power of her feminine nature,
which had so often enveloped him in a religious calm; recollections
of many a holy and passionate out-gush of her heart, when the pure
fountain had been unsealed from its depths, and made visible in its
transparency to his mental eye; recollections which, had Giovanni
known how to estimate them, would have assured him that all this
ugly mystery was but an earthly illusion, and that, whatever mist of
evil might seem to have gathered over her, the real Beatrice was a
heavenly angel. Incapable as he was of such high faith, still her presence had not utterly lost its magic. Giovanni's rage was quelled into
an aspect of sullen insensibility. Beatrice, with a quick spiritual sense,
immediately felt that there was a gulf of blackness between them,
which neither he nor she could pass. They walked on together, sad
and silent, and came thus to the marble fountain, and to its pool of
water on the ground, in the midst of which grew the shrub that bore
gem-like blossoms. Giovanni was affrighted at the eager enjoyment—
the appetite, as it were—with which he found himself inhaling the
fragrance of the flowers.

"Beatrice," asked he, abruptly, "whence came this shrub?"

"My father created it," answered she, with simplicity.

"Created it! created it!" repeated Giovanni. "What mean you,
Beatrice?"

"He is a man fearfully acquainted with the secrets of nature,"
replied Beatrice; "and, at the hour when I first drew breath, this plant
sprang from the soil, the offspring of his science, of his intellect, while
I was but his earthly child. Approach it not!" continued she, observing
with terror that Giovanni was drawing nearer to the shrub. "It has
qualities that you little dream of. But I, dearest Giovanni,—I grew up
and blossomed with the plant, and was nourished with its breath. It

was my sister, and I loved it with a human affection: for—alas! hast thou not suspected it?—there was an awful doom."

Here Giovanni frowned so darkly upon her that Beatrice paused and trembled. But her faith in his tenderness reassured her, and made her blush that she had doubted for an instant.

"There was an awful doom," she continued,—"the effect of my father's fatal love of science—which estranged me from all society of my kind. Until Heaven sent thee, dearest Giovanni, oh! how lonely was thy poor Beatrice!"

"Was it a hard doom?" asked Giovanni, fixing his eyes upon her.

"Only of late have I known how hard it was," answered she, tenderly. "Oh, yes; but my heart was torpid, and therefore quiet."

Giovanni's rage broke forth from his sullen gloom like a lightning-flash out of a dark cloud.

"Accursed one!" cried he, with venomous scorn and anger—"and finding thy solitude wearisome, thou hast severed me, likewise, from all the warmth of life, and enticed me into thy region of unspeakable horror!"

"Giovanni!" exclaimed Beatrice, turning her large bright eyes upon his face. The force of his words had not found its way into her mind; she was merely thunderstruck.

"Yes, poisonous thing!" repeated Giovanni, beside himself with passion—"thou hast done it! Thou hast blasted me! Thou hast filled my veins with poison! Thou hast made me as hateful, as ugly, as loathsome and deadly a creature as thyself,—a world's wonder of hideous monstrosity! Now—if our breath be happily as fatal to ourselves as to all others—let us join our lips in one kiss of unutterable hatred, and so die!"

"What has befallen me?" murmured Beatrice, with a low moan out of her heart. "Holy Virgin, pity me, a poor heart-broken child!"

"Thou! dost thou pray?" cried Giovanni, still with the same fiendish scorn. "Thy very prayers, as they come from thy lips, taint the atmosphere with death. Yes, yes; let us pray! Let us to church, and dip our fingers in the holy water at the portal! They that come after us will perish as by a pestilence. Let us sign crosses in the air! It will be scattering curses abroad in the likeness of holy symbols!"

"Giovanni," said Beatrice calmly, for her grief was beyond passion, "Why dost thou join thyself with me thus in those terrible words? I, it is true, am the horrible thing thou namest me. But thou!—what hast thou to do, save with one other shudder at my hideous misery, to go forth out of the garden, and mingle with thy race, and forget that there ever crawled on earth such a monster as poor Beatrice?"

"Dost thou pretend ignorance?" asked Giovanni, scowling upon her. "Behold! This power have I gained from the pure daughter of Rappaccini!"

There was a swarm of summer-insects flitting through the air, in search of the food promised by the flower-odours of the fatal garden. They circled round Giovanni's head, and were evidently attracted towards him by the same influence which had drawn them, for an instant, within the sphere of several of the shrubs. He sent forth a breath among them, and smiled bitterly at Beatrice, as at least a score of the insects fell dead upon the ground.

"I see it! I see it!" shrieked Beatrice. "It is my father's fatal science? No, no, Giovanni; it was not I! Never, never! I dreamed only to love thee, and be with thee a little time, and so to let thee pass away, leaving but thine image in mine heart. For, Giovanni—believe it—though my body be nourished with poison, my spirit is God's creature, and craves love as its daily food. But my father!—he has united us in this fearful sympathy. Yes; spurn me!—tread upon me!—kill me! Oh, what is death, after such words as thine? But it was not I! Not for a world of bliss would I have done it!"

Giovanni's passion had exhausted itself in its outburst from his lips. There now came across him a sense, mournful, and not without tenderness, of the intimate and peculiar relationship between Beatrice and himself. They stood, as it were, in an utter solitude, which would be made none the less solitary by the densest throng of human life. Ought not, then, the desert of humanity around them to press this insulated pair closer together? If they should be cruel to one another, who was there to be kind to them? Besides, thought Giovanni, might there not still be a hope of his returning within the limits of ordinary nature, and leading Beatrice—the redeemed Beatrice—by the hand? Oh, weak, and selfish, and unworthy spirit, that could dream of an earthly union and earthly happiness as possible, after such deep love had been so bitterly wronged as was Beatrice's love by Giovanni's blighting words! No, no; there could be no such hope. She must pass heavily, with that broken heart, across the borders—she must bathe her hurts in some fount of Paradise, and forget her grief in the light of immortality—and *there* be well!

But Giovanni did not know it.

"Dear Beatrice," said he, approaching her, while she shrank away, as always, at his approach, but now with a different impulse,—"dearest Beatrice, our fate is not yet so desperate. Behold! There is a medicine, potent, as a wise physician has assured me, and almost divine in its efficacy. It is composed of ingredients the most opposite to those by which thy awful father has brought this calamity upon thee and me. It is distilled of blessed herbs. Shall we not quaff it together, and thus be purified from evil?"

"Give it me!" said Beatrice, extending her hand to receive the little silver phial which Giovanni took from his bosom. She added, with a peculiar emphasis: "I will drink—but do thou await the result."

She put Baglioni's antidote to her lips; and, at the same moment, the figure of Rappaccini emerged from the portal, and came slowly towards the marble fountain. As he drew near, the pale man of science seemed to gaze with a triumphant expression at the beautiful youth and maiden, as might an artist who should spend his life in achieving a picture or a group of statuary, and finally be satisfied with his success. He paused—his bent form grew erect with conscious power, he spread out his hand over them, in the attitude of a father imploring a blessing upon his children. But those were the same hands that had thrown poison into the stream of their lives! Giovanni trembled. Beatrice shuddered very nervously, and pressed her hand upon her heart.

"My daughter," said Rappaccini, "thou art no longer lonely in the world! Pluck one of those precious gems from thy sister shrub, and bid thy bridegroom wear it in his bosom. It will not harm him now! My science, and the sympathy between thee and him, have so wrought within his system, that he now stands apart from common men, as thou dost, daughter of my pride and triumph, from ordinary women. Pass on, then, through the world, most dear to one another, and dreadful to all besides!"

"My father," said Beatrice, feebly—and still, as she spoke, she kept her hand upon her heart—"wherefore didst thou inflict this miserable doom upon thy child?"

"Miserable!" exclaimed Rappaccini. "What mean you, foolish girl? Dost thou deem it misery to be endowed with marvellous gifts, against which no power nor strength could avail an enemy? Misery, to be able to quell the mightiest with a breath? Misery, to be as terrible as thou art beautiful? Wouldst thou, then, have preferred the condition of a weak woman, exposed to all evil, and capable of none?"

"I would fain have been loved, not feared," murmured Beatrice, sinking down upon the ground. "But now it matters not; I am going, father, where the evil, which thou hast striven to mingle with my being, will pass away like a dream—like the fragrance of these poisonous flowers, which will no longer taint my breath among the flowers of Eden. Farewell, Giovanni! Thy words of hatred are like lead within my heart—but they, too, will fall away as I ascend. Oh, was there not, from the first, more poison in thy nature than in mine?"

To Beatrice—so radically had her earthly part been wrought upon by Rappaccini's skill—as poison had been life, so the powerful antidote was death. And thus the poor victim of man's ingenuity and of thwarted nature, and of the fatality that attends all such efforts of perverted wisdom, perished there, at the feet of her father and Giovanni. Just at that moment, Professor Pietro Baglioni looked forth from the window, and called loudly, in a tone of triumph, mixed with horror, to the thunder-stricken man of science:

"Rappaccini! Rappaccini! And is *this* the upshot of your experiment?"

THE FACTS IN THE CASE
OF M. VALDEMAR

Edgar Allan Poe

Another of the greats of the American Gothic tradition, Edgar Allan
Poe (1808–1849) is known for his development of a highly psychologi-
cal type of horror, as well as for his interest in science.

Mesmerism, a pseudoscientific process that can allegedly bring
a patient to a hypnagogic state (the transitional moment between
wakefulness and sleep) and which took its name from German physician Franz Mesmer (1734–1815), was not new to the Gothic by the time
Poe published 'The Facts in the Case of M. Valdemar' in 1845. E. T. A.
Hoffmann had published 'The Magnetiser' ('Der Magnetiseur') in
1814, where the practice is abused for selfish purposes, and Nathaniel
Hawthorne had referred to it repeatedly in his most celebrated novels.
Poe himself had dabbled in the various aspects of mesmerism in three
other stories: 'A Tale of the Ragged Mountains' (1844), 'Mesmeric
Revelation' (1845) and 'Some Words with a Mummy' (1845). It is, however, 'Valdemar' which provides the most memorable portrayal of this
practice in its retelling of the ordeal of a phthisic man mesmerized
at the point of death. Its ending is also one of the most gruesome in
the history of the Gothic.

O F COURSE I SHALL NOT PRETEND TO CONSIDER IT ANY MATTER for wonder, that the extraordinary case of M. Valdemar has excited discussion. It would have been a miracle had it not—especially under the circumstances. Through the desire of all parties concerned, to keep the affair from the public, at least for the present, or until we had farther opportunities for investigation—through our endeavours to effect this—a garbled or exaggerated account made its way into society, and became the source of many unpleasant misrepresentations; and, very naturally, of a great deal of disbelief.

It is now rendered necessary that I give the *facts*—as far as I comprehend them myself. They are, succinctly, these:

My attention, for the last three years, had been repeatedly drawn to the subject of Mesmerism; and, about nine months ago, it occurred to me, quite suddenly, that in the series of experiments made hitherto, there had been a very remarkable and most unaccountable omission:—no person had as yet been mesmerized *in articulo mortis*. It remained to be seen, first, whether, in such condition, there existed in the patient any susceptibility to the magnetic influence; secondly, whether, if any existed, it was impaired or increased by the condition; thirdly, to what extent, or for how long a period, the encroachments of Death might be arrested by the process. There were other points to be ascertained, but these most excited my curiosity—the last in especial, from the immensely important character of its consequences.

In looking around me for some subject by whose means I might test these particulars, I was brought to think of my friend, M. Ernest Valdemar, the well-known compiler of the "Bibliotheca Forensica," and author (under the *nom de plume* of Issachar Marx) of the Polish versions of "Wallenstein" and "Gargantua." M. Valdemar, who has resided principally at Harlem, N. Y., since the year 1839, is (or was) particularly noticeable for the extreme spareness of his person—his lower limbs much resembling those of John Randolph; and, also, for the whiteness of his whiskers, in violent contrast to the blackness of his hair—the latter, in consequence, being very generally mistaken for a wig. His temperament was markedly nervous, and rendered him a good subject for mesmeric experiment. On two or three occasions I had put him to sleep with little difficulty, but was disappointed in other results which his peculiar constitution had naturally led me to anticipate. His will was at no period positively, or thoroughly, under my control, and in regard to *clairvoyance*, I could accomplish with him nothing to be relied upon. I always attributed my failure at these points to the disordered state of his health. For some months previous to my becoming acquainted with him, his physicians had declared him in a confirmed phthisis. It was his custom, indeed, to speak calmly of his approaching dissolution, as of a matter neither to be avoided nor regretted.

When the ideas to which I have alluded first occurred to me, it was of course very natural that I should think of M. Valdemar. I knew the steady philosophy of the man too well to apprehend any scruples from *him*; and he had no relatives in America who would be likely to interfere. I spoke to him frankly upon the subject; and, to my surprise, his interest seemed vividly excited. I say to my surprise; for, although he had always yielded his person freely to my experiments, he had never before given me any tokens of sympathy with what I did. His disease was of that character which would admit of exact calculation in respect to the epoch of its termination in death; and it was finally arranged between us that he would send for me about twenty-four hours before the period announced by his physicians as that of his decease.

It is now rather more than seven months since I received, from M. Valdemar himself, the subjoined note:

> "My Dear P—,
>
> "You may as well come *now*. D— and F— are agreed that I cannot hold out beyond tomorrow midnight; and I think they have hit the time very nearly.
>
> "VALDEMAR."

I received this note within half an hour after it was written, and in fifteen minutes more I was in the dying man's chamber. I had not seen him for ten days, and was appalled by the fearful alteration which the brief interval had wrought in him. His face wore a leaden hue; the eyes were utterly lustreless; and the emaciation was so extreme, that the skin had been broken through by the cheek-bones. His expectoration was excessive. The pulse was barely perceptible. He retained, nevertheless, in a very remarkable manner, both his mental power and a certain degree of physical strength. He spoke with distinctness—took some palliative medicines without aid—and, when I entered the room, was occupied in pencilling memoranda in a pocket-book. He was propped up in the bed by pillows. Doctors D— and F— were in attendance.

After pressing Valdemar's hand, I took these gentlemen aside, and obtained from them a minute account of the patient's condition. The left lung had been for eighteen months in a semi-osseous or cartilaginous state, and was, of course, entirely useless for all purposes of vitality. The right, in its upper portion, was also partially, if not thoroughly, ossified, while the lower region was merely a mass of purulent tubercles, running one into another. Several extensive perforations existed; and, at one point, permanent adhesion to the ribs had taken place. These appearances in the right lobe were of comparatively recent date. The ossification had proceeded with very unusual rapidity; no sign of it had been discovered a month before, and the adhesion had only been observed during the three previous days. Independently of the phthisis, the patient was suspected of aneurism of the aorta; but on this point the osseous symptoms rendered an exact diagnosis impossible. It was the opinion of both physicians that M. Valdemar would die about midnight on the morrow (Sunday.) It was then seven o'clock on Saturday evening.

On quitting the invalid's bedside to hold conversation with myself, Doctors D— and F— had bidden him a final farewell. It had not been their intention to return; but, at my request, they agreed to look in upon the patient about ten the next night.

When they had gone, I spoke freely with M. Valdemar on the subject of his approaching dissolution, as well as, more particularly, of the experiment proposed. He still professed himself quite willing and even anxious to have it made, and urged me to commence it at once. A male and a female nurse were in attendance; but I did not feel myself altogether at liberty to engage in a task of this character with no more reliable witnesses than these people, in case of sudden accident, might prove. I therefore postponed operations until about eight the next night, when the arrival of a medical student, with whom I had some acquaintance, (Mr. Theodore L——l,) relieved me from farther embarrassment. It had been my design, originally, to wait for the physicians; but I was induced to proceed, first, by the urgent entreaties of M. Valdemar, and secondly, by my conviction that I had not a moment to lose, as he was evidently sinking fast.

Mr. L——l was so kind as to accede to my desire that he would take notes of all that occurred; and it is from his memoranda that what I now have to relate is, for the most part, either condensed or copied *verbatim*.

It wanted about five minutes of eight when, taking the patient's hand, I begged him to state, as distinctly as he could, to Mr. L——l, whether he (M. Valdemar,) was entirely willing that I should make the experiment of mesmerizing him in his then condition.

He replied feebly, yet quite audibly, "Yes, I wish to be mesmerized"—adding immediately afterwards, "I fear you have deferred it too long."

While he spoke thus, I commenced the passes which I had already found most effectual in subduing him. He was evidently influenced with the first lateral stroke of my hand across his forehead; but although I exerted all my powers, no farther perceptible effect was induced until some minutes after ten o'clock, when Doctors D— and F— called, according to appointment. I explained to them, in a few words, what I designed, and as they opposed no objection, saying that the patient was already in the death agony, I proceeded without hesitation—exchanging, however, the lateral passes for downward ones, and directing my gaze entirely into the right eye of the sufferer.

By this time his pulse was imperceptible and his breathing was stertorous, and at intervals of half a minute.

This condition was nearly unaltered for a quarter of an hour. At the expiration of this period, however, a natural although a very deep sigh escaped the bosom of the dying man, and the stertorous breathing ceased—that is to say, its stertorousness was no longer apparent; the intervals were undiminished. The patient's extremities were of an icy coldness.

At five minutes before eleven, I perceived unequivocal signs of the mesmeric influence. The glassy roll of the eye was changed for that expression of uneasy *inward* examination which is never seen except in cases of sleep-waking, and which it is quite impossible to mistake. With a few rapid lateral passes I made the lids quiver, as in incipient sleep, and with a few more I closed them altogether. I was not satisfied, however, with this, but continued the manipulations vigorously, and with the fullest exertion of the will, until I had completely stiffened the limbs of the slumberer, after placing them in a seemingly easy position. The legs were at full length; the arms were nearly so, and reposed on the bed at a moderate distance from the loins. The head was very slightly elevated.

When I had accomplished this, it was fully midnight, and I requested the gentlemen present to examine M. Valdemar's condition. After a few experiments, they admitted him to be in an unusually perfect state of mesmeric trance. The curiosity of both the physicians was greatly excited. Dr. D— resolved at once to remain with the patient all night, while Dr. F— took leave with a promise to return at daybreak. Mr. L——l and the nurses remained.

We left M. Valdemar entirely undisturbed until about three o'clock in the morning, when I approached him and found him in precisely the same condition as when Dr. F— went away—that is to say, he lay in the same position; the pulse was imperceptible; the breathing was gentle (scarcely noticeable, unless through the application of a mirror to the lips;) the eyes were closed naturally; and the limbs were as rigid and as cold as marble. Still, the general appearance was certainly not that of death.

As I approached M. Valdemar I made a kind of half effort to influence his right arm into pursuit of my own, as I passed the latter gently to and fro above his person. In such experiments with this patient, I had never perfectly succeeded before, and assuredly I had little thought of succeeding now; but to my astonishment, his arm very readily, although feebly, followed every direction I assigned it with mine. I determined to hazard a few words of conversation.

"M. Valdemar," I said, "are you asleep?" He made no answer, but I perceived a tremor about the lips, and was thus induced to repeat the question, again and again. At its third repetition, his whole frame was agitated by a very slight shivering; the eyelids unclosed themselves so far as to display a white line of a ball; the lips moved sluggishly, and from between them, in a barely audible whisper, issued the words:

"Yes;—asleep now. Do not wake me!—let me die so!"

I here felt the limbs and found them as rigid as ever. The right arm, as before, obeyed the direction of my hand. I questioned the sleep-waker again:

"Do you still feel pain in the breast, M. Valdemar?"

The answer now was immediate, but even less audible than before:

"No pain—I am dying."

I did not think it advisable to disturb him farther just then, and nothing more was said or done until the arrival of Dr. F——, who came a little before sunrise, and expressed unbounded astonishment at finding the patient still alive. After feeling the pulse and applying a mirror to the lips, he requested me to speak to the sleep-waker again. I did so, saying:

"M. Valdemar, do you still sleep?"

As before, some minutes elapsed ere a reply was made; and during the interval the dying man seemed to be collecting his energies to speak. At my fourth repetition of the question, he said very faintly, almost inaudibly:

"Yes; still asleep—dying."

It was now the opinion, or rather the wish, of the physicians, that M. Valdemar should be suffered to remain undisturbed in his present apparently tranquil condition, until death should supervene—and this, it was generally agreed, must now take place within a few minutes. I concluded, however, to speak to him once more, and merely repeated my previous question.

While I spoke, there came a marked change over the countenance of the sleep-waker. The eyes rolled themselves slowly open, the pupils disappearing upwardly; the skin generally assumed a cadaverous hue, resembling not so much parchment as white paper; and the circular hectic spots which, hitherto, had been strongly defined in the centre of each cheek, *went out* at once. I use this expression, because the suddenness of their departure put me in mind of nothing so much as the extinguishment of a candle by a puff of the breath. The upper lip, at the same time, writhed itself away from the teeth, which it had previously covered completely; while the lower jaw fell with an audible jerk, leaving the mouth widely extended, and disclosing in full view the swollen and blackened tongue. I presume that no member of the party then present had been unaccustomed to death-bed horrors; but so hideous beyond conception was the appearance of M. Valdemar at this moment, that there was a general shrinking back from the region of the bed.

I now feel that I have reached a point of this narrative at which every reader will be startled into positive disbelief. It is my business, however, simply to proceed.

There was no longer the faintest sign of vitality in M. Valdemar; and concluding him to be dead, we were consigning him to the charge of the nurses, when a strong vibratory motion was observable in the tongue. This continued for perhaps a minute. At the expiration of this period, there issued from the distended and motionless jaws a voice—such as it would be madness in me to attempt describing. There are, indeed, two or three epithets which might be considered as applicable to it in part; I might say, for example, that the sound was harsh, and broken and hollow; but the hideous whole is indescribable, for the simple reason that no similar sounds have ever jarred upon the ear of humanity. There were two particulars, nevertheless, which I thought then, and still think, might fairly be stated as characteristic of the intonation—as well adapted to convey some idea of its unearthly peculiarity. In the first place, the voice seemed to reach our ears—at least mine—from a vast distance, or from some deep cavern within the earth. In the second place, it impressed me (I fear, indeed, that it will be impossible to make myself comprehended) as gelatinous or glutinous matters impress the sense of touch.

I have spoken both of "sound" and of "voice." I mean to say that the sound was one of distinct—of even wonderfully, thrillingly distinct—syllabification. M. Valdemar *spoke*—obviously in reply to the question I had propounded to him a few minutes before. I had asked him, it will be remembered, if he still slept. He now said:

"Yes;—no;—I *have been* sleeping—and now—now—*I am dead.*"

No person present even affected to deny, or attempted to repress, the unutterable, shuddering horror which these few words, thus uttered, were so well calculated to convey. Mr. L——l (the student) swooned. The nurses immediately left the chamber, and could not be induced to return. My own impressions I would not pretend to render intelligible to the reader. For nearly an hour, we busied ourselves, silently—without the utterance of a word—in endeavours to revive Mr. L——l. When he came to himself, we addressed ourselves again to an investigation of M. Valdemar's condition.

It remained in all respects as I have last described it, with the exception that the mirror no longer afforded evidence of respiration. An attempt to draw blood from the arm failed. I should mention, too, that this limb was no farther subject to my will. I endeavoured in vain to make it follow the direction of my hand. The only real indication, indeed, of the mesmeric influence, was now found in the vibratory movement of the tongue, whenever I addressed M. Valdemar a question. He seemed to be making an effort to reply, but had no longer sufficient volition. To queries put to him by any other person than myself he seemed utterly insensible—although I endeavoured to place each member of the company in mesmeric *rapport* with him. I believe that I have now related all that is necessary to an understanding of the sleep-waker's state at this epoch. Other nurses were procured; and at ten o'clock I left the house in company with the two physicians and Mr. L——l.

In the afternoon we all called again to see the patient. His condition remained precisely the same. We had now some discussion as to the propriety and feasibility of awakening him; but we had little difficulty in agreeing that no good purpose would be served by so doing. It was evident that, so far, death (or what is usually termed death) had been arrested by the mesmeric process. It seemed clear to us all that to awaken M. Valdemar would be merely to insure his instant, or at least his speedy dissolution.

From this period until the close of last week—*an interval of nearly seven months*—we continued to make daily calls at M. Valdemar's house, accompanied, now and then, by medical and other friends. All this time the sleeper-waker remained *exactly* as I have last described him. The nurses' attentions were continual.

It was on Friday last that we finally resolved to make the experiment of awakening, or attempting to awaken him; and it is the (perhaps) unfortunate result of this latter experiment which has given rise to so much discussion in private circles—to so much of what I cannot help thinking unwarranted popular feeling.

For the purpose of relieving M. Valdemar from the mesmeric trance, I made use of the customary passes. These, for a time, were unsuccessful. The first indication of revival was afforded by a partial descent of the iris. It was observed, as especially remarkable, that this lowering of the pupil was accompanied by the profuse out-flowing of a yellowish ichor (from beneath the lids) of a pungent and highly offensive odour.

It was now suggested that I should attempt to influence the patient's arm, as heretofore. I made the attempt and failed. Dr. F— then intimated a desire to have me put a question. I did so, as follows:

"M. Valdemar, can you explain to us what are your feelings or wishes now?"

There was an instant return of the hectic circles on the cheeks; the tongue quivered, or rather rolled violently in the mouth (although the jaws and lips remained rigid as before;) and at length the same hideous voice which I have already described, broke forth:

"For God's sake!—quick!—quick!—put me to sleep—or, quick!—waken me!—quick!—*I say to you that I am dead!*"

I was thoroughly unnerved, and for an instant remained undecided what to do. At first I made an endeavour to re-compose the patient; but, failing in this through total abeyance of the will, I retraced my steps and as earnestly struggled to awaken him. In this attempt I soon saw that I should be successful—or at least I soon fancied that my success would be complete—and I am sure that all in the room were prepared to see the patient awaken.

For what really occurred, however, it is quite impossible that any human being could have been prepared.

As I rapidly made the mesmeric passes, amid ejaculations of "dead! dead!" absolutely *bursting* from the tongue and not from the lips of the sufferer, his whole frame at once—within the space of a single minute, or even less, shrunk—crumbled—absolutely *rotted* away beneath my hands. Upon the bed, before that whole company, there lay a nearly liquid mass of loathsome—of detestable putrescence.

THE SECRET OF THE SCAFFOLD

Auguste Villiers de l'Isle-Adam

The French symbolist Auguste Villiers de l'Isle-Adam (1838–1889) is perhaps best remembered today as the author of the science fiction novel *The Future Eve* (*L'Ève future*, 1886), which helped popularize the now common term 'android'. He was also an important writer of supernatural and horror fiction, and his short story collections *Contes cruels* (1883, translated as *Sardonic Tales* in 1927 and as *Cruel Tales* in 1963) and *Histories insolites* (1888) are important to the history of the genre, if virtually forgotten by contemporary audiences. In fact, the term 'conte cruel', used to define a story that exploits and extols the cruelties of fate for macabre purposes, took its name from the former collection.

'The Secret of the Scaffold', published originally in 1883 and first collected in *L'Amour suprême* (1886), is ostensibly a tale more preoccupied with the effects of the guillotine on the consciousness of the executed. It does, however, boast a rare instance of a mad scientist offering to collaborate on a gruesome experiment for the benefit of science. Real names are used in the story and it is possible that it was, at least in part, inspired by real events.

To Monsieur Edmond Goncourt

T HE RECENT EXECUTIONS REMINDED ME OF THE FOLLOWING extraordinary story:

At seven o'clock on the evening of June 5, 1864, Doctor Edmond-Désiré Couty de la Pommerais, recently transferred to the Conciergerie at la Roquette, was sitting in the dungeon allocated to those condemned to death, clad in a straitjacket. He leaned back in his chair, saying nothing, his eyes staring into space. A candle on the table illuminated the pallor of his frozen features. Two steps away, a guard stood watching him, arms crossed and back to the wall.

Prisoners were almost always required to do some daily labour, from whose wages the administration deducted in advance the price of the shrouds they would require if they were to die in custody, these not being furnished by public funds. Only those condemned to execution had no such work to do.

The prisoner was not one of those who play cards. His expression was devoid of the least trace of fear or hope. He was 34 years old, dark-haired, of medium height but very strongly built. His temples were greying a little; his eyes were half closed. He had the forehead of an intellectual; his voice was flat and curt, his hands saturnine and his features regular. His manners had the studied distinction of an eloquent specialist—or so it appeared.

You will remember the case at the Seine assizes. Messire Lachaud's plea for the defence, very constricted on this occasion, had not nullified in the minds of the jury, the triple effect produced by the proceedings themselves, the conclusions of Doctor Tardieu and the indictment of Monsieur Oscar de Vallée. Monsieur de la Pommerais had been convicted of having administered, for covetous motives and with premeditation, fatal doses of digitalis to the wife of one of his friends, Madame de Pauw—and had heard pronounced against him, according to articles 301 and 302 of the Penal Code, the sentence of capital punishment.

On the evening of June 5, he had not yet been informed of the rejection of his appeal and the refusal of the mercy hearing for which his close relatives had asked. The distracted Emperor had hardly bothered to listen to his defenders. The venerable Abbé Crozes, who wore himself out in supplications to the Tuileries before every execution, had returned without any response. Would commuting a sentence of death, in such circumstances as these, not be equivalent to the abolition of the penalty? The case was exemplary. In the estimation of Parquet, the rejection of the appeal was no longer in doubt. Without any undue delay, Monsieur Hendreich was notified that he would be required to take delivery of the condemned man on the morning of June 9, at five o'clock.

Suddenly, the noise of rifle-butts sounded on the flagstones of the corridor. The lock creaked dully and the door opened. Bayonets glittered in the half-light. The governor of la Roquette, Monsieur Beauquesne, appeared on the threshold, accompanied by a visitor. Monsieur de la Pommerais, having raised his head, immediately recognized this visitor as the eminent surgeon Armand Velpeau.

The governor gestured to the guard, who went out. Monsieur Beauquesne, after a silent introduction, also retired. The two colleagues found themselves alone, staring at one another as they stood face to face.

La Pommerais silently offered the doctor his own chair, then went to sit down on the *couchette* whose sleepers were not often long delayed in awakening from life with a sudden jolt.

As if he were seeing symptoms of a sickness, the great clinician drew nearer to the *invalid*, in order to observe him more closely and to talk to him in a hushed tone.

At that time, Velpeau was just entering his sixties. He was at the height of his fame, the inheritor of Larrey's chair at the Institute and the first professor of the surgical clinic of Paris. His work, whose logical rigour was so neat and so vivid, had made him one of the leading lights of practical pathological science. The retired practitioner was already established as one of the century's great men.

After a moment of frosty silence, he said: "Monsieur, we are both physicians and we do not need to bother with useless condolences. In any case, an infection of the prostate—of which I shall surely perish within two years, or two and a half at the most—places me alongside you in the category of those condemned to death, with a date of execution set for a few months hence. So let's come straight to the point, without further preamble."

"Then, in your opinion, Doctor, my legal situation is… hopeless?" La Pommerais put in.

"So it is feared," Velpeau replied, straightforwardly.

"The hour of my death is fixed?"

"I don't know—but as nothing has interrupted the process of your case thus far, you may be sure that the blow will fall within a few days."

La Pommerais passed the sleeve of his straitjacket over his livid brow. "So that's it. Thanks. I'll be ready—I already was. The sooner the better, now."

"Your appeal has not been rejected—at least, not yet," Velpeau replied. "The proposition I have to put to you is only conditional. If your reprieve arrives, so much the better. If not…"

The great surgeon paused.

"If not…?" La Pommerais asked.

Velpeau, without replying, took a little case from his pocket, opened it and took out a lancet. He cut through the left wrist of the straitjacket and applied his middle finger to the pulse of the condemned man. "Monsieur de Pommerais," he said, "your pulse reveals a coolness and a rare firmness. The step that I have taken in coming to you—which will be kept secret—has as its object a kind of offer which might seem an extravagant and criminal mockery, even when addressed to a physician of your vitality: to a mind steeped in the positive convictions of Science and quite immune to all fantastic anxieties about Death. I think we know one another well enough, though; you will surely give your attentive consideration to something that might seem troubling to you at first glance."

"You have my attention, Monsieur," La Pommerais replied.

"As you know very well," Velpeau continued, "one of the most interesting questions of modern physiology is that of whether some glimmer of memory, thought or actual sensibility persists in the brain of a man after the severance of his head."

At this unexpected overture, the condemned man shivered. Then, collecting himself, he said: "When you came in, Doctor, I was preoccupied by that problem myself—quite justifiably, since it is doubly interesting for me."

"You are familiar with the works written on this subject, from those of Soemmering, Sue, Sédillot and Bichat to those of our contemporaries?"

"I have even assisted, at one time, in one of your dissections of the remains of an executed man."

"Really? Let's go on, then. Have you a precise opinion, from the surgical point-of-view, as to the effects of the guillotine?"

La Pommerais, having looked coldly at Velpeau, said: "No, Monsieur."

"I have made a scrupulous study of the apparatus, which is still ongoing," Doctor Velpeau continued, without any sign of emotion. "It is, in my estimation, a perfect instrument. The blade, acting at one and the same time as a wedge, a fulcrum and a mass, passes through the neck of the patient in a third of a second. The decapitated person, under the shock of that fulgurant passage, can no more feel pain thereafter than a soldier on the battlefield can when his arm is carried away by a cannonball. The sensation, lacking the time to make itself felt, is obscured and nullified."

"There might perhaps be an *afterpain*; its consequence is, after all, two wounds! Wasn't it Julia Fontenelle who, giving her reasons, raised the question of whether that same swiftness might actually be more painful than execution by the rope or the axe?"

"Bérard has provided an adequate answer to that idea!" Velpeau replied. "For myself, I am firmly convinced—based on a hundred experiences and my particular observations—that the instantaneous ablation of the head instantaneously produces in the truncated individual the most absolute anaesthetic oblivion. The shock alone, provoked by the abrupt loss of four or five litres of blood—which erupts from the vessels with enough circulatory pressure to project it a meter and a half—would suffice to reassure the most timorous in that respect. As for the unconscious convulsions of the carnal machine, so suddenly arrested in its operation, they no more constitute an indication of suffering than... the palpitation of an amputated leg, for example, whose muscles and nerves contract but which cannot suffer any longer.

"In my opinion, the nervous fever of uncertainty, the solemnity of the preparations and the jolt of awakening on the fatal morning constitute the sum of the alleged suffering in this sort of case. Amputation can only be imperceptible; the real pain is only imaginary. A violent blow on the head not only is not felt but leaves no trace of consciousness of its shock. A simple lesion of the vertebrae is followed by ataxic insensibility—and the lifting of the head, the bisection of the spine and the interruption of organic rapport between the heart and the brain would surely be sufficient to paralyse any sensation of death—however vague—in the most intimate depths of human being. Pain, in such circumstance, is impossible and inadmissible! You know that as well as I do."

"I hope so, at least—rather more than you, Monsieur!" La Pommerais replied. "In reality, though, it isn't some gross and rapid physical suffering—hardly conceived in the midst of sensory disarray, and very quickly choked by the invading ascendance of Death—that I dread. It's something else."

"Would you care to try to explain what you mean?" Velpeau said.

"Listen," murmured La Pommerais, after a pause. "The organs of memory and the will—if they are located in man in the same lobes in which we have discovered them in, say, a dog—are spared by the passage of the blade! Too many equivocal precedents have been set, as disquieting as they are incomprehensible, to allow me to be easily persuaded of the immediate unconsciousness of a decapitated head. According to legend, how many severed heads, called upon to tell the truth, have turned their gaze upon their questioner? Neural memory? Reflexive movements? Empty words!

"Remember the head of the sailor which, at the clinic in Brest, an hour and a quarter after removal, by a possibly voluntary movement of the jaws, cut through a pencil placed between them! Having chosen that example alone from among a thousand, the real question at issue here becomes a matter of knowing whether or not that man's self acted upon the muscles of its exsanguinated head after the cessation of blood flow."

"The self is a property of the whole," said Velpeau.

"The spinal cord is an extension of the cerebellum," replied Monsieur de la Pommerais. "After that lapse of time, where would the sensitive whole be? How could it be reawakened? Before the week is out, I shall certainly have found that out… and forgotten it!"

"It may depend on you whether Humanity can obtain an answer to this question, once and for all," Velpeau said, slowly, his eyes fixed on those of his interlocutor. "Speaking frankly, that's why I'm here. I have been delegated to approach you by a committee of our most eminent colleagues of the Faculty of Paris, and here is my letter of permission from the Emperor. It contains powers sufficiently extensive even to obtain, if necessary, a stay of execution."

"I'm not following you any longer," La Pommerais said. "Explain yourself."

"Monsieur de la Pommerais, I come in the name of Science—which is forever dear to men like us, who no longer count the number of her magnanimous martyrs—in the hope that some practical experiment, to be agreed between us, will confirm or deny this hypothesis, which I myself find more than doubtful. I come to claim from you the greatest sum of energy and intrepidity that can be expected of the human species. If your appeal for mercy is rejected, you will find yourself, as a physician, in a position to become the foremost authority on the supreme operation that you must undergo. Your co-operation in a tentative experiment in communication would therefore be invaluable. All the evidence seems to attest in advance that the result will be negative—but if you are willing to offer yourself as a test case, it might be finally settled. If we accept the hypothesis that continued experience is not absurd, in principle, we have a chance in ten thousand to enlighten modern physiology—miraculously, as it were. The opportunity must be seized this time—and in the case of a sign of intelligence victoriously exchanged after execution, you will leave a name whose scientific glory will efface forever the memory of your social lapse."

"Ah," murmured La Pommerais, becoming pale, but with a resolute smile. "Ah—I begin to understand. In fact, torture has already revealed the phenomena of digestion, Michelot informs us. But... what will be the nature of your experiment? Galvanic convulsions? Ciliary incitements? Injections of arterial blood? All that is hardly conclusive!"

"It goes without saying that immediately after the sad ceremony, your remains will go to rest in peace in the earth, and that no scalpels will touch you," Velpeau told him. "Definitely not! But as the blade falls I shall be standing there in person, facing you and the machine. As quickly as possible, your head will be passed from the hands of the executioner into mine. And then—the experiment is all the more serious and conclusive by reason of its simplicity—I will cry out to you, very distinctly, in your ear: 'Monsieur Couty de la Pommerais, in memory of our conversations during life, can you, at this moment, lower your right eyelid three times in succession while keeping the other eye wide open?' If, at that moment, whatever other contractions of the features there might be, you are able by means of that triple wink to notify me that you have heard and understood me, and thus prove to me, in producing that effect by the action of your memory and permanent will, your facial nerves and your eyelids—overcoming all horror and the surge of all other impressions of your being—that will suffice for the illumination of Science and the revolutionizing of our convictions. And I would be able, without any doubt, to identify the manner in which you would be remembered in future: not as a criminal, but as a hero."

As these strange words were spoken, Monsieur de la Pommerais appeared to be struck by a seizure so profound that he remained silent, as if petrified, for a full minute, his pupils dilated and fixed on the surgeon. Then, without saying a word, he got up and took a few steps, very pensively. Eventually, he shook his head sadly.

"The horrible violence of the blow would throw me out of myself," he said. "To realize this appears to me beyond the power of any will or human effort. Besides, it's said that the chances of vitality are not the same for us, the guillotined. However... come to me again, Monsieur, on the morning of the execution. I will tell you then whether or not I shall be a party to this tentative endeavour, which is frightful, revolting and illusory at the same time. If I say no, I shall count on your discretion to let my bloody head lie tranquilly in the tin bucket set to receive it, yielding up its last vitality."

"So—until then, Monsieur de la Pommerais?" Velpeau said, as he also got up. "Think about it."

They bowed to one another. Immediately afterwards, Doctor Velpeau left the cell. The guard came back in, and the condemned man stretched himself out resignedly on his meagre bed, to sleep or to dream.

Four days later, at 5:30 in the morning, Monsieur Beauquesne, Abbé Crozes, Monsieur Claude and Monsieur Potier, the clerk of the Imperial Court, came into the cell. Monsieur de la Pommerais was already awake. At the news that the hour had come, he sat up in bed, very pale. He got dressed quickly, then spoke for ten minutes with Abbé Crozes, from whom he had already received several visits. The priest administered the extreme unction that makes the final hour more bearable. After that, seeing Doctor Velpeau arrive, the condemned man said: "I've been practising—look!" And while the order of execution was being read out, he held his right eyelid shut, while fixing the surgeon with the gaze of his wide-open left eye.

Velpeau bowed deeply. Then, turning towards Hendreich, who had come in with his assistants, he made a brief gesture to the executioner, which was reciprocated.

The preparations were rapid. It was observed that the phenomenon of the hair becoming visibly whiter in the shadow of the blade did not occur. A letter of farewell from his wife, read in a low voice by the almoner, moistened Monsieur de la Pommerais' eyes with tears, which the priest piously wiped away with piece of cloth gathered from the hem of his chemise.

Once he was standing up, with his frock coat thrown over his shoulders, the shackles were removed from the condemned man's wrists. He refused the proffered glass of brandy, and the escort marched him into the corridor. As he went through the door, passing his colleague at the threshold, he said to him: "It's time—goodbye!"

Soon the vast iron gates were opening before him.

The morning wind blew into the prison. Dawn was breaking. The great plaza extended into the distance, encircled by a double cordon of cavalry. Facing Monsieur de la Pommerais, at a distance of ten paces, the scaffold loomed over a semicircle of mounted police, who drew their sabres noisily as he appeared. His arrival caused a stir among the groups of newspaper reporters standing some distance away.

Further away, behind the trees, the murmurous swell of the enervated crowd could be heard. On the roofs of the pleasure-houses, in the attic windows, a few pale girls in crumpled silks were watching, some of them still holding bottles of champagne and leaning on the arms of sad black suits. Swallows were flying this way and that across the square, buoyed up by the early morning air.

The solitary guillotine, filling the empty space and marking out the boundary of the sky, seemed to throw the shadow of its two lifted arms all the way to the horizon. Between them, up there in the blueness of the dawn, one last star was twinkling in the distance.

The condemned man shivered before this funereal spectacle, then walked, resolutely, towards the foot of the steps. He climbed them without pausing. The triangular blade shone upon the black chassis now, veiling the star. As he stood before the fatal machine, he kissed a lock of his own hair that had been cut while he made his preparations by Abbé Crozes. In touching it to his lips, he said: "For *her*!"

Five people stood out in silhouette upon the scaffold. The silence, in that moment, was so profound that the noise of a distant branch breaking under the weight of a spectator carried as far the tragic group, accompanied by a cry of alarm and a few vague and hideous bursts of laughter. Then, as the clock chimed the hour appointed for the administration of the last blow, Monsieur de la Pommerais saw his fellow experimenter, facing him on the far side of the scaffold. Velpeau was studying him, with one hand resting on the platform. He collected himself for a moment, and closed his eyes.

The apparatus was brusquely brought into play. The collar came down. The button was pressed. The gleaming blade fell.

A terrible shock shook the platform. The horses reared at the magnetic odour of blood, and the echoes reverberated. Already, the bloody head of the victim was palpitating between the impassive hands of the surgeon of the Pitié, sending waves of red across his fingers, cuffs and clothes.

It was a sombre face, horribly white; the eyes rolling as if bewildered; the eyebrows twisted as if clenched by a rictus. The teeth chattered; the chin was indented at the extremity of the lower jaw.

Velpeau quickly bent over the head and pronounced the pre-arranged question in the right ear. As strong as the man's constitution was, the result made him shiver with a kind of cold fear.

The lid of the right eye lowered, while the distended left eye looked at him.

"In the name of God and humanity, give me the sign twice more!" Velpeau cried, in some distress.

The eyelashes came apart, as if by an internal effort—but the eyelid did not raise itself again. As the moments passed, the visage became rigid, frozen and immobile. It was over.

Doctor Velpeau gave the dead head to Monsieur Hendreich—who, reopening the basket, placed it between the legs of the already-stiffened trunk, as is the custom.

The great surgeon bathed his hands in one of the buckets designated for the washing of the machine, which had already begun. Around him, the crowd dispersed, anxiously, without quite knowing why. He wiped himself dry, still silent. Then, at a slow pace, his face pensive and grave, he went back to his carriage, which was parked at the corner of the prison. As he climbed into it, he noticed the cart of justice moving off at a fast trot towards Montparnasse.

THE BODY SNATCHER

Robert Louis Stevenson

Alongside Victor Frankenstein, the vivisectionist Moreau and the invisible man, Henry Jekyll has to be one of the most famous fictional mad scientists of all time. Hardly could his creator, Scottish writer Robert Louis Stevenson (1850–1894), have predicted upon the publication of his novel *Strange Case of Dr Jekyll and Mr Hyde* in 1886 that his gentle doctor and dark double would go on to become one of the main figures in the Gothic's literary and cinematic pantheons. This novel was not, however, Stevenson's only foray into mad science.

'The Body Snatcher', published in 1884, is a horror tale about a doctor who will stop at nothing to ensure his studies into human anatomy are not hindered by a shortage in dissection bodies. Taking inspiration from the real West Port Murders of 1828 and from the figures of Doctor Robert Knox and 'corpse suppliers' William Burke and William Hare, Stevenson crafted a complex story full of suspense and crime whose denouement is truly hair-raising. 'The Body Snatcher' would eventually become the basis for the stellar 1945 film of the same title, directed by Val Lewton and starring horror stars Boris Karloff and Bela Lugosi.

E VERY NIGHT IN THE YEAR, FOUR OF US SAT IN THE SMALL parlour of the George at Debenham—the undertaker, and the landlord, and Fettes, and myself. Sometimes there would be more; but blow high, blow low, come rain or snow or frost, we four would be each planted in his own particular armchair. Fettes was an old drunken Scotchman, a man of education obviously, and a man of some property, since he lived in idleness. He had come to Debenham years ago, while still young, and by a mere continuance of living had grown to be an adopted townsman. His blue camlet cloak was a local antiquity, like the church-spire. His place in the parlour at the George, his absence from church, his old, crapulous, disreputable vices, were all things of course in Debenham. He had some vague Radical opinions and some fleeting infidelities, which he would now and again set forth and emphasize with tottering slaps upon the table. He drank rum—five glasses regularly every evening; and for the greater portion of his nightly visit to the George sat, with his glass in his right hand, in a state of melancholy alcoholic saturation. We called him the Doctor, for he was supposed to have some special knowledge of medicine, and had been known, upon a pinch, to set a fracture or reduce a dislocation; but beyond these slight particulars, we had no knowledge of his character and antecedents.

One dark winter night—it had struck nine some time before the landlord joined us—there was a sick man in the George, a great neighbouring proprietor suddenly struck down with apoplexy on his way to Parliament; and the great man's still greater London doctor had been telegraphed to his bedside. It was the first time that such a thing had happened in Debenham, for the railway was but newly open, and we were all proportionately moved by the occurrence.

"He's come," said the landlord, after he had filled and lighted his pipe.

"He?" said I. "Who?—not the doctor?"

"Himself," replied our host.

"What is his name?"

"Doctor Macfarlane," said the landlord.

Fettes was far through his third tumbler, stupidly fuddled, now nodding over, now staring mazily around him; but at the last word he seemed to awaken, and repeated the name "Macfarlane" twice, quietly enough the first time, but with sudden emotion at the second.

"Yes," said the landlord, "that's his name, Doctor Wolfe Macfarlane."

Fettes became instantly sober; his eyes awoke, his voice became clear, loud, and steady, his language forcible and earnest. We were all startled by the transformation, as if a man had risen from the dead.

"I beg your pardon," he said, "I am afraid I have not been paying much attention to your talk. Who is this Wolfe Macfarlane?" And then, when he had heard the landlord out, "It cannot be, it cannot be," he added; "and yet I would like well to see him face to face."

"Do you know him, Doctor?" asked the undertaker, with a gasp.

"God forbid!" was the reply. "And yet the name is a strange one; it were too much to fancy two. Tell me, landlord, is he old?"

"Well," said the host, "he's not a young man, to be sure, and his hair is white; but he looks younger than you."

"He is older, though; years older. But," with a slap upon the table, "it's the rum you see in my face—rum and sin. This man, perhaps, may have an easy conscience and a good digestion. Conscience! Hear me speak. You would think I was some good, old, decent Christian, would you not? But no, not I; I never canted. Voltaire might have canted if he'd stood in my shoes; but the brains"—with a rattling fillip on his bald head—"the brains were clear and active, and I saw and made no deductions."

"If you know this doctor," I ventured to remark, after a somewhat awful pause, "I should gather that you do not share the landlord's good opinion."

Fettes paid no regard to me.

"Yes," he said, with sudden decision, "I must see him face to face."

There was another pause, and then a door was closed rather sharply on the first floor, and a step was heard upon the stair.

"That's the doctor," cried the landlord. "Look sharp, and you can catch him."

It was but two steps from the small parlour to the door of the old George Inn; the wide oak staircase landed almost in the street; there was room for a Turkey rug and nothing more between the threshold and the last round of the descent; but this little space was every evening brilliantly lit up, not only by the light upon the stair and the great signal-lamp below the sign, but by the warm radiance of the barroom window. The George thus brightly advertised itself to passers-by in the cold street. Fettes walked steadily to the spot, and we, who were hanging behind, beheld the two men meet, as one of them had phrased it, face to face. Dr. Macfarlane was alert and vigorous. His white hair set off his pale and placid, although energetic, countenance. He was richly dressed in the finest of broadcloth and the whitest of linen, with a great gold watch-chain, and studs and spectacles of the same precious material. He wore a broad-folded tie, white and speckled with lilac, and he carried on his arm a comfortable driving-coat of fur. There was no doubt but he became his years, breathing, as he did, of wealth and consideration; and it was a surprising contrast to see our parlour sot—bald, dirty, pimpled, and robed in his old camlet cloak—confront him at the bottom of the stairs.

"Macfarlane!" he said somewhat loudly, more like a herald than a friend.

The great doctor pulled up short on the fourth step, as though the familiarity of the address surprised and somewhat shocked his dignity.

"Toddy Macfarlane!" repeated Fettes.

The London man almost staggered. He stared for the swiftest of seconds at the man before him, glanced behind him with a sort of scare, and then in a startled whisper, "Fettes!" he said, "you!"

"Ay," said the other, "me! Did you think I was dead too? We are not so easy shut of our acquaintance."

"Hush, hush!" exclaimed the doctor. "Hush, hush! this meeting is so unexpected—I can see you are unmanned. I hardly knew you, I confess, at first; but I am overjoyed—overjoyed to have this opportunity. For the present it must be how-d'ye-do and goodbye in one, for my fly is waiting, and I must not fail the train; but you shall—let me see—yes—you shall give me your address, and you can count on early news of me. We must do something for you, Fettes. I fear you are out at elbows; but we must see to that for auld lang syne, as once we sang at suppers."

"Money!" cried Fettes; "money from you! The money that I had from you is lying where I cast it in the rain."

Dr. Macfarlane had talked himself into some measure of superiority and confidence, but the uncommon energy of this refusal cast him back into his first confusion.

A horrible, ugly look came and went across his almost venerable countenance. "My dear fellow," he said, "be it as you please; my last thought is to offend you. I would intrude on none. I will leave you my address, however—"

"I do not wish it—I do not wish to know the roof that shelters you," interrupted the other. "I heard your name; I feared it might be you; I wished to know if, after all, there were a God; I know now that there is none. Begone!"

He still stood in the middle of the rug, between the stair and doorway; and the great London physician, in order to escape, would be forced to step to one side. It was plain that he hesitated before the thought of this humiliation. White as he was, there was a dangerous glitter in his spectacles; but while he still paused uncertain, he became aware that the driver of his fly was peering in from the street at this unusual scene and caught a glimpse at the same time of our little body from the parlour, huddled by the corner of the bar. The presence of so many witnesses decided him at once to flee. He crouched together, brushing on the wainscot, and made a dart like a serpent, striking for the door. But his tribulation was not yet entirely at an end, for even as he was passing Fettes clutched him by the arm and these words came in a whisper, and yet painfully distinct, "Have you seen it again?"

The great rich London doctor cried out aloud with a sharp, throttling cry; he dashed his questioner across the open space, and, with his hands over his head, fled out of the door like a detected thief. Before it had occurred to one of us to make a movement the fly was already rattling toward the station. The scene was over like a dream, but the dream had left proofs and traces of its passage. Next day the servant found the fine gold spectacles broken on the threshold, and that very night we were all standing breathless by the barroom window, and Fettes at our side, sober, pale, and resolute in look.

"God protect us, Mr. Fettes!" said the landlord, coming first into possession of his customary senses. "What in the universe is all this? These are strange things you have been saying."

Fettes turned toward us; he looked us each in succession in the face. "See if you can hold your tongues," said he. "That man Macfarlane is not safe to cross; those that have done so already have repented it too late."

And then, without so much as finishing his third glass, far less waiting for the other two, he bade us goodbye and went forth, under the lamp of the hotel, into the black night.

We three turned to our places in the parlour, with the big red fire and four clear candles; and as we recapitulated what had passed, the first chill of our surprise soon changed into a glow of curiosity. We sat late; it was the latest session I have known in the old George. Each man, before we parted, had his theory that he was bound to prove; and none of us had any nearer business in this world than to track out the past of our condemned companion, and surprise the secret that he shared with the great London doctor. It is no great boast, but I believe I was a better hand at worming out a story than either of my fellows at the George; and perhaps there is now no other man alive who could narrate to you the following foul and unnatural events.

In his young days Fettes studied medicine in the schools of Edinburgh. He had talent of a kind, the talent that picks up swiftly what it hears and readily retails it for its own. He worked little at home; but he was civil, attentive, and intelligent in the presence of his masters. They soon picked him out as a lad who listened closely and remembered well; nay, strange as it seemed to me when I first heard it, he was in those days well favoured, and pleased by his exterior. There was, at that period, a certain extramural teacher of anatomy, whom I shall here designate by the letter K. His name was subsequently too well known. The man who bore it skulked through the streets of Edinburgh in disguise, while the mob that applauded at the execution of Burke called loudly for the blood of his employer.

But Mr. K— was then at the top of his vogue; he enjoyed a popularity due partly to his own talent and address, partly to the incapacity of his rival, the university professor. The students, at least, swore by his name, and Fettes believed himself, and was believed by others, to have laid the foundations of success when he had acquired the favour of this meteorically famous man. Mr. K— was a *bon vivant* as well as an accomplished teacher; he liked a sly illusion no less than a careful preparation. In both capacities Fettes enjoyed and deserved his notice, and by the second year of his attendance he held the half-regular position of second demonstrator or sub-assistant in his class.

In this capacity the charge of the theatre and lecture-room devolved in particular upon his shoulders. He had to answer for the cleanliness of the premises and the conduct of the other students, and it was a part of his duty to supply, receive, and divide the various subjects. It was with a view to this last—at that time very delicate—affair that he was lodged by Mr. K— in the same wynd, and at last in the same building, with the dissecting-rooms. Here, after a night of turbulent pleasures, his hand still tottering, his sight still misty and confused, he would be called out of bed in the black hours before the winter dawn by the unclean and desperate interlopers who supplied the table. He would open the door to these men, since infamous throughout the land. He would help them with their tragic burden, pay them their sordid price, and remain alone, when they were gone, with the unfriendly relics of humanity. From such a scene he would return to snatch another hour or two of slumber, to repair the abuses of the night, and refresh himself for the labours of the day.

Few lads could have been more insensible to the impressions of a life thus passed among the ensigns of mortality. His mind was closed against all general considerations. He was incapable of interest in the fate and fortunes of another, the slave of his own desires and low ambitions. Cold, light, and selfish in the last resort, he had that modicum of prudence, miscalled morality, which keeps a man from inconvenient drunkenness or punishable theft. He coveted, besides, a measure of consideration from his masters and his fellow-pupils, and he had no desire to fail conspicuously in the external parts of life. Thus he made it his pleasure to gain some distinction in his studies, and day after day rendered unimpeachable eye-service to his employer, Mr. K—. For his day of work he indemnified himself by nights of roaring, blackguardly enjoyment; and when that balance had been struck, the organ that he called his conscience declared itself content.

The supply of subjects was a continual trouble to him as well as to his master. In that large and busy class, the raw material of the anatomists kept perpetually running out; and the business thus rendered necessary was not only unpleasant in itself, but threatened dangerous consequences to all who were concerned. It was the policy of Mr. K— to ask no questions in his dealings with the trade. "They bring the body, and we pay the price," he used to say, dwelling on the alliteration—"*quid pro quo*." And, again, and somewhat profanely, "Ask no questions," he would tell his assistants, "for conscience' sake." There was no understanding that the subjects were provided by the crime of murder. Had that idea been broached to him in words, he would have recoiled in horror; but the lightness of his speech upon so grave a matter was, in itself, an offence against good manners, and a temptation to the men with whom he dealt. Fettes, for instance, had often remarked to himself upon the singular freshness of the bodies. He had been struck again and again by the hang-dog, abominable looks of the ruffians who came to him before the dawn; and putting things together clearly in his private thoughts, he perhaps attributed a meaning too immoral and too categorical to the unguarded counsels of his master. He understood his duty, in short, to have three branches:

to take what was brought, to pay the price, and to avert the eye from any evidence of crime.

One November morning this policy of silence was put sharply to the test. He had been awake all night with a racking toothache—pacing his room like a caged beast or throwing himself in fury on his bed—and had fallen at last into that profound, uneasy slumber that so often follows on a night of pain, when he was awakened by the third or fourth angry repetition of the concerted signal. There was a thin, bright moonshine; it was bitter cold, windy, and frosty; the town had not yet awakened, but an indefinable stir already preluded the noise and business of the day. The ghouls had come later than usual, and they seemed more than usually eager to be gone. Fettes, sick with sleep, lighted them upstairs. He heard their grumbling Irish voices through a dream; and as they stripped the sack from their sad merchandise he leaned dozing, with his shoulder propped against the wall; he had to shake himself to find the men their money. As he did so his eyes lighted on the dead face. He started; he took two steps nearer, with the candle raised.

"God Almighty!" he cried. "That is Jane Galbraith!"

The men answered nothing, but they shuffled nearer the door.

"I know her, I tell you," he continued. "She was alive and hearty yesterday. It's impossible she can be dead; it's impossible you should have got this body fairly."

"Sure, sir, you're mistaken entirely," said one of the men.

But the other looked Fettes darkly in the eyes, and demanded the money on the spot.

It was impossible to misconceive the threat or to exaggerate the danger. The lad's heart failed him. He stammered some excuses, counted out the sum, and saw his hateful visitors depart. No sooner were they gone than he hastened to confirm his doubts. By a dozen unquestionable marks he identified the girl he had jested with the day before. He saw, with horror, marks upon her body that might well betoken violence. A panic seized him, and he took refuge in his room. There he reflected at length over the discovery that he had made; considered soberly the bearing of Mr. K—'s instructions and the danger to himself of interference in so serious a business, and at last, in sore perplexity, determined to wait for the advice of his immediate superior, the class assistant.

This was a young doctor, Wolfe Macfarlane, a high favourite among all the reckless students, clever, dissipated, and unscrupulous to the last degree. He had travelled and studied abroad. His manners were agreeable and a little forward. He was an authority on the stage, skilful on the ice or the links with skate or golf-club; he dressed with nice audacity, and, to put the finishing touch upon his glory, he kept a gig and a strong trotting-horse. With Fettes he was on terms of intimacy; indeed, their relative positions called for some community of life; and when subjects were scarce the pair would drive far into the country in Macfarlane's gig, visit and desecrate some lonely graveyard, and return before dawn with their booty to the door of the dissecting-room.

On that particular morning Macfarlane arrived somewhat earlier than his wont. Fettes heard him, and met him on the stairs, told him his story, and showed him the cause of his alarm. Macfarlane examined the marks on her body.

"Yes," he said with a nod, "it looks fishy."

"Well, what should I do?" asked Fettes.

"Do?" repeated the other. "Do you want to do anything? Least said soonest mended, I should say."

"Some one else might recognize her," objected Fettes. "She was as well known as the Castle Rock."

"We'll hope not," said Macfarlane, "and if anybody does—well, you didn't, don't you see, and there's an end. The fact is, this has been going on too long. Stir up the mud, and you'll get K— into the most unholy trouble; you'll be in a shocking box yourself. So will I, if you come to that. I should like to know how any one of us would look, or what the devil we should have to say for ourselves, in any Christian witness-box. For me, you know, there's one thing certain—that, practically speaking, all our subjects have been murdered."

"Macfarlane!" cried Fettes.

"Come now!" sneered the other. "As if you hadn't suspected it yourself!"

"Suspecting is one thing—"

"And proof another. Yes, I know; and I'm as sorry as you are this should have come here," tapping the body with his cane. "The next best thing for me is not to recognize it; and," he added coolly, "I don't. You may, if you please. I don't dictate, but I think a man of the world would do as I do; and I may add, I fancy that is what K— would look for at our hands. The question is, Why did he choose us two for his assistants? And I answer, because he didn't want old wives."

This was the tone of all others to affect the mind of a lad like Fettes. He agreed to imitate Macfarlane. The body of the unfortunate girl was duly dissected, and no one remarked or appeared to recognize her.

One afternoon, when his day's work was over, Fettes dropped into a popular tavern and found Macfarlane sitting with a stranger. This was a small man, very pale and dark, with coal-black eyes. The cut of his features gave a promise of intellect and refinement which was but feebly realized in his manners, for he proved, upon a nearer acquaintance, coarse, vulgar, and stupid. He exercised, however, a very remarkable control over Macfarlane; issued orders like the Great Bashaw; became inflamed at the least discussion or delay, and commented rudely on the servility with which he was obeyed. This most offensive person took a fancy to Fettes on the spot, plied him with drinks, and honoured him with unusual confidences on his past career. If a tenth part of what he confessed were true, he was a very loathsome rogue; and the lad's vanity was tickled by the attention of so experienced a man.

"I'm a pretty bad fellow myself," the stranger remarked, "but Macfarlane is the boy—Toddy Macfarlane I call him. Toddy, order your friend another glass." Or it might be, "Toddy, you jump up and shut the door." "Toddy hates me," he said again. "Oh yes, Toddy, you do!"

"Don't you call me that confounded name," growled Macfarlane.

"Hear him! Did you ever see the lads play knife? He would like to do that all over my body," remarked the stranger.

"We medicals have a better way than that," said Fettes. "When we dislike a dead friend of ours, we dissect him."

Macfarlane looked up sharply, as though this jest were scarcely to his mind.

The afternoon passed. Gray, for that was the stranger's name, invited Fettes to join them at dinner, ordered a feast so sumptuous that the tavern was thrown into commotion, and when all was done commanded Macfarlane to settle the bill. It was late before they separated; the man Gray was incapably drunk. Macfarlane, sobered by his fury, chewed the cud of the money he had been forced to squander and the slights he had been obliged to swallow. Fettes, with various liquors singing in his head, returned home with devious footsteps and a mind entirely in abeyance. Next day Macfarlane was absent from the class, and Fettes smiled to himself as he imagined him still squiring the intolerable Gray from tavern to tavern. As soon as the hour of liberty had struck, he posted from place to place in quest of his last night's companions. He could find them, however, nowhere; so returned early to his rooms, went early to bed, and slept the sleep of the just.

At four in the morning he was awakened by the well-known signal. Descending to the door, he was filled with astonishment to find Macfarlane with his gig, and in the gig one of those long and ghastly packages with which he was so well acquainted.

"What?" he cried. "Have you been out alone? How did you manage?"

But Macfarlane silenced him roughly, bidding him turn to business. When they had got the body upstairs and laid it on the table, Macfarlane made at first as if he were going away. Then he paused and seemed to hesitate; and then, "You had better look at the face," said he, in tones of some constraint. "You had better," he repeated, as Fettes only stared at him in wonder.

"But where, and how, and when did you come by it?" cried the other.

"Look at the face," was the only answer.

Fettes was staggered; strange doubts assailed him. He looked from the young doctor to the body, and then back again. At last, with a start, he did as he was bidden. He had almost expected the sight that met his eyes, and yet the shock was cruel. To see, fixed in the rigidity of death and naked on that coarse layer of sackcloth, the man whom he had left well clad and full of meat and sin upon the threshold of a tavern, awoke, even in the thoughtless Fettes, some of the terrors of the conscience. It was a *cras tibi* which re-echoed in his soul, that two whom he had known should have come to lie upon these icy tables. Yet these were only secondary thoughts. His first concern regarded Wolfe. Unprepared for a challenge so momentous, he knew not how to look his comrade in the face. He durst not meet his eye, and he had neither words nor voice at his command.

It was Macfarlane himself who made the first advance. He came up quietly behind and laid his hand gently but firmly on the other's shoulder.

"Richardson," said he, "may have the head."

Now, Richardson was a student who had long been anxious for that portion of the human subject to dissect. There was no answer, and the murderer resumed: "Talking of business, you must pay me; your accounts, you see, must tally."

Fettes found a voice, the ghost of his own: "Pay you!" he cried. "Pay you for that?"

"Why, yes, of course you must. By all means and on every possible account, you must," returned the other. "I dare not give it for nothing, you dare not take it for nothing; it would compromise us both. This is another case like Jane Galbraith's. The more things are wrong, the more we must act as if all were right. Where does old K— keep his money?"

"There," answered Fettes hoarsely, pointing to a cupboard in the corner.

"Give me the key, then," said the other calmly, holding out his hand.

There was an instant's hesitation, and the die was cast. Macfarlane could not suppress a nervous twitch, the infinitesimal mark of an immense relief, as he felt the key between his fingers. He opened the cupboard, brought out pen and ink and a paper-book that stood in one compartment, and separated from the funds in a drawer a sum suitable to the occasion.

"Now, look here," he said, "there is the payment made—first proof of your good faith: first step to your security. You have now to clinch it by a second. Enter the payment in your book, and then you for your part may defy the devil."

The next few seconds were for Fettes an agony of thought; but in balancing his terrors it was the most immediate that triumphed. Any future difficulty seemed almost welcome if he could avoid a present quarrel with Macfarlane. He set down the candle which he had been carrying all this time, and with a steady hand entered the date, the nature, and the amount of the transaction.

"And now," said Macfarlane, "it's only fair that you should pocket the lucre. I've had my share already. By-the-bye, when a man of the world falls into a bit of luck, has a few shillings extra in his pocket— I'm ashamed to speak of it, but there's a rule of conduct in the case. No treating, no purchase of expensive class-books, no squaring of old debts; borrow, don't lend."

"Macfarlane," began Fettes, still somewhat hoarsely, "I have put my neck in a halter to oblige you."

"To oblige me?" cried Wolfe. "Oh, come! You did, as near as I can see the matter, what you downright had to do in self-defence. Suppose I got into trouble, where would you be? This second little matter flows clearly from the first. Mr. Gray is the continuation of Miss Galbraith. You can't begin and then stop. If you begin, you must keep on beginning; that's the truth. No rest for the wicked."

A horrible sense of blackness and the treachery of fate seized hold upon the soul of the unhappy student.

"My God!" he cried, "but what have I done? and when did I begin? To be made a class assistant—in the name of reason, where's the harm in that? Service wanted the position; Service might have got it. Would *he* have been where *I* am now?"

"My dear fellow," said Macfarlane, "what a boy you are! What harm *has* come to you? What harm *can* come to you if you hold your tongue? Why, man, do you know what this life is? There are two squads of us—the lions and the lambs. If you're a lamb, you'll come to lie upon these tables like Gray or Jane Galbraith; if you're a lion, you'll live and drive a horse like me, like K—, like all the world with any wit or courage. You're staggered at the first. But look at K—! My dear fellow, you're clever, you have pluck. I like you, and K— likes you. You were born to lead the hunt; and I tell you, on my honour and my experience of life, three days from now you'll laugh at all these scarecrows like a High School boy at a farce."

And with that Macfarlane took his departure and drove off up the wynd in his gig to get under cover before daylight. Fettes was thus left alone with his regrets. He saw the miserable peril in which he stood involved. He saw, with inexpressible dismay, that there was no limit to his weakness, and that, from concession to concession, he had fallen from the arbiter of Macfarlane's destiny to his paid and helpless accomplice. He would have given the world to have been a little braver at the time, but it did not occur to him that he might still be brave. The secret of Jane Galbraith and the cursed entry in the day-book closed his mouth.

Hours passed; the class began to arrive; the members of the unhappy Gray were dealt out to one and to another, and received without remark. Richardson was made happy with the head; and before the hour of freedom rang, Fettes trembled with exultation to perceive how far they had already gone toward safety.

For two days he continued to watch, with increasing joy, the dreadful process of disguise.

On the third day Macfarlane made his appearance. He had been ill, he said; but he made up for lost time by the energy with which he directed the students. To Richardson in particular he extended the most valuable assistance and advice, and that student, encouraged by the praise of the demonstrator, burned high with ambitious hopes, and saw the medal already in his grasp.

Before the week was out Macfarlane's prophecy had been ful-filled. Fettes had outlived his terrors and had forgotten his baseness. He began to plume himself upon his courage, and had so arranged the story in his mind that he could look back on these events with an unhealthy pride. Of his accomplice he saw but little. They met, of course, in the business of the class; they received their orders together from Mr. K—. At times they had a word or two in private, and Macfarlane was from first to last particularly kind and jovial. But it was plain that he avoided any reference to their common secret; and even when Fettes whispered to him that he had cast in his lot with the lions and forsworn the lambs, he only signed to him smilingly to hold his peace.

At length an occasion arose which threw the pair once more into a closer union. Mr. K— was again short of subjects; pupils were eager, and it was a part of this teacher's pretensions to be always well supplied. At the same time there came the news of a burial in the rustic graveyard of Glencorse. Time has little changed the place in question. It stood then, as now, upon a crossroad, out of call of human habitations, and buried fathom deep in the foliage of six cedar trees. The cries of the sheep upon the neighbouring hills, the streamlets upon either hand, one loudly singing among pebbles, the other dripping furtively from pond to pond, the stir of the wind in mountainous old flowering chestnuts, and once in seven days the voice of the bell and the old tunes of the precentor, were the only sounds that disturbed the silence around the rural church. The Resurrection Man—to use a byname of the period—was not to be deterred by any of the sanctities of customary piety. It was part of his trade to despise and desecrate the scrolls and trumpets of old tombs, the paths worn by the feet of worshippers and mourners, and the offerings and the inscriptions of bereaved affection. To rustic neighbourhoods, where love is more than commonly tenacious, and where some bonds of blood or fellowship unite the entire society of a parish, the body-snatcher, far from being repelled by natural respect, was attracted by the ease and safety of the task. To bodies that had been laid in earth, in joyful expectation of a far different awakening, there came that hasty, lamp-lit, terror-haunted resurrection of the spade and mattock. The coffin was forced, the cerements torn, and the melancholy relics, clad in sackcloth, after being rattled for hours on moonless byways, were at length exposed to uttermost indignities before a class of gaping boys.

Somewhat as two vultures may swoop upon a dying lamb, Fettes and Macfarlane were to be let loose upon a grave in that green and quiet resting-place. The wife of a farmer, a woman who had lived for sixty years, and been known for nothing but good butter and a godly conversation, was to be rooted from her grave at midnight and carried, dead and naked, to that far-away city that she had always honoured with her Sunday's best; the place beside her family was to be empty till the crack of doom; her innocent and almost venerable members to be exposed to that last curiosity of the anatomist.

Late one afternoon the pair set forth, well wrapped in cloaks and furnished with a formidable bottle. It rained without remission—a cold, dense, lashing rain. Now and again there blew a puff of wind, but these sheets of falling water kept it down. Bottle and all, it was a sad and silent drive as far as Penicuik, where they were to spend the evening. They stopped once, to hide their implements in a thick bush not far from the churchyard, and once again at the Fisher's Tryst, to have a toast before the kitchen fire and vary their nips of whisky with a glass of ale. When they reached their journey's end the gig was housed, the horse was fed and comforted, and the two young doctors in a private room sat down to the best dinner and the best wine the house afforded. The lights, the fire, the beating rain upon the window, the cold, incongruous work that lay before them, added zest to their enjoyment of the meal. With every glass their cordiality increased. Soon Macfarlane handed a little pile of gold to his companion.

"A compliment," he said. "Between friends these little d——d accommodations ought to fly like pipe-lights."

Fettes pocketed the money, and applauded the sentiment to the echo. "You are a philosopher," he cried. "I was an ass till I knew you. You and K— between you, by the Lord Harry! but you'll make a man of me."

"Of course we shall," applauded Macfarlane. "A man? I tell you, it required a man to back me up the other morning. There are some big, brawling, forty-year-old cowards who would have turned sick at the look of the d——d thing; but not you—you kept your head. I watched you."

"Well, and why not?" Fettes thus vaunted himself. "It was no affair of mine. There was nothing to gain on the one side but disturbance, and on the other I could count on your gratitude, don't you see?" And he slapped his pocket till the gold pieces rang.

Macfarlane somehow felt a certain touch of alarm at these unpleasant words. He may have regretted that he had taught his young companion so successfully, but he had no time to interfere, for the other noisily continued in this boastful strain:

"The great thing is not to be afraid. Now, between you and me, I don't want to hang—that's practical; but for all cant, Macfarlane, I was born with a contempt. Hell, God, Devil, right, wrong, sin, crime, and all the old gallery of curiosities—they may frighten boys, but men of the world, like you and me, despise them. Here's to the memory of Gray!"

It was by this time growing somewhat late. The gig, according to order, was brought round to the door with both lamps brightly shining, and the young men had to pay their bill and take the road. They announced that they were bound for Peebles, and drove in that direction till they were clear of the last houses of the town; then, extinguishing the lamps, returned upon their course, and followed a by-road toward Glencorse. There was no sound but that of their own passage, and the incessant, strident pouring of the rain. It was pitch dark; here and there a white gate or a white stone in the wall guided them for a short space across the night; but for the most part it was at a foot pace, and almost groping, that they picked their way through that resonant blackness to their solemn and isolated destination. In the sunken woods that traverse the neighbourhood of the burying-ground the last glimmer failed them, and it became necessary to kindle a match and re-illumine one of the lanterns of the gig. Thus, under the dripping trees, and environed by huge and moving shadows, they reached the scene of their unhallowed labours.

They were both experienced in such affairs, and powerful with the spade; and they had scarce been twenty minutes at their task before they were rewarded by a dull rattle on the coffin lid. At the same moment Macfarlane, having hurt his hand upon a stone, flung it carelessly above his head. The grave, in which they now stood almost to the shoulders, was close to the edge of the plateau of the graveyard; and the gig lamp had been propped, the better to illuminate their labours, against a tree, and on the immediate verge of the steep bank descending to the stream. Chance had taken a sure aim with the stone. Then came a clang of broken glass; night fell upon them; sounds alternately dull and ringing announced the bounding of the lantern down the bank, and its occasional collision with the trees. A stone or two, which it had dislodged in its descent, rattled behind it into the profundities of the glen; and then silence, like night, resumed its sway; and they might bend their hearing to its utmost pitch, but naught was to be heard except the rain, now marching to the wind, now steadily falling over miles of open country.

They were so nearly at an end of their abhorred task that they judged it wisest to complete it in the dark. The coffin was exhumed and broken open; the body inserted in the dripping sack and carried between them to the gig; one mounted to keep it in its place, and the other, taking the horse by the mouth, groped along by wall and bush until they reached the wider road by the Fisher's Tryst. Here was a faint, diffused radiancy, which they hailed like daylight; by that they pushed the horse to a good pace and began to rattle along merrily in the direction of the town.

They had both been wetted to the skin during their operations, and now, as the gig jumped among the deep ruts, the thing that stood propped between them fell now upon one and now upon the other. At every repetition of the horrid contact each instinctively repelled it with the greater haste; and the process, natural although it was, began to tell upon the nerves of the companions. Macfarlane made some ill-favoured jest about the farmer's wife, but it came hollowly from his lips, and was allowed to drop in silence. Still their unnatural burden bumped from side to side; and now the head would be laid, as if in confidence, upon their shoulders, and now the drenching sackcloth would flap icily about their faces. A creeping chill began to possess the soul of Fettes. He peered at the bundle, and it seemed somehow larger than at first. All over the country-side, and from every degree of distance, the farm dogs accompanied their passage with tragic ululations; and it grew and grew upon his mind that some unnatural miracle had been accomplished, that some nameless change had befallen the dead body, and that it was in fear of their unholy burden that the dogs were howling.

"For God's sake," said he, making a great effort to arrive at speech, "for God's sake, let's have a light!"

Seemingly Macfarlane was affected in the same direction; for, though he made no reply, he stopped the horse, passed the reins to his companion, got down, and proceeded to kindle the remaining lamp. They had by that time got no farther than the crossroad down to Auchenclinny. The rain still poured as though the deluge were returning, and it was no easy matter to make a light in such a world of wet and darkness. When at last the flickering blue flame had been transferred to the wick and began to expand and clarify, and shed a wide circle of misty brightness round the gig, it became possible for the two young men to see each other and the thing they had along with them. The rain had moulded the rough sacking to the outlines of the body underneath; the head was distinct from the trunk, the shoulders plainly modelled; something at once spectral and human riveted their eyes upon the ghastly comrade of their drive.

For some time Macfarlane stood motionless, holding up the lamp. A nameless dread was swathed, like a wet sheet, about the body, and tightened the white skin upon the face of Fettes; a fear that was meaningless, a horror of what could not be, kept mounting to his brain. Another beat of the watch, and he had spoken. But his comrade forestalled him.

"That is not a woman," said Macfarlane, in a hushed voice.

"It was a woman when we put her in," whispered Fettes.

"Hold that lamp," said the other. "I must see her face."

And as Fettes took the lamp his companion untied the fastenings of the sack and drew down the cover from the head. The light fell very clear upon the dark, well-moulded features and smooth-shaven cheeks of a too familiar countenance, often beheld in dreams of both of these young men. A wild yell rang up into the night; each leaped from his own side into the roadway: the lamp fell, broke, and was extinguished; and the horse, terrified by this unusual commotion, bounded and went off toward Edinburgh at a gallop, bearing along with it, sole occupant of the gig, the body of the dead and long-dissected Gray.

THE BLUE LABORATORY

L. T. Meade

L. T. Meade, or Elizabeth Thomasina Meade Smith (1844–1914), was an incredibly prolific Irish novelist who authored over 300 books, many of them intended for young readers. She also published mystery and detective stories, some of which appeared in *The Strand*, the magazine which carried Arthur Conan Doyle's Sherlock Holmes stories.

Although less well known than others in this collection, 'The Blue Laboratory' is a great modern Gothic story that mixes the female heroinism of Ann Radcliffe with touches of the Bluebeard fairy tale, the detective story and science fiction. It tells the tale of an English governess who ends up involved in her employer's experiments on the photography of thought. But what, for Madeline, begins as genuine interest in science soon turns to fear after she hears agonizing screams coming from Dr. Chance's secret workshop.

'The Blue Laboratory' first appeared in *Cassell's Family Magazine* in 1897, but was reprinted in Meade's collection *Silenced* (1904) and more recently in Mike Ashley's *The Dreaming Sex: Early Tales of Scientific Imagination by Women* (2010). It is a great reminder that there were many excellent female writers of science fiction working throughout the nineteenth and twentieth centuries who have been unduly forgotten.

W HEN I DECIDED TO ACCEPT THE OFFER OF A SITUATION AS
governess in a Russian family, I bought, amongst other
things, a small silver-mounted revolver, and fifty cartridges.

But before proceeding to tell this story, I had better say one or two
words about myself. My name is Madeline Rennick; I am an orphan,
and have no near relations. When Dr. Chance, an Englishman, but
a naturalized Russian, offered me a hundred per annum to educate
his two daughters, I determined to accept the situation without
a moment's hesitation. I bade my friends adieu, and reached St.
Petersburg without any sort of adventure. Dr. Chance met me at
the station. He was a somewhat handsome but near-sighted man on
quite the shady side of fifty. He was coldly polite to me, gave directions about my luggage, and took me straight to his house on the
Ligovka Canal. There I was received by Mrs. Chance, a lady in every
respect the antipodes of her husband. She was of mixed Russian
and German extraction, and had a manner full of curiosity, and yet
thoroughly unsympathetic. My pupils were rather pretty girls. The
elder was tall, and had the dark eyes of her father; she had a fine open
expression—her name was Olga. The younger was small in stature,
with a piquante face—she was called Maroussa. The girls could speak
English tolerably well, and the warmth of their greeting made up for
their mother's indifference.

"You must find it dreadfully dull here," said Maroussa, on a certain
afternoon when I had been a month in Russia.

"Not at all," I replied. "I have long had a great desire to see
Russia."

"You know, of course, that father is English. He has lived here ever since he was thirty years of age. He is a great scientist. How your eyes sparkle, Madeline! Are you interested in science?"

"I took a science tripos at Girton," I answered.

As I spoke I bent over the Russian novel which I was trying to read. The next moment a coldly polite voice spoke almost in my ear. I looked up, and saw to my astonishment that Dr. Chance, who seldom or never favoured the ladies of his family with his presence, had come into the salon.

"Did I hear aright?" he said. "Is it possible that you, a young lady, are interested in science?"

"I like it immensely," I replied.

"Your information pleases me. The fact is this, I came up just now to ask you to grant me a favour. At times I have intolerable pain in the right eye. To use it on such occasions makes it worse. Today I suffer torture. Will you come downstairs and be my secretary for the nonce?"

"Of course, I will," I answered. The moment I spoke, Dr. Chance moved towards the door, beckoning to me with a certain imperious gesture to follow him. I felt myself, as it were, whirled from the room. In a moment or two I was alone with the Doctor in his cabinet. A gentleman's study in Russian houses is always called by this name. The Doctor's cabinet was a nobly proportioned room—two-thirds of the walls being lined from ceiling to floor with books—a large double window giving abundant light, and a door at the further end letting in a peep of a somewhat mysterious room beyond.

"My laboratory," said the Doctor, noticing my glance. "Some day I shall have pleasure in showing it to you. Now, can you take down from dictation?"

"Yes, in shorthand."

"Capital! Pray give me your very best attention. The paper I am about to dictate to you is to be posted to England tonight. It will appear in the *Science Gazette*. As you are interested in such matters I do not mind confiding its subject to you. Miss Rennick, I have discovered a *method of photographing thought.*"

I stared at him in astonishment; he met my gaze fully. His deep-set, glittering eyes looked something like little sparks of fire.

"You do not believe me," he said, "and you represent to a great extent the public to whom I am about to appeal. I shall doubtless be scoffed at in England, but wait awhile. I can prove my words, but not yet—not yet. Are you ready?"

"I am all attention," I answered.

His brow cleared, he sank back on his divan. He began to dictate, and I took down his words assiduously. At the end of an hour he stopped.

"That will do," he said. "Now, will you kindly transcribe in your best and fairest writing what I have been saying to you?"

"Yes," I answered.

"And please accept ten roubles for the pleasure and help you have given me. Not a word of refusal. Be assured that you have my very best thanks."

He gave me a long and earnest look, and slowly left the room.

It took me from two to three hours to transcribe what had fallen so glibly from the Doctor's lips. Having finished my paper, I went upstairs.

When I entered the salon, Olga and Maroussa rushed to meet me.

"Tell us what has happened," they cried.

"But I have nothing to tell."

"Nonsense, you have been away for five hours."

"Yes, and during that time your father dictated a lecture to me, which I took down in shorthand. I have just transcribed it for him, and left it on his desk."

"Please, Madeline," said Olga, "tell us what was the subject of father's paper."

"I am not at liberty to do that, Olga."

Olga and Maroussa glanced at each other.

Then Olga took my hand.

"Listen," she said, "we have something to say to you. In the future you will be often in the laboratories."

"Are there more than one?"

"Yes. Now pray give me your attention. Please understand that father will ask you to help him again and again. He may even get you to assist him with his chemistry. It is about father's other laboratory, the one you have not yet seen—the Blue laboratory, that we want to speak. The fact is, Olga and I have a secret on our minds in connection with it. It weighs on us—sometimes it weighs heavily."

As Maroussa spoke she shuddered, and Olga's olive-tinted face grew distinctly paler.

"We long to confide in someone," said Olga. "From the moment we saw you we felt that we would be *en rapport* with you. Now will you listen?"

"Certainly, and I also promise to respect your secret."

"Well then, I will tell you in as few words as possible.

"A couple of months ago some gentlemen came to dinner—they were Germans and were very learned. One of them was called Dr. Schopenhauer; he is a great savant. When the wine was on the table, they began to talk about something which made father angry. Soon they were all quarrelling. It was fun to listen to them. They got red and father pale, and father said, 'I can prove my words.' I am sure they forgot all about our existence. Suddenly father sprang up and said, 'Come this way, gentlemen. I am in a position to make my point abundantly plain.' They all swept out of the dining-room and went into the cabinet. Mother said she had a headache, and she went upstairs to her boudoir, but Maroussa and I were quite excited, and we slipped into the cabinet after them. I don't think any of them noticed us. They went from the cabinet into the laboratory, a glimpse of which you saw today. He opened a door at the further end, and walked down a long passage. The scientists and father, absorbed in their own interests, went on in front, and Maroussa and I followed. Father took a key out of his pocket and opened a door in the wall, and as he did so he touched a spring, and behold, Madeline, we found ourselves on the threshold of another laboratory, double, treble as large as the one we had left. There was an extraordinary sort of dome in one of the corners standing up out of the floor. Maroussa and I noticed it the moment we entered the room. We were dreadfully afraid of being banished, and we slipped at once behind a big screen and waited there while father and the savants talked their secrets together. Suddenly Maroussa, who is always up to a bit of fun, suggested to me that we should stay behind and examine the place for ourselves after father and the Germans had gone. I do not know how we thought of such a daring scheme, for, of course, father would lock us in, but we forgot that part. After a time he seemed to satisfy the gentlemen, and they left the room as quickly as they had come in. Father turned off the electric light, and we were in darkness.

"We heard the footsteps dying away down the long corridor. We felt full of fun and mischief, and I said to Maroussa, 'Now let us turn on the light.'

"We had not gone half way across the room when, oh Madeline! what do you think happened? There came a knock which sounded as if it proceeded from the floor under our feet; it was in the direction of the queer dome which I have already mentioned to you. A voice cried piteously three times, 'Help, help, help!' We were terrified, all our little spirit of bravado ran out of us. I think Maroussa fell flop on the floor, and I know I gave about the loudest scream that could come from a human throat. It was so loud that it reached father's ears. The knocking underneath ceased, and we heard father's footsteps hurrying back. There was Maroussa moaning on the floor and pointing at the dome; she was too frightened to speak, but I said, 'There is someone underneath, away by that dome in the corner. I heard someone knocking distinctly, and a voice cried "Help!" three times.'

"'Folly!' said father; 'there is nothing underneath. Come away; this moment.'

"He hurried us out of the room and locked the door, and told us to go up to mother. We told mother all about it, but she too said we were talking nonsense, and seemed quite angry; and Maroussa could not help crying, and I had to comfort her.

"But, Madeline, that night we heard the cry again in our dreams, and it has haunted us ever since. Madeline, if you go on helping father, he will certainly take you into the Blue laboratory. If ever he does, pray listen and watch and tell us—oh, tell us!—if you hear that terrible, that awful voice again."

Olga stopped speaking; her face was white, and there were drops of moisture on her forehead.

I tried to make light of what she had said, but from that hour I felt that I had a mission in life. There was something in Olga's face when she told me her story which made me quite certain that she was speaking the truth. I determined to be wary and watchful, to act cautiously, and, if possible, to discover the secret of the Blue laboratory. For this purpose I made myself agreeable and useful to Dr. Chance. Many times when he complained of his eyes he asked me to be his secretary, and on each of these occasions he paid me ten roubles for my trouble. But during our intercourse—and I now spent a good deal of my time with the Doctor—I never really went the smallest way into his confidence. He never, for a moment, lifted the veil which hid his real nature from my gaze. Never, except once; and to tell of that awful time is the main object of this story. To an ordinary observer, Dr. Chance was a gentle-mannered, refined, but cold man. Now and then, it is true, I did see his eyes sparkle as if they were flints which had been suddenly struck to emit fire. Now and then, too, I noticed an anxious look about the tense lines of his mouth, and I have seen the dew coming out on his forehead when an experiment which I was helping him to conduct promised to prove exceptionally interesting. At last on a certain afternoon it was necessary for him to do some very important work in the Blue laboratory. He required my aid, and asked me to follow him there. It was, indeed, a splendidly equipped room. A teak bench ran round three sides of the wall, fitted with every conceivable apparatus and appliance, glazed fume chambers, stoneware sinks, Bunsen burners, porcelain dishes, balances, microscopes, burettes, mortars, retorts, and, in fact, every instrument devoted to the rites of the mephitic divinity. In one corner, as the girls had described to me, was a mysterious-looking, dome-shaped projection, about three or four feet high, and covered with a black cloth that looked like a pall.

This was the first occasion on which I worked with the Doctor in the Blue laboratory, but from that afternoon I went with him there on many occasions and learned to know the room well.

At last, on a certain day, my master was obliged to leave me for a few minutes alone in the laboratory. I have by nature plenty of courage, and I did not lose an instant in availing myself of this unlooked-for opportunity. The moment he left the room I hurried across to the mysterious dome, and, raising the black cloth, saw that it covered a frame of glass, doubtless communicating with some chamber below.

I struck my knuckles loudly on the glass. The effect was almost instantaneous. I was immediately conscious of a dim face peering up at me from beneath, and I now saw that there was an inner and much thicker partition of glass between us. The face was a horrible one—terrible with suffering—haggard, lean, and ghastly; there was a look about the mouth and the eyes which I had never before seen, and I hope to God I may never witness again on human countenance. This face so unexpected, so appalling, glanced at me for a second, then my master's steps were heard returning, a shadowy hand was raised as if to implore, and the ghoul-like vision vanished into the dark recesses beneath. I pulled the covering back over the dome and returned quickly to my work. Dr. Chance was near-sighted; he came bustling in with a couple of phials in his hand.

"Come here," he said. "I want you to hold these. What is the matter?" He glanced at me suspiciously. "You look pale. Are you ill?"

"I have a slight headache," I replied, "but I shall be all right in a moment."

"Would you like to leave off work? I have no desire to injure your health."

"I can go on," I answered, placing immense control upon myself. The shock was past; it was an awful one, but it was over. My suspicions were now realities: the girls had really heard that cry of pain. There was someone confined in a dungeon below the Blue laboratory—God only knew for what awful purpose. My duty was plain as daylight.

"Dr. Chance," I said, when my most important work was over, "why have you that peculiar dome in the corner of the floor?"

"I warned you to ask no questions," he said, his back was slightly to me as he spoke. "There is nothing in this room," he continued, "which is not of use. If you become curious and spying, I shall need your services no longer."

"You must please yourself about that," I replied with spirit; "but it is not an English girl's habit to spy."

"I believe you are right," said Dr. Chance, coming close and staring into my face. "Well, on this occasion I shall have pleasure in gratifying your curiosity. That dome is part of an apparatus by which I make a vacuum. Now you are doubtless as wise as you were before."

"I am no wiser," I answered.

The Doctor smiled in a sardonic manner.

"I have finished my experiment," he said; "let us come away."

I ran straight up to my room and shut and locked myself in. I could not face the girls—I must not see them again until I had so completely controlled my features that they would not guess that their suspicions were confirmed. I sat down and thought. No danger should now deter me on the course which I had marked out for myself. The miserable victim of Dr. Chance's cruelty should be rescued, even if my life were the penalty. But I knew well that my only chance of success was by putting the Doctor off his guard.

Having planned a certain line of action, I proceeded to act upon it. That evening I dressed for dinner in my choicest. I possessed an old black velvet dress which had belonged to my grandmother. The velvet was superb, but the make was old-fashioned. This very old-fashion would, doubtless, add to its charm in the eyes of the Doctor; he might, when he saw the dress, remember some of the beauties he had met when he was young. Accordingly, I put on the black velvet dress, pinned a lace kerchief in artistic folds round my throat, piled my hair high on my head, and then daringly powdered it. I had black hair—black as ink—a clear complexion, a good deal of colour in my cheeks, and very dark eyes and eyebrows. The effect of the powdered hair immediately removed me from the conventional girl of the period and gave me that old-picture look which men especially admire.

When I went into the salon, Olga and Maroussa rushed to meet me with cries of rapture.

"How beautiful you look, Madeline!" they exclaimed; "but why have you dressed so much?"

"I took a fancy to wear this," I said; "it belonged to my grandmother."

"But why have you powdered your hair?"

"Because it suits the dress."

"Well, you certainly do look lovely. I wonder what mamma will say?"

When Mrs. Chance appeared, she stared at me in some astonishment, but vouchsafed no remark. We all went down to dinner, and I saw Dr. Chance raise his eyes and observe my picturesque dress with a puzzled glance, followed immediately by a stare of approval.

"You remind me of someone," he said, after a pause. "My dear," turning to his wife, "of whom does Miss Rennick remind you?"

Mrs. Chance favoured me with her round, curious, unsympathetic stare.

"Miss Rennick is somewhat like the picture of Marie Antoinette just before she was guillotined," she remarked after a pause.

"True, there is certainly a resemblance," answered the Doctor, nodding his head.

I drew my chair a little closer to him and began to talk. I talked more brilliantly than I had ever done before; he listened to me in surprise. Soon I saw that I was pleasing him; I began to draw him out. He told me stories of his early youth, of a time when his fat German wife had not appeared on the horizon of his existence. He even described his conquests in those early days, and laughed merrily over his own exploits. Our conversation was in English, and Mrs. Chance evidently could not follow the Doctor's brilliant remarks and my somewhat smart replies. She stared at me in some astonishment, then, gently sighing, she lay back in her chair and began to doze. The girls talked to one another; they evidently suspected nothing.

"Shall we go up to the salon?" said Mrs. Chance at last.

"You may, my dear," was the Doctor's quick reply, "and the fact is, the sooner you and the girls do so the better, for Miss Rennick has to get through some work this evening for me. Did I not tell you so, Miss Rennick? Will you have the goodness to follow me now to the cabinet? If you finish your work quickly, I will do something for you. I see by your manner that you are devoured by curiosity. Yes, don't attempt to deny it. I will gratify you. You shall ask me this evening to tell you one of my secrets. Whatever you ask I shall do my best to comply with. The fact is, I am in the humour to be gracious."

"Miss Rennick looks tired," said Mrs. Chance; "don't keep her downstairs too long, Alexander. Come, girls."

The girls smiled and nodded to me, they followed their mother upstairs, and I went with the Doctor to his cabinet. The moment we were alone he turned and faced me.

"I repeat what I have just said," he began. "You are full of curiosity. That which ruined our mother Eve is also your bane. I see this evening defiance and a strong desire to wring my secrets from me in your eye. Now let me ask you a question. What has a young, unformed creature like you to do with science?"

"I love science," I said; "I respect her; her secrets are precious. But what can I do for you, Dr. Chance?"

"You speak in the right spirit, Miss Rennick. Yes, I require your services: follow me at once to the Blue laboratory."

He tripped on in front, genial and pleased. He opened the door in the wall, switched on the electric light, and we found ourselves in the ghastly place with its ghastly human secret. I went and stood close to the dome-shaped roof on the floor. Dr. Chance crossed the room and began to examine some microbes which he was carefully bringing to perfection.

"After all," he said, "this experiment is not in a sufficiently advanced stage to do anything further tonight. I shall not require you to help me until tomorrow. What, then, can I do for you?"

"You can keep your promise and tell me your secret," I answered.

"Certainly: what do you want to know?"

"Do you remember the first day I helped you?"

"Well."

"I wrote a paper for you on that day; the subject was the Photography of Thought. You promised your English public that in a month or six weeks at farthest you would be able to prove your words. The time is past. Prove your words to me now. Show me how you photograph thought."

Dr. Chance stared at me for a moment. Then he grinned from ear to ear. His glittering teeth showed, then vanished. His eyes looked like sparks of living fire; they contracted and seemed to sink into his head, they shone like the brightest diamonds. His emaciated, pale, high forehead became full of wrinkles. He stretched out his hand and grasped me by my shoulder.

"Are you prepared?" he asked; "do you know what you ask? I *could* tell you that secret. God knows I would tell it to you, if I thought you could bear it."

"I can bear anything," I said, steadying myself. "At the present moment I am all curiosity. I have no fear. Is your secret a fearful one? Is it a terrible thing to photograph thought?"

"The ways and means by which these secrets have been wrung from Nature are fraught with terror," was the slow reply; "but you have asked me, and you shall know—on a condition."

"What is that?"

"That you wait until tomorrow evening."

I was about to reply, when a servant came softly up the room, bearing a card on a salver.

He presented it to the Doctor. Dr. Chance looked at me.

"Dr. Schopenhauer has called," he said abruptly; "he wants to see me on something important. I shall be back with you in a few moments."

He left me alone. I could scarcely believe my senses. I was by myself in the Blue laboratory. Such an unlooked-for opportunity was indeed providential. I went straight like an arrow shot from a bow to the dome-shaped roof. I withdrew the covering and bent over it, peering into the utter darkness below. Of course, I could see nothing. I rapped with my knuckles on the glass; there was no sound, no reply of any sort. Had the victim been removed into a still further dungeon? I did not despair. I knocked again. This time my efforts were rewarded by a faint, far-away, terrible groan. I was desperate now, and, in spite of the risk I ran of being heard by Dr. Chance, began to shout down through the glass.

"If there is anyone within, speak!" I cried.

A voice, faint and hollow, a long way off—dim as if these were its last and dying utterances—answered me.

"I am an Englishman—unjustly imprisoned." There was a long pause; the next words came fainter: "Put to torture." Another silence; then the voice again: "In the shadow of death—help, save!"

"You shall be released within twenty-four hours: I swear it by God," I answered back. My next act was indeed daring, and the inspiration of a moment. I ran to the door, took out the key, and, hurrying to the bench where Dr. Chance's large microscope stood, took one of the pieces of hard paraffin which he used for regulating the temperature of his stage, and taking a careful impression of the key, returned it to its place, slipping the paraffin impression into my pocket. Having done this, I wandered about for a moment or two, trembling violently and trying to resume my self-control. The Doctor did not return. I resolved to stay in the Blue laboratory no longer. I turned off the electric light, took the key out of the lock, went up the long passage, and knocked at the door of the other laboratory. It was quickly opened by the Doctor. I gave him the key without glancing at him, and hurried to my room.

How I spent that dreadful night I can never now recall. I had no personal fear, but each thought in my brain, was centred upon one feverish goal. I would rescue that tortured Englishman, even at the risk of my life. At the present moment I could not determine clearly how to act, but before the morning two steps became clear to me. One was to have a duplicate key made immediately of the laboratory, the second to go and see the English Consul. I did not even know the name of the Consul, but I was aware that the Ambassador and Consul were bound to protect English subjects. Dr. Chance was himself a naturalized Russian, but the imprisoned man was an Englishman. I would appeal to my own country for his release.

Having nerved myself to this point, I dressed as usual and attended to my duties during the morning hours. All my splendour of the night before was laid aside, and I was once again the plain, sensible-looking English governess. At half-past twelve we all assembled for the mid-day meal. Dr. Chance sat at the foot of his table. He was particularly agreeable in his manner, but I observed that he gave me some stealthy and covert glances. For a moment I thought he might suspect something; then, believing this to be impossible, I tried to remain cool and quiet. Towards the end of the meal, and just when I was about to rise from table, he laid his hand on mine, and spoke.

"I am sorry to see you looking so pale," he said; "are you suffering from headache?"

"Yes."

"Ah, Miss Rennick, you allow your emotions to get the better of you. That headache is due to excitement."

"I have no cause to be excited," I replied.

"Pardon me, you have cause. You remember what I promised to tell you tonight?"

I stared him full in the eyes.

"I remember," I answered.

"It grieves me to have to disappoint you. An unexpected matter of business calls me from St. Petersburg; I shall be absent for a couple of days."

"But, my dear Alexander, I know nothing of this," said the wife.

"I will explain the matter to you later, my dear," he said. "The principal thing now is that I am unable to fulfil a promise made to Miss Rennick. See how she droops; her passion for science grows with what it is fed upon. Miss Rennick, I must leave home at eight o'clock this evening; I shall not be back before Saturday, but for the greater part of this day I shall require your services. Will you meet me in my cabinet not later than half-past two?"

I promised, and left the room with the two girls. At this hour we always went upstairs and devoted ourselves to lessons: we generally sat in the salon. It was all-important, all essential to my plans, that I should have the hour on this occasion, the one precious hour left to me—for it was now half-past one—at my disposal.

The moment I was alone with the girls I locked the door and turned and faced them.

"Listen to me," I said. "I have something most important to do. I mean to trust you, but only to a certain extent; I have no time to tell you everything."

"Oh, Madeline, Madeline! have you discovered something?" cried Olga.

"Yes, but I cannot breathe a word now; you can both help me to an invaluable extent."

"I shall be only too delighted," said Maroussa, beginning to skip about.

"Try to keep quiet, Maroussa; this is a matter of life or death. It is now half-past one. In an hour's time I must be in your father's cabinet; in the meantime I have much to do. I want to visit a locksmith's; he must make me a key. I shall ask him to have it ready by the afternoon, and will beg of you, Olga and Maroussa, to call for it when you go out later in the day. Do not let anyone know; contrive to do this in secret, and bring the key carefully back to me."

"Nurse will come with us," said Olga; "we can easily manage. What locksmith will you go to?"

I mentioned the name of a man whose shop I had noticed in a street near. Olga took a little pocket-book and made a note of the address, looked at me again as if she wanted to question further, but I told her I had not a moment to spare. She kissed me, and she and Maroussa ran to their own rooms.

Now, indeed, I must put wings to my feet. I sat down and wrote the following letter to the Consul.

Chance House, Ligovka Canal.

Sir,—I urgently implore your immediate assistance. I have discovered that an Englishman is imprisoned in an underground cellar in this house, and put to torture. I am an English girl residing here as governess. I have made up my mind to rescue the Englishman, but cannot do so without assistance. Dr. Chance leaves Petersburg this evening at eight o'clock. At nine o'clock I shall be in the large laboratory in the garden, known by the name of the Blue laboratory. I will give one of the servants directions to bring you there, if you will be kind enough to come to my aid. In God's name do not fail me, for the case is urgent. Both the Englishman and I are likely to be in extreme danger. I claim assistance for us both as British subjects.

Yours faithfully,
MADELINE RENNICK.

This letter written, I hastily addressed it and slipped it into my pocket. I wrapped myself in my warm furs and went out. No one saw me go. At this hour Mrs. Chance slept, and the girls and I were supposed to be engaged over our work. On my way to the Consul's house I stopped at the locksmith's, and gave him directions to make a key from the wax impression. I told him that the key must be ready in two or three hours. He objected, expostulating at the shortness of time, and stared me all over. I was firm, telling him that Miss Chance would call for the key between five and six o'clock that evening. He then promised that it should be ready for her, and I left him to hurry to the Consul's. The Consul's servant opened the door; I put the letter into his hands, charged him to take it immediately to his master, and hurried home. I had then in truth set a match to the mine. What the result would be God only knew!

At half-past two o'clock I knocked at the door of Dr. Chance's cabinet. He called to me to come in. I entered and went through my usual duties. The Doctor gave me plenty of work. I had letters to copy, to take down paragraphs for different science papers at his dictation, to transcribe and copy them—in short, to work hard as his clerk for several hours. Tea was brought to us between five and six, but at the meal he scarcely spoke, and sat with his back half-turned to me. At seven o'clock he left the room.

"I must prepare for my journey," he said. "I shall find you here for last directions just before I start."

When he was gone I rested my face in my hands, and wondered with a palpitating heart what the Consul would do for the relief of the wretched victim whose life I was determined to save. At ten minutes to eight Dr. Chance, dressed from head to foot in his warm furs, entered the cabinet.

"Goodbye, Miss Rennick," he said. His wife accompanied him, and so did both the girls. "You will have a couple of days' holiday while I am absent. This is Wednesday evening; I trust to be back by Saturday at farthest."

He shook hands with me and went into the hall, accompanied by his wife and daughters. In two minutes' time Olga danced into my presence.

"Here is the key," she said, dropping her voice. She glanced behind her. "Madeline, how white you look—but it is all right: I called for the key, leaving Maroussa and nurse outside. We often go to that shop to have locks repaired and altered, and no one suspects anything. Madeline, won't you tell me now what you have discovered?"

"Not yet, Olga. Olga, you have helped me much; and now, if you wish really to do more, will you and Maroussa, as you pity those in sore misery and given over unto death, offer up your prayers for what I am about to do during the next few hours?"

"I will," said Olga, tears springing to her eyes. "Oh, Madeline, how brave and good you are!" She flung her arms round my neck, kissed me and left the cabinet.

I went up to my room, resolving to visit the Blue laboratory between eight and nine o'clock. At nine o'clock, if all went well, the Consul would come to my aid. I had already prepared one of the servants to receive the Englishman on his arrival and to bring him to me straight to the Blue laboratory. The man said he quite understood. I slipped three roubles into his hand; his countenance became blandly agreeable, he put the money into his pocket and promised to attend faithfully to my directions. When I reached my room I glanced at the clock on my table; it pointed to five-and-twenty minutes past eight. The time had come. I hastily slipped my revolver into my pocket, and, with the duplicate key also concealed about my person, ran downstairs. I did not meet a soul; I went into the cabinet, passed through the first laboratory, sped down the stone passage, and reached the door in the garden wall. Would my key open it? Yes, the lock yielded smoothly and easily to the touch of the duplicate key. I swung the door back and did not even trouble to shut it. I felt no fear whatever now. Dr. Chance was miles away by this time. I switched on the electric light and walked across the room. My difficulties were, however, by no means over. It was one thing to have entered the laboratory, but it was quite another to go down into that dim dungeon where the victim was incarcerated. The face had peered at me through the glass dome, but how was that dome opened? By what means was the dungeon reached? I carefully examined the floor, and quickly perceived a trap-door concealed by a mat. In the centre of this door was a ring. I tugged at it with all my might and main; the door gave way. I saw that it was shut down by a spring and was only capable of being opened from the top. The moment I opened the door I saw steps underneath. I had provided myself with a candle and some matches. I now lit the candle and went slowly and cautiously down the stone stairs. There were about seven or eight stairs in all.

My candle gave but small light, and I was rather in despair how to act, when a button in the wall attracted my attention. Doubtless this place was also lit by electricity. I pressed the button, and lo! a small incandescent globe shone out on the wall beside me. I now saw that I was in a somewhat large underground chamber, the deep arches of its groined roof receding farther and farther away into total darkness. Not a living soul could I see. I looked around me much puzzled, and then a faint, very faint, groan fell upon my ears. I directed my steps in the direction of this sound, and I saw the dim outline of further groined arches, and deeper shadows. I went on a few more steps, and then discovered the object of my search. A man, tightly bound, lay upon the floor. His eyes stared fully at me; his face was cadaverous, of that yellow hue which one has seen now and then on the face of a corpse. His hands were tied, so were his feet; he could not move an inch. His lips moved, but no sound came from them. Only the eyes could speak, and they told me volumes. I fell on my knees and touched him tenderly.

"I said I would rescue you," I cried, "and I have come within the time. Now, fear nothing. I shall soon manage to untie your bonds and set you free."

The lips again moved faintly, and the eyes tried to express something negative: what, I could never guess. I laid my hand on the man's brow—it was wet with perspiration. My blood began to boil. Why had I ever worked for such a demon as Dr. Chance? But surely Providence had set me this task in order to rescue the miserable creature who lay at my feet? I was just about to raise the head of the wretched man, when I felt a touch on my shoulder. Had the Consul already arrived? Surely it was not yet nine o'clock? The next moment I started upright as if I had been shot. Dr. Chance stood before me! There was not the least surprise in his gaze; neither was there the faintest touch of anger in his small, deeply-set, short-sighted eyes. He peered forward as if he would examine me closely, and then stepped back.

"Miss Rennick," he said, "when I began my journey, the thought came over me that it was cruel to disappoint you. I had faithfully promised to impart one of my gravest—my very gravest—secrets to you tonight. After all, a gentleman's word to a lady ought to come before every other consideration. I have therefore postponed my journey. My servant told me that I should find you in the Blue laboratory. I came straight here. The moment I entered the room I saw that the trap-door was raised; the faint light beneath further guided my footsteps. I have found you: I am now prepared to tell you my secret."

I did not reply, but my heart beat loud and hard in great heavy thumps which must surely have been heard; the man was a monster—his very civility was laden with omen.

"You are doubtless overpowered by my polite consideration for you," he continued. He never once glanced at his victim. I tried to moisten my lips—I tried to say something, but not a word would escape me.

"You are anxious to know how I photograph thought. I am prepared to enlighten you. Stand here, will you?"

He came forward and pushed me into a different position. From where I now stood I could see both the victim and the devil in human shape who had tortured him.

"By means of that man who lies on the floor at your feet," continued Dr. Chance, "I have photographed thought. He was once my secretary. I quickly perceived that his character was feeble. I used mesmerism to get him into my power. By slow degrees he became my servant, I his master. By still slower, but also sure, degrees he became my slave, and I his tyrant. He is now absolutely subjective to my will, and consequently of immense use to me. By means of that bodily frame of his I have been able to peer deeper into certain secrets of Nature than any other man of my day. Yes, Miss Rennick, I am the greatest scientist at present in existence. What are the tortures of one man in comparison with so stupendous a result? Now listen. I always knew that you were inspired with the vein of curiosity to a marked degree: you are a clever girl, and might have done well, but as you sow, you must reap. When I left you in the Blue laboratory for a short time yesterday, I did so without suspicion, but the moment I returned I guessed that you had discovered something. Your face was full of wonder, despair, incredulity, horror. I then carefully laid a trap for you. It would never do for you to know my secrets, and then to go abroad and possibly divulge them. I took you into the laboratory again in the evening; I desired my servant to announce Dr. Schopenhauer; he never really came at all. I left the room, and from the passage outside watched you. I heard you cry out to that man; I saw you take an impression of the key. I determined that you should have your way. Today I kept you by my side on purpose, for I did not really require your services. I went away tonight more completely to blind you. I came back when I thought I had given you sufficient time to enter the laboratory. All has happened as I expected. Never for a single moment did you really deceive me. Now listen. I will keep my word: I will tell you my secret.

"It is a known scientific fact in physiology that in the dark the retina of some animals displays a pigment called the 'visual purple.' If, for instance, a frog is killed in the dark, and the eye after death is exposed to an object in the light, the image of this object becomes stamped on the retina, and can be fixed there by a solution of alum. Proceeding upon this basis, I have further discovered that by fixing my own gaze for a lengthened time on an object, and then going into a dark room and gazing at an exposed photo graphic plate the object

I have been looking at appears on the negative when developed. Do you follow me so far?"

I nodded. My tongue was dry, cleaving to the roof of my mouth; not a word could I utter.

"I doubt if you will understand me further," continued Dr. Chance, "but I will try to make the matter as plain to you as I can. I have conceived on a sound scientific basis that even *thought itself* may thus be photographed. This is what really takes place. Subjective impressions of thought cause molecular changes in the cells of the brain; why, then, may these not also be capable of decomposing this 'visual purple,' and then giving a distinct impression on a negative when exposed sufficiently long to its influence? I have made experiments and discovered that such is the case. In dreams especially this impression becomes terribly vivid. No more fascinating problem has ever absorbed a scientist than this. Behold my victim! Ought he not to congratulate himself on suffering in so vast a cause? Night after night I fasten back his eyelids with specula, and as he sleeps his eyes are wide open, staring straight for many hours in the dark at an exposed plate. This plate is destined to receive the impressions made by his dreams. Night after night I make different experiments. These can be easily done by giving my victim certain drugs, such as cocaine, Indian hemp, opium, and others. It is well known that the action of these drugs causes vivid and extraordinary dreams. This is my secret. During the day time I am merciful. I feed my patient well; he is not likely to die, although there is a possibility that he may reach madness owing to the sufferings which I cause his nervous system. Now, would you like to see some of the developed photographs?"

I shuddered and covered my face with my hands. A short scream burst from my lips.

"Nothing more," I cried. "I pray and beseech of you not to say another word. You are a devil in human shape. I will not listen to any more."

Dr. Chance came close to me.

"Women are hyper-sensitive," he said in a low tone. "Remember you wished to know. Remember I warned you that the secret was fraught with terror, with horror to many. I had hoped that you would rise above this horror, but I see that you are distinctly human."

"I am, and I rejoice in the fact," I replied. A small clock standing on a bench by my side showed me that it wanted seven minutes to nine. Would the English Consul come to my rescue? All now depended on him. Dr. Chance noticed the direction in which my eyes were travelling.

"You are tired of this room," he said: "little wonder! But remember you forced your way in against my will. Now listen to me. You know my secret. I have taken a pleasure in enlightening you. I could experiment on you. You are strongly imaginative, and would make a good victim."

"No, kill me rather," I cried, falling on my knees.

"That is what I propose to do," said Dr. Chance in a slow calm voice. "It would interfere vastly with my experiments were you to proclaim my secret to anybody else. Women, even the best women, are not to be trusted with such an important matter. I have no intention of having the grand dream of my life destroyed by the caprice of a girl. I propose, therefore, having imparted to you my secret, to seal it for ever on your lips by death. In five minutes you will die."

"Five minutes?" I answered. His very words braced me. In five minutes it would be nine o'clock.

"In the meantime," continued the Doctor, "is there anything I can do for you?"

I thought. Awful as my predicament was, I yet was able to think. If only I could gain time! I looked at the victim on the floor. His eyes were shining, dimly; they were full of tears. He tried to speak. Once I saw him writhe and struggle in his bonds.

"Never mind," I said bending over him. "Remember while there is life there is hope. If I can rescue you—"

"That is impossible," interrupted Dr. Chance. "It is unkind to raise sensations which can never by any possibility be realized. How shall we employ ourselves during the remaining minutes? You have now but four minutes to live. I should recommend you during the very short time which still remains to prepare your soul to meet your Maker. What, you will not?"

"My Maker will take care of my soul," I replied. "I am giving up my life in the cause of the oppressed. I have no fear of death. You can do your worst."

"You really are a most interesting character. It is a sad pity that you cannot devote your life to the science you would so vastly help. Give me your hand. I should like to walk round this dungeon with you."

He stretched out his hand and took mine. I did not refuse to walk with him. He took me from end to end of the dismal place. The little clock sounded nine strokes in a silvery voice.

"Your time is up," said Dr. Chance; "come!" He turned, and then walked quickly, still holding my hand, across the room. What was he going to do! Oh, great God! why was not the Consul punctual? I strained my ears to listen for a sound, but none came. I was standing exactly under the dome in the glass roof. I had just put out my foot to ascend the stairs when a sudden noise startled me. Before I could move a huge bell-shaped glass with great swiftness descended completely around me, and sank into a circular groove on the stone flags at my feet. What could this mean? Dr. Chance was looking at me from outside the wall of glass. He was grinning with a fiendish expression of triumph. I shouted to him—he took not the slightest notice; he turned round and pressed a lever beside the wall. There was a sudden loud thumping as of a piston working to and fro, and a valve at my feet opened and shut rapidly with a hissing sound. The truth flashed across me in a moment. I was under the receiver of an enormous exhaust pump, which had fitted into the dome above my head. Dr. Chance had told me that the dome was used for causing a vacuum. In a vacuum I knew no one could live. I gasped for breath and screamed to him for mercy, but the piston thumped on and on quicker and quicker. Frantic with terror, I dashed madly against the glass and tried with all my puny strength to burst it. It was very thick, and defied all my efforts. My eyes seemed to start from my head, my whole body seemed to be swelling. I fought for my breath madly. Suddenly there was a noise like the rushing of waters in my ears, my brain reeled and I fell. During the agonies of my death struggles I could just catch sight of the fiendish face of my master peering in at me. It was the face of a devil. What providential inspiration came to my aid at that last extreme moment I know not, but suddenly I remembered my revolver; with my last remaining strength I drew it from my pocket, and, pointing it upwards, pressed the trigger. There was a terrific crash of falling glass, a sudden in-rush of air, and I became unconscious.

When I came to myself a strange face was bending over me, and a kind hand was wiping something warm from my face, which doubtless was bleeding from the glass which had fallen upon it. I promptly guessed that the Consul had arrived, and that I was saved. I opened my eyes and caught sight of the face and figure of Dr. Chance. Handcuffs encircled his wrists, a man in the dress of the police officers of St. Petersburg was standing close to him; I further saw a shadowy figure—doubtless that of the victim whom I had come to rescue—he was supported by two other men.

"Don't speak, rest quiet; all your sufferings are over," said the kind voice which I afterwards knew to be that of the British Consul. Then I passed into deep oblivion, and it was many days before I remembered anything more. It may have been a fortnight later when I came to myself in a pleasant bedroom in the Consul's house. His wife was bending over me. She told me in a few words what had occurred. The victim of Dr. Chance's cruelty had been sent to the hospital, and was rapidly getting better. Dr. Chance himself was imprisoned, and would doubtless be sent to Siberia for his crimes. The whole place was talking of what I had done, of the horror which had been discovered in the Blue laboratory.

"Your letter came just in time," said Mrs. Seymour. "My husband acted on it immediately; he went to see the Ambassador, who gave him a note to the Prefect of Police. But how did it come into your head to act so promptly, so bravely?"

Tears filled my eyes, I was too weak to reply.

I am now back again in England. I have not seen Olga and Maroussa again. I wonder what will become of them, what their future history will be? For myself, I can never return to St. Petersburg.

THE FIVE SENSES

E. Nesbit

English writer E. (Edith) Nesbit (1858–1924) is best-known for her books for children, especially *Five Children and It* (1902) and *The Railway Children* (1906). Yet she also wrote fiction for adults, and even published a number of horror collections, such as *Grim Tales* (1893), which includes the classic uncanny story 'Man-Size in Marble', *Something Wrong* (1893) and *Fear* (1910). The latter reprinted 'The Five Senses', first published in *The London Magazine* in 1909.

Nesbit had a strong interest in science, especially in the unforeseeable effects of new technological discoveries. Her stories 'The Third Drug' (1908, also known as 'The Three Drugs') and 'The Haunted House' (1913), for example, explore the consequences of achieving immortality and a super-human mental state through blood transfusion and special draughts.

'The Five Senses' is of particular interest to this volume because it paints a richer picture of the mad scientist. Professor Boyd Thompson is preoccupied with intensifying the five senses because he believes this way 'worlds beyond the grasp of his tired mind' will open. But his personal vision is also driven by a keen wish to make a contribution to the discipline he loves so deeply. Regardless of his well-meaning intentions, this is a mad science story, so the professor's formula is bound to have unexpected and disturbing side effects.

P ROFESSOR BOYD THOMPSON'S SERVICES TO THE CAUSE OF SCI-
ence are usually spoken of as inestimable, and so indeed they
probably are, since in science, as in the rest of life, one thing leads
to another, and you never know where anything is going to stop.
At any rate, inestimable or not, they are world-renowned, and he
with them. The discoveries which he gave to his time are a matter
of common knowledge among biological experts, and the sudden
ending of his experimental activities caused a few days' wonder in
even lay circles. Quite unintelligent people told each other that it
seemed a pity, and persons on omnibuses exchanged commonplaces
starred with his name.

But the real meaning and cause of that ending have been studi-
ously hidden, as well as the events which immediately preceded it. A
veil has been drawn over all the things that people would have liked
to know, and it is only now that circumstances so arrange themselves
as to make it possible to tell the whole story. I propose to avail myself
of this possibility.

It will serve no purpose for me to explain how the necessary
knowledge came into my possession; but I will say that the story
was only in part pieced together by me. Another hand is responsible
for much of the detail, and for a certain occasional emotionalism
which is, I believe, wholly foreign to my own style. In my original
statement of the following facts I dealt fully, as I am, I may say
without immodesty, qualified to do, with all the scientific points of
the narrative. But these details were judged, unwisely as I think, to
be needless to the expert, and unintelligible to the ordinary reader,

and have therefore been struck out; the merest hints being left as necessary links in the story. This appears to me to destroy most of its interest, but I admit that the elisions are perhaps justified. I have no desire to assist or encourage callow students in such experiments as those by which Professor Boyd Thompson brought his scientific career to an end.

Incredible as it may appear, Professor Boyd Thompson was once a little boy who wore white embroidered frocks and blue sashes; in that state he caught flies and pulled off their wings to find out how they flew. He did not find out, and Lucilla, his little girl-cousin, also in white frocks, cried over the dead, dismembered flies, and buried them in little paper coffins. Later, he wore a holland blouse with a belt of leather, and watched the development of tadpoles in a tin bath in the stable yard. A microscope was, on his eighth birthday, presented to him by an affluent uncle. The uncle showed him how to surprise the secrets of a drop of pond water, which, limpid to the eye, confessed under the microscope to a whole cosmogony of strenuous and undesirable careers. At the age of ten, Arthur Boyd Thompson was sent to a private school, its Headmaster an acolyte of Science, who esteemed himself to be a high priest of Huxley and Tyndal, a devotee of Darwin. Thence to the choice of medicine as a profession was, when the choice was insisted on by the elder Boyd Thompson, a short, plain step. Inorganic chemistry failed to charm, and under the cloak of Medicine and Surgery the growing fever of scientific curiosity could be sated on bodies other than the cloak-wearer's. He became a medical student and an enthusiast for vivisection.

The bow of Apollo was not always bent. In a rest-interval, the summer vacation, to be exact, he met again the cousin—second, once removed—Lucilla, and loved her. They were betrothed. It was a long, bright summer full of sunshine, garden-parties, picnics,

archery—a decaying amusement—and croquet, then coming to its
own. He exulted in the distinction already crescent in his career
but some half-formed, wholly-unconscious desire to shine with
increased lustre in the eyes of the beloved, caused him to invite, for
the holidays' ultimate week, a fellow student, one who knew and
could testify to the quality of the laurels already encircling the head
of the young scientist. The friend came, testified, and in a vibrat-
ing interview under the lime-trees of Lucilla's people's garden, Mr.
Boyd Thompson learned that Lucilla never could, never would love
or marry a vivisectionist.

The moon hung low and yellow in the spacious calm of the sky;
the hour was propitious, the lovers fond. Mr. Boyd Thompson vowed
that his scientific research should henceforth deal wholly with depart-
ments into which the emotions of the non-scientific cannot enter.
He went back to London, and within the week bought four dozen
frogs, twelve guinea-pigs, five cats, and a spaniel. His scientific aspira-
tions met his love-longings, and did not fight them. You cannot fight
beings of another world. He took part in a debate on blood pressure,
which created some little stir in medical circles, spoke eloquently, and
distinction surrounded him with a halo.

He wrote to Lucilla three times a week, took his degree, and
published that celebrated paper of his which set the whole scientific
world by the ears, "The Action of Choline on the Nervous System,"
I think its name was.

Lucilla surreptitiously subscribed to a press-cutting agency for all
snippets of print relating to her lover. Three weeks after the publication of that paper, which really was the beginning of Professor Boyd
Thompson's fame, she wrote to him from her home in Kent.

"Arthur, you have been doing it again. You know how I love you,
and I believe you love me; but you must choose between loving me

and torturing dumb animals. If you don't choose right, then it's goodbye, and God forgive you.

"Your poor Lucilla, who loved you very dearly."

He read the letter, and the human heart in him winced and whined. Yet not so deeply now, nor so loudly, but that he bethought himself to seek out a friend and pupil, who would watch certain experiments, attend to the cutting of certain sections, before he started for Tenterden, where she lived. There was no station at Tenterden in those days, but a twelve mile walk did not dismay him.

Lucilla's home was one of those houses of brave proportions and an inalienable bourgeois stateliness, which stand back a little from the noble High Street of that most beautiful of Kentish towns. He came there pleasantly exercised, his boots dusty, and his throat dry, and stood on the snowy doorstep, beneath the Jacobean lintel. He looked down the wide, beautiful street, raised eyebrows and shrugged uneasy shoulders within his professional frock-coat.

"It's all so difficult," he said to himself.

Lucilla received him in a drawing-room scented with last year's rose leaves, and fresh with chintz that had been washed a dozen times. She stood, very pale and frail; her blonde hair was not teased into fluffiness, and rounded over the chignon of the period, but banded Madonna-wise, crowning her with heavy burnished plaits. Her gown was of white muslin, and round her neck black velvet passed, supporting a gold locket. He knew whose picture it held. The loose bell sleeves fell away from the slender arms with little black velvet bracelets, and she leaned one hand on a chiffonier of carved rosewood, on whose marble top stood, under a glass case, a Chinese pagoda, carved in ivory, and two Bohemian glass vases with medallions representing young women nursing pigeons. There were white curtains of darned net, in the fireplace white ravelled muslin spread a cascade brightened with threads of tinsel. A canary sang in a green cage, wainscotted with yellow tarlatan, and two red rosebuds stood in lank specimen glasses on the mantelpiece.

Every article of furniture in the room spoke eloquently of the sheltered life, the iron obstinacy of the well-brought-up.

It was a scene that invaded his mental vision many a time, in the laboratory, in the lecture-room. It symbolized many things, all dear, and all impossible.

They talked awkwardly, miserably. And always it came round to this same thing.

"But you don't mean it," he said, and at last came close to her.

"I do mean it," she said, very white, very trembling, very determined.

"But it's my life," he pleaded, "it's the life of thousands. You don't understand."

"I understand that dogs are tortured. I can't bear it."

He caught at her hand.

"Don't," she said. "When I think what that hand does!"

"Dearest," he said very earnestly, "which is the more important, a dog or a human being?"

"They're all God's creatures," she flashed, unorthodoxly orthodox. "They're all God's creatures," with much more that he heard, and pitied, and smiled at miserably in his heart.

"You don't understand," he kept saying, stemming the flood of her rhetorical pleadings. "Spencer Wells alone has found out wonderful things, just with experiments on rabbits."

"Don't tell me," she said, "I don't want to hear."

The conventions of their day forbade that he should tell her anything plainly. He took refuge in generalities. "Spencer Wells, that operation he perfected, it's restored thousands of women to their husbands—saved thousands of women for their children."

"I don't care what he's done—it's wrong if it's done in that way."

It was on that day that they parted, after more than an hour and more than two, of mutual misunderstood reiteration. He, she said, was brutal. And besides it was plain that he did not love her. To him, she seemed unreasonable, narrow, prejudiced, blind to the high ideals of the new science.

"Then it's goodbye," he said at last. "If I gave way, you'd only despise me. Because I should despise myself. It's no good. Goodbye, dear."

"Goodbye," she said. "I know I'm right. You'll know I am, some day."

"Never," he answered, more moved and in a more diffused sense than he had ever believed he could be. "I can't set my pleasure in you against the good of the whole world."

"If that's all you think of me," she said, and her silk and her muslin whirled from the room.

He walked back to Staplehurst, thrilled with the conflict. The thrill died down, went out, and left as ashes a cold resolve.

That was the end of Mr. Boyd Thompson's engagement.

It was quite by accident that he made his greatest discovery. There are those who hold that all great discoveries are accident—or Providence. The terms are in this connection, interchangeable. He plunged into work to wash away the traces of his soul's wounds, as a man plunges into water to wash off red blood. And he swam there, perhaps, a little blindly. The injection with which he treated that white rabbit was not compounded of the drugs he had intended to use. He could not lay his hand on the thing he wanted, and in that sort of frenzy of experiment, to which no scientific investigator is wholly a stranger, he cast about for a new idea. The thing that came to his hand was a drug that he had never in his normal mind intended to use—an unaccredited, wild, magic, medicine obtained by a missionary from some savage South Sea tribe and brought home as an example of the ignorance of the heathen.

And it worked a miracle.

He had been fighting his way through the unbending opposition of known facts, he had been struggling in the shadows, and this discovery was like the blinding light that meets a man's eyes when his pickaxe knocks a hole in a dark cave, and he finds himself face to face with the sun. The effect was undoubted. Now it behoved him to make sure of the cause, to eliminate all those other factors to which that effect might have been due. He experimented cautiously, slowly. These things take years, and the years he did not grudge. He was never tired, never impatient; the slightest variations, the least indications, were eagerly observed, faithfully recorded.

His whole soul was in his work, Lucilla was the one beautiful memory of his life. But she was a memory. The reality was this discovery, the accident, the Providence.

Day followed day, all alike, and yet each taking, almost unperceived, one little step forward; or stumbling into sudden sloughs, those losses and lapses that take days and weeks to retrieve. He was Professor, and his hair was grey at the temples before his achievement rose before him, beautiful, inevitable, austere in its completed splendour, as before the triumphant artist rises the finished work of his art.

He had found out one of the secrets with which Nature has crammed her dark hiding-places. He had discovered the hidden possibilities of sensation. In plain English, his researches had led him thus far: he had found—by accident or by Providence—the way to intensify sensation. Vaguely, incredulously, he had perceived his discovery; the rabbits and guinea-pigs had demonstrated it plainly enough. Then there was a night when he became aware that those results must be checked by something else. He must work out in marble the form he had worked out in clay. He knew that by this drug, which had, so to speak, thrust itself upon him, he could intensify the five senses of any of the inferior animals. Could he intensify those senses in man? If so, worlds beyond the grasp of his tired mind opened themselves before him. If so, he would have achieved a discovery, made a contribution to the science he had loved so well and followed at such a cost, a discovery equal to any that any man had ever made.

Ferrier, and Leo, and Horsley; those he would outshine. Galileo, Newton, Harvey; he would rank with these.

Could he find a human rabbit to submit to the test?

The soul of the man Lucilla had loved, turned and revolted. No: he had experimented on guinea-pigs and rabbits, but when it came to experimenting on men, there was only one man on whom he chose to use his new-found powers. Himself.

At least she would not have it to say that he was a coward, or unfair, when it came to the point of what a man could do and dare, could suffer and endure.

His big laboratory was silent and deserted. His assistants were gone, his private pupils dispersed. He was alone with the tools of his trade. Shelf on shelf of smooth stoppered bottles, drugs and stains, the long bench gleaming with beakers, test tubes, and the glass mansions of costly apparatus. In the shadows at the far end of the room, where the last going assistant had turned off the electric lights, strange shapes lurked, wicker-covered carboys, kinographs, galvanometers, the faintly threatening aspect of delicate complex machines all wires and coils and springs, the gaunt form of the pendulum myograph, and certain well-worn tables and copper troughs, for which the moment had no use.

He knew that this drug with others, diversely compounded and applied, produced in animals an abnormal intensification of the senses; that it increased—nay, as it were magnified a thousandfold, the hearing, the sight, the touch—and he was almost sure the senses of taste and smell. But of the extent of the increase he could form no exact estimate.

Should he tonight put himself in the position of one able to speak on these points with authority? Or should he go to the Royal Society's meeting, and hear that ass Netherby maunder yet once again about the Secretion of Lymph?

He pulled out his notebook and laid it open on the bench. He went to the locked cupboard, unfastened it with the bright key that hung instead of seal or charm at his watch-chain. He unfolded a paper and laid it on the bench where no one coming in could fail to see it. Then he took out little bottles, three, four, five, polished a graduated glass and dropped into it slow, heavy drops. A larger bottle yielded a medium in which all mingled. He hardly hesitated at all before turning up his sleeve and slipping the tiny needle into his arm. He pressed the end of the syringe. The injection was made.

Its effect, though not immediate, was sudden. He had to close his eyes, staggered indeed and was glad of the stool near him; for the drug coursed through him as a hunt in full cry might sweep over untrodden plains. Then suddenly everything seemed to settle; he was no longer the helpless scene of incredible meetings, but Professor Boyd Thompson who had injected a mixture of certain drugs, and was experiencing their effect.

His fingers, still holding the glass syringe, sent swift messages to his brain. When he looked down at his fingers, he saw that what they grasped was the smooth, slender tube of clear glass. What he felt that they held was a tremendous cylinder, rough to the touch. He wondered, even at the moment, why, if his sense of touch were indeed magnified to this degree, everything did not appear enormous—his ring, his collar. He examined the new phenomenon with cold care. It seemed that only that was enlarged on which his attention, his mind, was fixed. He kept his hand on the glass syringe, and thought of his ring, got his mind away from the tube, back again in time to feel it small between his fingers, grow, increase, and become big once more.

"So *that's* a success," he said, and saw himself lay the thing down. It lay just in front of the rack of test tubes, to the eye just that little glass cylinder. To the touch it was like a water-pipe on a house side, and the test tubes, when he touched them, like the pipes of a great organ.

"Success," he said again, and mixed the antidote. For he had found the antidote in one of those flashes of intuition, imagination, genius, that light the ways of science as stars light the way of a ship in dark waters. The action of the antidote was enough for one night. He locked the cupboard, and, after all, was glad to listen to the maunderings of Netherby. It had been lonely there, in the atmosphere of complete success.

One by one, day by day, he tested the action of his drugs on his other senses. Without being technical, I had perhaps better explain that the compelling drug was, in each case, one and the same. Its action was directed to this set of nerves or that by means of the other drugs mixed with it. I trust this is clear?

The sense of smell was tested, and its laboratory, with its mingled odours, became abominable to him. Hardly could he stay himself from rushing forth into the outer air, to wash his nostrils in the clear coolness of Hampstead Heath. The sense of taste gave him, magnified a thousand times, the flavour of his after-dinner coffee, and other tastes, distasteful almost beyond the bearing point.

"But success," he said, rinsing his mouth at the laboratory sink after the drinking of the antidote, "all along the line, success."

Then he tested the action of his discovery on the sense of hearing. And the sound of London came like the roar of a giant, yet when he fixed his attention on the movements of a fly, all other sounds ceased, and he heard the sound of the fly's feet on the shelf when it walked. Thus, in turn, he heard the creak of boards expanding in the heat, the movement of the glass stoppers that kept imprisoned in their proper bottles the giants of acid and alkali.

"Success!" he cried aloud, and his voice sounded in his ears like the shout of a monster overcoming primeval forces. "Success! success!"

There remained only the eyes, and here, strangely enough, the Professor hesitated, faint with a sudden heart-sickness. Following all intensification there must be reaction. What if the reaction exceeded that from which it reacted, what if the wave of tremendous sight, stemmed by the antidote ebbing, left him blind? But the spirit of the explorer in science is the spirit that explores African rivers, and sails amid white bergs to seek the undiscovered Pole.

He held the syringe with a firm hand, made the required puncture, and braced himself for the result. His eyes seemed to swell to great globes, to dwindle to microscopic globules, to swim in a flood of fire, to shrivel high and dry on a beach of hot sand. Then he saw, and the glass fell from his hand. For the whole of the stable earth seemed to be suddenly set in movement, even the air grew thick with vast overlapping shapeless shapes. He opined later that these were the microbes and bacilli that cover and fill all things, in this world that looks so clean and bright.

Concentrating his vision, he saw in the one day's little dust on the bottles myriads of creatures, crawling and writhing, alive. The proportions of the laboratory seemed but little altered. Its large lines and forms remained practically unchanged. It was the little things that were no longer little, the invisible things that were now invisible no longer. And he felt grateful for the first time in his life, for the limits set by Nature to the powers of the human body. He had increased those powers. If he let his eyes stray idly about, as one does in the waltz for example, all was much as it used to be. But the moment he looked steadily at any one thing, it became enormous.

He closed his eyes. Success here had gone beyond his wildest dreams. Indeed he could not but feel that success, taking the bit between its teeth, had perhaps gone just the least little bit too far.

And on the next day he decided to examine the drug in all its aspects, to court the intensification of all his senses which should set him in the position of supreme power over men and things, transform him from a Professor into a demi-god.

The great question was, of course, how the five preparations of his drug would act on or against each other. Would it be intensification, or would they neutralize each other? Like all imaginative scientists, he was working with stuff perilously like the spells of magic, and certain things were not possible to be foretold. Besides, this drug came from a land of mystery and the knowledge of secrets which we call magic. He did not anticipate any increase in the danger of the experiment. Nevertheless he spent some hours in arranging and destroying papers, among others certain pages of the yellow note-book. After dinner he detained his man as, laden with the last tray, he was leaving the room.

"I may as well tell you, Parker," the Professor said, moved by some impulse he had not expected, "that you will benefit to some extent by my will. On conditions. If any accident should cut short my life, you will at once communicate with my solicitor; whose name you will now write down."

The model man, trained by fifteen years of close personal service, drew forth a notebook neat as the Professor's own, wrote in it neatly the address the Professor gave.

"Anything more, sir?" he asked, looking up, pencil in hand.

"No," said the Professor, "nothing more. Good-night, Parker."

"Good-night, sir," said the model man.

The next words the model man opened his lips to speak were breathed into the night tube of the nearest doctor.

"My master, Professor Boyd Thompson; could you come round at once, sir. I'm afraid it's very serious."

It was half past six when the nearest doctor—Jones was his unimportant name—stooped over the lifeless body of the Professor.

He shook his head as he stood up and looked round the private laboratory on whose floor the body lay.

"His researches are over," he said. "Yes, he's dead. Been dead some hours. When did you find him?"

"I went to call my master as usual," said Parker; "he rises at six, summer and winter, sir. He was not in his room, and the bed had not been slept in. So I came in here, sir. It is not unusual for my master to work all night when he has been very interested in his experiments, and then he likes his coffee at six."

"I see," said Doctor Jones. "Well, you'd better rouse the house and fetch his own doctor. It's heart failure, of course, but I daresay he'd like to sign the certificate himself."

"Can nothing be done?" said Parker, much affected.

"Nothing," said Dr. Jones. "It's the common lot. You'll have to look out for another situation."

"Yes, sir," said Parker; "he told me only last night what I was to do in case of anything happening to him. I wonder if he had any idea?"

"Some premonition, perhaps," the doctor corrected.

The funeral was a very quiet one. So the late Professor Boyd Thompson had decreed in his will. He had arranged all details. The body was to be clothed in flannel, placed in an open coffin covered only with a linen sheet, and laid in the family mausoleum, a moss-grown building in the midst of a little park which surrounded Boyd Grange, the birthplace of the Boyd Thompsons. A little property in Sussex it was. The professor sometimes went there for week-ends. He had left this property to Lucilla, with a last love-letter, in which he begged her to give his body the hospitality of the death-house, now hers with the rest of the estate. To Parker he left an annuity of two hundred pounds, on the condition that he should visit and enter the mausoleum once in every twenty-four hours for fourteen days after the funeral.

To this end the late Professor's solicitor decided that Parker had better reside at Boyd Grange for the said fortnight, and Parker, whose nerves seemed to be shaken, petitioned for company. This made easy the arrangement which the solicitor desired to make—of a witness to the carrying out by Parker of the provisions of the dead man's will. The solicitor's clerk was quite good company, and arm-in-arm with him Parker paid his first visit to the mausoleum. The little building stands in a glade of evergreen oaks. The trees are old and thick, and the narrow door is deep in shadow even on the sunniest day. Parker went to the mausoleum, peered through its square grating, but he did not go in. Instead, he listened, and his ears were full of silence.

"He's dead, right enough," he said, with a doubtful glance at his companion.

"You ought to go in, oughtn't you?" said the solicitor's clerk.

"Go in yourself, if you like, Mr. Pollack," said Parker, suddenly angry; "anyone who likes can go in, but it won't be me. If he was alive, it 'ud be different. I'd have done anything for *him*. But I ain't going in among all them dead and mouldering Thompsons. See? If we both say I did, it'll be just the same as me doing it."

"So it will," said the clerk; "but where do I come in?"

Parker explained to him where he came in, to their mutual content.

"Right you are," said the clerk; "on those terms I'm fly. And if we both say you did it, we needn't come to the beastly place again," he added, shivering and glancing over his shoulder at the door with the grating.

"No more we need," said Parker.

Behind the bars of the narrow door lay deeper shadows than those of the ilexes outside. And in the blackest of the shadows lay a man whose every sense was intensified as though by a magic potion. For when the Professor swallowed the five variants of his great discovery, each acted as he had expected it to act. But the union of the five vehicles conveying the drug to the nerves, which served his five senses, had paralysed every muscle. His hearing, taste, touch, scent and sight were intensified a thousandfold—as they had been in the individual experiments—but the man who felt all this exaggerated increase of sensation was powerless as a cat under kurali. He could not raise a finger, stir an eyelash. More, he could not breathe, nor did his body advise him of any need of breathing. And he had lain thus immobile and felt his body slowly grow cold, had heard in thunder the voices of Parker and the doctor; had felt the enormous hands of those who made his death-toilet, had smelt intolerably the camphor and lavender that they laid round him in the narrow, black bed; had tasted the mingled flavours of the drug and its five mediums; and, in an ecstasy of magnified sensation, had made the lonely train journey which coffins make, and known himself carried into the mausoleum and left there alone. And every sense was intensified, even his sense of time, so that it seemed to him that he had lain there for many years. And the effect of the drugs showed no sign of any diminution or reaction. Why had he not left directions for the injection of the antidote? It was one of those slips which wreck campaigns, cause the discovery of hidden crimes. It was a slip, and he had made it. He had thought of death, but in all the results he had anticipated, death's semblance had found no place. Well, he had made his bed, and he must lie on it. This narrow bed, whose scent of clean oak and French polish was distinct among the musty, intolerable odours of the charnel house.

It was perhaps twenty hours that he had lain there, powerless, immobile, listening to the sounds of unexplained movements about him, when he felt with a joy, almost like delirium, a faint quivering in the eyelids.

They had closed his eyes, and till now, they had remained closed. Now, with an effort as of one who lifts a grave-stone, he raised his eyelids. They closed again quickly, for the roof of the vault, at which he gazed earnestly, was alive with monsters; spiders, earwigs, crawling beetles and flies, far too small to have been perceived by normal eyes, spread giant forms over him. He closed his eyes and shuddered. It felt like a shudder, but no one who had stood beside him could have noted any movement.

It was then that Parker came—and went.

Professor Boyd Thompson heard Parker's words, and lay listening to the thunder of Parker's retreating feet. He tried to move—to call out. But he could not. He lay there helpless, and somehow he thought of the dark end of the laboratory, where the assistant before leaving had turned out the electric lights.

He had nothing but his thoughts. He thought how he would lie there, and die there. The place was sequestered; no one passed that way. Parker had failed him, and the end was not hard to picture. He might recover all his faculties, might be able to get up, able to scream, to shout, to tear at the bars. The bars were strong, and Parker would not come again. Well, he would try to face with a decent bravery whatever had to be faced.

Time, measureless, spread round. It seemed as though someone had stopped all the clocks in the world, as though he were not in time but in eternity. Only by the waxing and waning light he knew of the night and the day.

His brain was weary with the effort to move, to speak, to cry out. He lay, informed with something like despair—or fortitude. And then Parker came again. And this time a key grated in the lock. The Professor noted with rapture that it sounded no louder than a key should sound, turned in a lock that was rusty. Nor was the voice other than he had been used to hear it, when he was man alive and Parker's master. And—

"You can go in, of course, if you wish it, Miss," said Parker disapprovingly; "but it's not what I should advise myself. For me it's different," he added on a sudden instinct of self-preservation; "I've *got* to go in. Every day for a fortnight," he added, pitying himself.

"I will go in, thank you," said a voice. "Yes, give me the candle, please. And you need not wait. I will lock the door when I come out." Thus the voice spoke. And the voice was Lucilla's.

In all his life the Professor had never feared death or its trappings. Neither its physical repulsiveness, nor the supernatural terrors which cling about it, had he either understood or tolerated. But now, in one little instant, he did understand.

He heard Lucilla come in. A light held near him shone warm and red through his closed eyelids. And he knew that he had only to unclose those eyelids to see her face bending over him. And he could unclose them. Yet he would not. He lay there, still and straight in his coffin, and life swept through him in waves of returning power. Yet he lay like death. For he said, or something in him said:

"She believes me dead. If I open my eyes it will be like a dead man looking at her. If I move it will be a dead man moving under her eyes. People have gone mad for less. Lie still, lie still," he told himself; "take any risks yourself. There must be none for her."

She had taken the candle away, set it down somewhere at a distance, and now she was kneeling beside him and her hand was under his head. He knew he could raise his arm and clasp her—and Parker would come back perhaps, when she did not return to the house, come back to find a man in grave-clothes, clasping a mad woman. He lay still. Then her kisses and tears fell on his face, and she murmured broken words of love and longing. But he lay still. At any cost he must lie still. Even at the cost of his own sanity, his own life. And the warmth of her hand under his head, her face against his, her kisses, her tears, set his blood flowing evenly and strongly. Her other arm lay on his breast, softly pressing over his heart. He would not move. He would be strong. If he were to be saved, it must be by some other way, not this.

Suddenly tears and kisses ceased; her every breath seemed to have stopped with these. She had drawn away from him. She spoke. Her voice came from above him. She was standing up.

"Arthur!" she said, "Arthur!" Then he opened his eyes, the narrowest chink. But he could not see her. Only he knew she was moving towards the door. There had been a new quality in her tone, a thrill of fear, or hope was it? or at least of uncertainty? Should he move; should he speak? He dared not. He knew too well the fear that the normal human being has of death and the grave, the fear transcending love, transcending reason. Her voice was further away now. She was by the door. She was leaving him. If he let her go, it was an end of hope for him. If he did not let her go, an end, perhaps, of reason, for her. No.

"Arthur," she said, "I don't believe... I believe you can hear me. I'm going to get a doctor. If you *can* speak, speak to me."

Her speaking ended, cut off short as a cord is cut by a knife. He did not speak. He lay in a conscious, forced rigidity.

"Speak if you can," she implored, "just one word!"

Then he said, very faintly, very distinctly, in a voice that seemed to come from a great way off, "Lucilla!"

And at the word she screamed aloud, pitifully, and leapt for the entrance; and he heard the rustle of her cape in the narrow door. Then he opened his eyes wide, and raised himself on his elbow. Very weak he was, and trembling exceedingly. To his ears her scream held the note of madness. Vainly he had refrained. Selfishly he had yielded. The cold hand of a mortal faintness clutched at his heart.

"I don't want to live now," he told himself, and fell back in the straight bed.

Her arms were round him.

"I'm going to get help," she said, her lips to his ear; "brandy and things. Only I came back. I didn't want you to think I was frightened. Oh, my dear! thank God, thank God!" He felt her kisses even through the swooning mist that swirled about him. Had she really fled in terror? He never knew. He knew that she had come back to him.

That is the real, true, and authentic narrative of the events which caused Professor Boyd Thompson to abandon a brilliant career, to promise anything that Lucilla might demand, and to devote himself entirely to a gentlemanly and unprofitable farming, and to his wife. From the point of view of the scientific world it is a sad ending to much promise, but at any rate there are two happy people hand in hand at the story's ending.

There is no doubt that for several years Professor Boyd Thompson had had enough of science, and, by a natural revulsion, flung himself into the full tide of commonplace sentiment. But genius, like youth, cannot be denied. And I, for one, am doubtful whether the Professor's renunciation of research will be a lasting one. Already I have heard whispers of a laboratory which is being built on to the house, beyond the billiard-room.

But I am inclined to believe the rumours which assert that, for the future, his research will take the form of extending paths already well trodden; that he will refrain from experiments with unknown drugs, and those dreadful researches which tend to merge the chemist and biologist in the alchemist and the magician. And he certainly does not intend to experiment further on the nerves of any living thing, even his own. The Professor had already done enough work to make the reputation of half a dozen ordinary scientists. He may be pardoned if he rests on his laurels, entwining them, to some extent, with roses.

The bottle containing the drug from the South Seas was knocked down on the day of his death and swept up in bits by the laboratory boy. It is a curious fact that the Professor has wholly forgotten the formulae of his great discovery, the notes of which he destroyed just before his experiment which so nearly was his last. This is a great satisfaction to his wife, and possibly to the Professor. But of this I cannot be sure; the scientific spirit survives much.

To the unscientific reader the strangest part of this story will perhaps be the fact that Parker is still with his old master, a wonderful example of the perfect butler. Professor Boyd Thompson was able to forgive Parker because he understood him. And he learned to understand Parker in those moments of agony, when his keen intellect and his awakened heart taught him, through his love for Lucilla, the depth of that gulf of fear which lies between the quick and the dead.

FROM BEYOND

H. P. Lovecraft

The American H. P. Lovecraft (1890–1937) is easily one of the most influential horror writers of the twentieth century. His cosmic horror, especially the stories in the so-called Cthulhu Mythos, helped develop the modern weird tale. Although his writing is varied and, in some places, strongly influenced by the Gothic tradition and by Poe, Lovecraft's work is best epitomized by a gradual build-up to a moment of horrific encounter with creatures or events that defy or exceed the parameters of ordinary human experience.

Like the professor in 'The Five Senses', Crawford Tillinghast, the mad scientist in 'From Beyond' (1934), is consumed by the idea that what we know of the world is very partial and that we need to gain access to its 'absolute nature'. For him, the way to achieve this is to stimulate the pineal gland, 'the great sense-organ of organs', with resonance waves. Is the human mind ready for the 'truth', though? Readers are more likely to recognize the ghastly shenanigans of the medical student in Lovecraft's 'Herbert West—Reanimator' (1922), but 'From Beyond' is certainly on a par when it comes to atmosphere and intensity.

H ORRIBLE BEYOND CONCEPTION WAS THE CHANGE WHICH HAD taken place in my best friend, Crawford Tillinghast. I had not seen him since that day, two months and a half before, when he had told me toward what goal his physical and metaphysical researches were leading; when he had answered my awed and almost frightened remonstrances by driving me from his laboratory and his house in a burst of fanatical rage. I had known that he now remained mostly shut in the attic laboratory with that accursed electrical machine, eating little and excluding even the servants, but I had not thought that a brief period of ten weeks could so alter and disfigure any human creature. It is not pleasant to see a stout man suddenly grown thin, and it is even worse when the baggy skin becomes yellowed or greyed, the eyes sunken, circled, and uncannily glowing, the forehead veined and corrugated, and the hands tremulous and twitching. And if added to this there be a repellent unkemptness; a wild disorder of dress, a bushiness of dark hair white at the roots, and an unchecked growth of pure white beard on a face once clean-shaven, the cumulative effect is quite shocking. But such was the aspect of Crawford Tillinghast on the night his half-coherent message brought me to his door after my weeks of exile; such the spectre that trembled as it admitted me, candle in hand, and glanced furtively over its shoulder as if fearful of unseen things in the ancient, lonely house set back from Benevolent Street.

That Crawford Tillinghast should ever have studied science and philosophy was a mistake. These things should be left to the frigid and impersonal investigator, for they offer two equally tragic alternatives to the man of feeling and action; despair if he fail in his quest, and terrors unutterable and unimaginable if he succeed. Tillinghast had once been the prey of failure, solitary and melancholy; but now I knew, with nauseating fears of my own, that he was the prey of success. I had indeed warned him ten weeks before, when he burst forth with his tale of what he felt himself about to discover. He had been flushed and excited then, talking in a high and unnatural, though always pedantic, voice.

"What do we know," he had said, "of the world and the universe about us? Our means of receiving impressions are absurdly few, and our notions of surrounding objects infinitely narrow. We see things only as we are constructed to see them, and can gain no idea of their absolute nature. With five feeble senses we pretend to comprehend the boundlessly complex cosmos, yet other beings with a wider, stronger, or different range of senses might not only see very differently the things we see, but might see and study whole worlds of matter, energy, and life which lie close at hand yet can never be detected with the senses we have. I have always believed that such strange, inaccessible worlds exist at our very elbows, *and now I believe I have found a way to break down the barriers.* I am not joking. Within twenty-four hours that machine near the table will generate waves acting on unrecognized sense-organs that exist in us as atrophied or rudimentary vestiges. Those waves will open up to us many vistas unknown to man, and several unknown to anything we consider organic life. We shall see that at which dogs howl in the dark, and that at which cats prick up their ears after midnight. We shall see these things, and other things which no breathing creature has yet seen. We shall overleap time, space, and dimensions, and without bodily motion peer to the bottom of creation."

When Tillinghast said these things I remonstrated, for I knew him well enough to be frightened rather than amused; but he was a fanatic, and drove me from the house. Now he was no less a fanatic, but his desire to speak had conquered his resentment, and he had written me imperatively in a hand I could scarcely recognize. As I entered the abode of the friend so suddenly metamorphosed to a shivering gargoyle, I became infected with the terror which seemed stalking in all the shadows. The words and beliefs expressed ten weeks before seemed bodied forth in the darkness beyond the small circle of candle light, and I sickened at the hollow, altered voice of my host. I wished the servants were about, and did not like it when he said they had all left three days previously. It seemed strange that old Gregory, at least, should desert his master without telling as tried a friend as I. It was he who had given me all the information I had of Tillinghast after I was repulsed in rage.

Yet I soon subordinated all my fears to my growing curiosity and fascination. Just what Crawford Tillinghast now wished of me I could only guess, but that he had some stupendous secret or discovery to impart, I could not doubt. Before I had protested at his unnatural pryings into the unthinkable; now that he had evidently succeeded to some degree I almost shared his spirit, terrible though the cost of victory appeared. Up through the dark emptiness of the house I followed the bobbing candle in the hand of this shaking parody on man. The electricity seemed to be turned off, and when I asked my guide he said it was for a definite reason.

"It would be too much... I would not dare," he continued to mutter. I especially noted his new habit of muttering, for it was not like him to talk to himself. We entered the laboratory in the attic, and I observed that detestable electrical machine, glowing with a sickly, sinister, violet luminosity. It was connected with a powerful chemical battery, but seemed to be receiving no current; for I recalled that in its experimental stage it had sputtered and purred when in action. In reply to my question Tillinghast mumbled that this permanent glow was not electrical in any sense that I could understand.

He now seated me near the machine, so that it was on my right, and turned a switch somewhere below the crowning cluster of glass bulbs. The usual sputtering began, turned to a whine, and terminated in a drone so soft as to suggest a return to silence. Meanwhile the luminosity increased, waned again, then assumed a pale, outré colour or blend of colours which I could neither place nor describe. Tillinghast had been watching me, and noted my puzzled expression.

"Do you know what that is?" he whispered. "*That is ultra-violet.*" He chuckled oddly at my surprise. "You thought ultra-violet was invisible, and so it is—but you can see that and many other invisible things *now.*

"Listen to me! The waves from that thing are waking a thousand sleeping senses in us; senses which we inherit from aeons of evolution from the state of detached electrons to the state of organic humanity. I have seen *truth,* and I intend to shew it to you. Do you wonder how it will seem? I will tell you." Here Tillinghast seated himself directly opposite me, blowing out his candle and staring hideously into my eyes. "Your existing sense-organs—ears first, I think—will pick up many of the impressions, for they are closely connected with the dormant organs. Then there will be others. You have heard of the pineal gland? I laugh at the shallow endocrinologist, fellow-dupe and fellow-parvenu of the Freudian. That gland is the great sense-organ of organs—*I have found out.* It is like sight in the end, and transmits visual pictures to the brain. If you are normal, that is the way you ought to get most of it... I mean get most of the evidence from *beyond.*"

I looked about the immense attic room with the sloping south wall, dimly lit by rays which the every-day eye cannot see. The far corners were all shadows, and the whole place took on a hazy unreality which obscured its nature and invited the imagination to symbolism and phantasm. During the interval that Tillinghast was silent I fancied myself in some vast and incredible temple of long-dead gods; some vague edifice of innumerable black stone columns reaching up from a floor of damp slabs to a cloudy height beyond the range of my vision. The picture was very vivid for a while, but gradually gave way to a more horrible conception; that of utter, absolute solitude in infinite, sightless, soundless space. There seemed to be a void, and nothing more, and I felt a childish fear which prompted me to draw from my hip pocket the revolver I always carried after dark since the night I was held up in East Providence. Then, from the farthermost regions of remoteness, the *sound* softly glided into existence. It was infinitely faint, subtly vibrant, and unmistakably musical, but held a quality of surpassing wildness which made its impact feel like a delicate torture of my whole body. I felt sensations like those one feels when accidentally scratching ground glass. Simultaneously there developed something like a cold draught, which apparently swept past me from the direction of the distant sound. As I waited breathlessly I perceived that both sound and wind were increasing; the effect being to give me an odd notion of myself as tied to a pair of rails in the path of a gigantic approaching locomotive. I began to speak to Tillinghast, and as I did so all the unusual impressions abruptly vanished. I saw only the man, the glowing machine, and the dim apartment. Tillinghast was grinning repulsively at the revolver which I had almost unconsciously drawn, but from his expression I was sure he had seen and heard as much as I, if not a great deal more. I whispered what I had experienced, and he bade me to remain as quiet and receptive as possible.

"Don't move," he cautioned, "for in these rays *we are able to be seen as well as to see.* I told you the servants left, but I didn't tell you *how.* It was that thick-witted housekeeper—she turned on the lights downstairs after I had warned her not to, and the wires picked up sympathetic vibrations. It must have been frightful—I could hear the screams up here in spite of all I was seeing and hearing from another direction, and later it was rather awful to find those empty heaps of clothes around the house. Mrs. Updike's clothes were close to the front hall switch—that's how I know she did it. It got them all. But so long as we don't move we're fairly safe. Remember we're dealing with a hideous world in which we are practically helpless... *Keep still!"*

The combined shock of the revelation and of the abrupt command gave me a kind of paralysis, and in my terror my mind again opened to the impressions coming from what Tillinghast called *"beyond"*. I was now in a vortex of sound and motion, with confused pictures before my eyes. I saw the blurred outlines of the room, but from some point in space there seemed to be pouring a seething column of unrecognizable shapes or clouds, penetrating the solid roof at a point ahead and to the right of me. Then I glimpsed the temple-like effect again, but this time the pillars reached up into an aërial ocean of light, which sent down one blinding beam along the path of the cloudy column I had seen before. After that the scene was almost wholly kaleidoscopic, and in the jumble of sights, sounds, and unidentified sense-impressions I felt that I was about to dissolve or in some way lose the solid form. One definite flash I shall always remember. I seemed for an instant to behold a patch of strange night sky filled with shining, revolving spheres, and as it receded I saw that the glowing suns formed a constellation or galaxy of settled shape; this shape being the distorted face of Crawford Tillinghast. At another time I felt the huge animate things brushing past me and occasionally *walking or drifting through my supposedly solid body,* and thought I saw Tillinghast look at them as though his better trained senses could catch them visually.

I recalled what he had said of the pineal gland, and wondered what he saw with this preternatural eye.

Suddenly I myself became possessed of a kind of augmented sight. Over and above the luminous and shadowy chaos arose a picture which, though vague, held the elements of consistency and permanence. It was indeed somewhat familiar, for the unusual part was superimposed upon the usual terrestrial scene much as a cinema view may be thrown upon the painted curtain of a theatre. I saw the attic laboratory, the electrical machine, and the unsightly form of Tillinghast opposite me; but of all the space unoccupied by familiar material objects not one particle was vacant. Indescribable shapes both alive and otherwise were mixed in disgusting disarray, and close to every known thing were whole worlds of alien, unknown entities. It likewise seemed that all the known things entered into the composition of other unknown things, and vice versa. Foremost among the living objects were great inky, jellyish monstrosities which flabbily quivered in harmony with the vibrations from the machine. They were present in loathsome profusion, and I saw to my horror that they *overlapped*; that they were semi-fluid and capable of passing through one another and through what we know as solids. These things were never still, but seemed ever floating about with some malignant purpose. Sometimes they appeared to devour one another, the attacker launching itself at its victim and instantaneously obliterating the latter from sight. Shudderingly I felt that I knew what had obliterated the unfortunate servants, and could not exclude the things from my mind as I strove to observe other properties of the newly visible world that lies unseen around us. But Tillinghast had been watching me, and was speaking.

"You see them? You see them? You see the things that float and flop about you and through you every moment of your life? You see the creatures that form what men call the pure air and the blue sky? Have I not succeeded in breaking down the barrier; have I not shewn you worlds that no other living men have seen?" I heard him scream through the horrible chaos, and looked at the wild face thrust so offensively close to mine. His eyes were pits of flame, and they glared at me with what I now saw was overwhelming hatred. The machine droned detestably.

"You think those floundering things wiped out the servants? Fool, they are harmless! But the servants *are* gone, aren't they? You tried to stop me; you discouraged me when I needed every drop of encouragement I could get; you were afraid of the cosmic truth, you damned coward, but now I've got you! What swept up the servants? What made them scream so loud?… Don't know, eh? You'll know soon enough! Look at me—listen to what I say—do you suppose there are really any such things as time and magnitude? Do you fancy there are such things as form or matter? I tell you, I have struck depths that your little brain can't picture! I have seen beyond the bounds of infinity and drawn down daemons from the stars… I have harnessed the shadows that stride from world to world to sow death and madness… Space belongs to me, do you hear? Things are hunting me now—the things that devour and dissolve—but I know how to elude them. It is you they will get, as they got the servants. Stirring, dear sir? I told you it was dangerous to move. I have saved you so far by telling you to keep still—saved you to see more sights and to listen to me. If you had moved, they would have been at you long ago. Don't worry, they won't *hurt* you. They didn't hurt the servants—it was *seeing* that made the poor devils scream so. My pets are not pretty, for they come out of places where aesthetic standards are—*very different.* Disintegration is quite painless, I assure you—but *I want you to see them.* I almost saw them, but I knew how to stop. You are not curious? I always knew you were no scientist! Trembling, eh? Trembling with anxiety to see the ultimate things I have discovered? Why don't you move, then? Tired? Well, don't worry, my friend, *for they are coming…* Look! Look, curse you, look!… It's just over your left shoulder…"

What remains to be told is very brief, and may be familiar to you from the newspaper accounts. The police heard a shot in the old Tillinghast house and found us there—Tillinghast dead and me unconscious. They arrested me because the revolver was in my hand, but released me in three hours, after they found it was apoplexy which had finished Tillinghast and saw that my shot had been directed at the noxious machine which now lay hopelessly shattered on the laboratory floor. I did not tell very much of what I had seen, for I feared the coroner would be sceptical; but from the evasive outline I did give, the doctor told me that I had undoubtedly been hypnotized by the vindictive and homicidal madman.

I wish I could believe that doctor. It would help my shaky nerves if I could dismiss what I now have to think of the air and the sky about and above me. I never feel alone or comfortable, and a hideous sense of pursuit sometimes comes chillingly on me when I am weary. What prevents me from believing the doctor is this one simple fact—that the police never found the bodies of those servants whom they say Crawford Tillinghast murdered.

THE FLY

George Langelaan

Fans of David Cronenberg's body horror *The Fly* (1986) may know it was based on a 1958 film of the same title. They are less likely to know that Kurt Neumann's film was itself adapted from a short story by the French-born Brit George Langelaan (1908–1972). Langelaan wrote a few novels and short stories, but only a handful of his writings are still read today: 'Strange Miracle' (1958), a story which was adapted into an episode of the popular American television series *Alfred Hitchcock Presents* in 1962; 'The Other Hand' (1961), also adapted for another anthology programme, *Night Gallery*, in 1971; and, above all, 'The Fly' (1957).

Unlike the films, 'The Fly' is told from the point of view of François, the brother of the mad scientist, and through a manuscript written by his wife. This narrative device adds to the story's overall effect and masterful pace. Its plot is well known: a man creates a machine capable of transferring matter through space and, emboldened by this success, decides to try it on himself. Unbeknownst to him, a house fly enters the transmitter pod at the same time and induces a catastrophic instance of genetic splicing. This tale is horrific and moving in equal measure, and certainly one of the best mad science stories ever written.

To Jean Rostand, who knows such strange things.

TELEPHONES AND TELEPHONE BELLS HAVE ALWAYS MADE ME uneasy. Years ago, when they were mostly wall fixtures, I disliked them, but nowadays, when they are planted in every nook and corner, they are a downright intrusion. We have a saying in France that a coalman is master in his own house; with the telephone that is no longer true, and I suspect that even the Englishman is no longer king in his own castle.

At the office, the sudden ringing of the telephone annoys me. It means that, no matter what I am doing, in spite of the switchboard operator, in spite of my secretary, in spite of doors and walls, some unknown person is coming into the room and onto my desk to talk right into my very ear, confidentially—and that whether I like it or not. At home, the feeling is still more disagreeable, but the worst is when the telephone rings in the dead of night. If anyone could see me turn on the light and get up blinking to answer it, I suppose I would look like any other sleepy man annoyed at being disturbed. The truth in such a case, however, is that I am struggling against panic, fighting down a feeling that a stranger has broken into the house and is in my bedroom. By the time I manage to grab the receiver and say: *"Ici Monsieur Delambre. Je vous ecoute,"* I am outwardly calm, but I only get back to a more normal state when I recognize the voice at the other end and when I know what is wanted of me.

This effort at dominating a purely animal reaction and fear had become so effective that when my sister-in-law called me at two in the morning, asking me to come over, but first to warn the police that she had just killed my brother, I quietly asked her how and why she had killed André.

"But, François!… I can't explain all that over the telephone. Please call the police and come quickly."

"Maybe I had better see you first, Hélène?"

"No, you'd better call the police first; otherwise they will start asking you all sorts of awkward questions. They'll have enough trouble as it is to believe that I did it alone… And, by the way, I suppose you ought to tell them that André… André's body, is down at the factory. They may want to go there first."

"Did you say that André is at the factory?"

"Yes… under the steam-hammer."

"Under the what!"

"The steam-hammer! But don't ask so many questions. Please come quickly, François! Please understand that I'm afraid… that my nerves won't stand it much longer!"

Have you ever tried to explain to a sleepy police officer that your sister-in-law has just phoned to say that she has killed your brother with a steam-hammer? I repeated my explanation, but he would not let me.

"*Oui, Monsieur, oui*, I hear… but who are you? What is your name? Where do you live? I said, where do you live!"

It was then that Commissaire Charas took over the line and the whole business. He at least seemed to understand everything. Would I wait for him? Yes, he would pick me up and take me over to my brother's house. When? In five or ten minutes.

I had just managed to pull on my trousers, wriggle into a sweater and grab a hat and coat, when a black Citroën, headlights blazing, pulled up at the door.

"I assume you have a night watchman at your factory, Monsieur Delambre. Has he called you?" asked Commissaire Charas, letting in the clutch as I sat down beside him and slammed the door of the car.

"No, he hasn't. Though of course my brother could have entered the factory through his laboratory where he often works late at night... all night sometimes."

"Is Professor Delambre's work connected with your business?"

"No, my brother is, or was, doing research work for the Ministère de l'Air. As he wanted to be away from Paris and yet within reach of where skilled workmen could fix up or make gadgets big and small for his experiments, I offered him one of the old workshops of the factory and he came to live in the first house built by our grandfather on the top of the hill at the back of the factory."

"Yes, I see. Did he talk about his work? What sort of research work?"

"He rarely talked about it, you know; I suppose the Air Ministry could tell you. I only know that he was about to carry out a number of experiments he had been preparing for some months, something to do with the disintegration of matter, he told me."

Barely slowing down, the Commissaire swung the car off the road, slid it through the open factory gate and pulled up sharp by a policeman apparently expecting him.

I did not need to hear the policeman's confirmation. I knew now that my brother was dead, it seemed that I had been told years ago. Shaking like a leaf, I scrambled out after the Commissaire.

Another policeman stepped out of a doorway and led us toward one of the shops where all the lights had been turned on. More policemen were standing by the hammer, watching two men setting up a camera. It was tilted downward, and I made an effort to look.

It was far less horrid than I had expected. Though I had never seen my brother drunk, he looked just as if he were sleeping off a terrific binge, flat on his stomach across the narrow line on which the white-hot slabs of metal were rolled up to the hammer. I saw at a glance that his head and arm could only be a flattened mess, but that seemed quite impossible; it looked as if he had somehow pushed his head and arm right into the metallic mass of the hammer.

Having talked to his colleagues, the Commissaire turned toward me:

"How can we raise the hammer, Monsieur Delambre?"

"I'll raise it for you."

"Would you like us to get one of your men over?"

"No, I'll be all right. Look, here is the switchboard. It was originally a steam-hammer, but everything is worked electrically here now. Look, Commissaire, the hammer has been set at fifty tons and its impact at zero."

"At zero...?"

"Yes, level with the ground if you prefer. It is also set for single strokes, which means that it has to be raised after each blow. I don't know what Hélène, my sister-in-law, will have to say about all this, but one thing I am sure of: she certainly did not know how to set and operate the hammer."

"Perhaps it was set that way last night when work stopped?"

"Certainly not. The drop is never set at zero, Monsieur le Commissaire."

"I see. Can it be raised gently?"

"No. The speed of the upstroke cannot be regulated. But in any case it is not very fast when the hammer is set for single strokes."

"Right. Will you show me what to do? It won't be very nice to watch, you know."

"No, no, Monsieur le Commissaire. I'll be all right."

"All set?" asked the Commissaire of the others. "All right then, Monsieur Delambre. Whenever you like."

Watching my brother's back, I slowly but firmly pushed the upstroke button.

The unusual silence of the factory was broken by the sigh of compressed air rushing into the cylinders, a sigh that always makes me think of a giant taking a deep breath before solemnly socking another giant, and the steel mass of the hammer shuddered and then rose swiftly. I also heard the sucking sound as it left the metal base and thought I was going to panic when I saw André's body heave forward as a sickly gush of blood poured all over the ghastly mess bared by the hammer.

"No danger of it coming down again, Monsieur Delambre?"

"No, none whatever," I mumbled as I threw the safety switch and, turning around, I was violently sick in front of a young green-faced policeman.

For weeks after, Commissaire Charas worked on the case, listening, questioning, running all over the place, making out reports, telegraphing and telephoning right and left. Later, we became quite friendly and he owned that he had for a long time considered me as suspect number one, but had finally given up that idea because, not only was there no clue of any sort, but not even a motive.

Hélène, my sister-in-law, was so calm throughout the whole business that the doctors finally confirmed what I had long considered the only possible solution: that she was mad. That being the case, there was of course no trial.

My brother's wife never tried to defend herself in any way and even got quite annoyed when she realized that people thought her mad, and this of course was considered proof that she was indeed mad.

She owned up to the murder of her husband and proved easily that she knew how to handle the hammer; but she would never say why, exactly how, or under what circumstances she had killed my brother. The great mystery was how and why had my brother so obligingly stuck his head under the hammer, the only possible explanation for his part in the drama.

The night watchman had heard the hammer all right; he had even heard it twice, he claimed. This was very strange, and the stroke-counter which was always set back to naught after a job, seemed to prove him right, since it marked the figure two. Also, the foreman in charge of the hammer confirmed that after cleaning up the day before the murder, he had as usual turned the stroke-counter back to naught. In spite of this, Hélène maintained that she had only used the hammer once, and this seemed just another proof of her insanity.

Commissaire Charas who had been put in charge of the case at first wondered if the victim were really my brother. But of that there was no possible doubt, if only because of the great scar running from his knee to his thigh, the result of a shell that had landed within a few feet of him during the retreat in 1940; and there were also the fingerprints of his left hand which corresponded to those found all over his laboratory and his personal belongings up at the house.

A guard had been put on his laboratory and the next day half a dozen officials came down from the Air Ministry. They went through all his papers and took away some of his instruments, but before leaving, they told the Commissaire that the most interesting documents and instruments had been destroyed.

The Lyons police laboratory, one of the most famous in the world, reported that André's head had been wrapped up in a piece of velvet when it was crushed by the hammer, and one day Commissaire Charas showed me a tattered drapery which I immediately recognized as the brown velvet cloth I had seen on a table in my brother's laboratory, the one on which his meals were served when he could not leave his work.

After only a very few days in prison, Hélène had been transferred to a near-by asylum, one of the three in France where insane criminals are taken care of. My nephew Henri, a boy of six, the very image of his father, was entrusted to me, and eventually all legal arrangements were made for me to become his guardian and tutor.

Hélène, one of the quietest patients of the asylum, was allowed visitors and I went to see her on Sundays. Once or twice the Commissaire had accompanied me and, later, I learned that he had also visited Hélène alone. But we were never able to obtain any information from my sister-in-law who seemed to have become utterly indifferent. She rarely answered my questions and hardly ever those of the Commissaire. She spent a lot of her time sewing, but her favourite pastime seemed to be catching flies which she invariably released unharmed after having examined them carefully.

Hélène only had one fit of raving—more like a nervous breakdown than a fit said the doctor who had administered morphia to quieten her—the day she saw a nurse swatting flies.

The day after Hélène's one and only fit, Commissaire Charas came to see me.

"I have a strange feeling that there lies the key to the whole business, Monsieur Delambre," he said.

I did not ask him how it was that he already knew all about Hélène's fit.

"I do not follow you, Commissaire. Poor Madame Delambre could have shown an exceptional interest for anything else, really. Don't you think that flies just happen to be the border-subject of her tendency to raving?"

"Do you believe she is really mad?" he asked.

"My dear Commissaire, I don't see how there can be any doubt. Do you doubt it?"

"I don't know. In spite of all the doctors say, I have the impression that Madame Delambre has a very clear brain… even when catching flies."

"Supposing you were right, how would you explain her attitude with regard to her little boy? She never seems to consider him as her own child."

"You know, Monsieur Delambre, I have thought about that also. She may be trying to protect him. Perhaps she fears the boy or, for all we know, hates him?"

"I'm afraid I don't understand, my dear Commissaire."

"Have you noticed, for instance, that she never catches flies when the boy is there?"

"No. But come to think of it, you are quite right. Yes, that is strange… Still, I fail to understand."

"So do I, Monsieur Delambre. And I'm very much afraid that we shall never understand, unless perhaps your sister-in-law should *get better*."

"The doctors seem to think that there is no hope of any sort, you know."

"Yes. Do you know if your brother ever experimented with flies?"

"I really don't know, but I shouldn't think so. Have you asked the Air Ministry people? They knew all about the work."

"Yes, and they laughed at me."

"I can understand that."

"You are very fortunate to understand anything, Monsieur Delambre. I do not… but I hope to some day."

★

"Tell me, Uncle, do flies live a long time?"

We were just finishing our lunch and, following an established tradition between us, I was just pouring some wine into Henri's glass for him to dip a biscuit in.

Had Henri not been staring at his glass gradually being filled to the brim, something in my look might have frightened him.

This was the first time that he had ever mentioned flies, and I shuddered at the thought that Commissaire Charas might quite easily have been present. I could imagine the glint in his eye as he would have answered my nephew's question with another question. I could almost hear him saying:

"I don't know, Henri. Why do you ask?"

"Because I have again seen the fly that *Maman* was looking for."

And it was only after drinking off Henri's own glass of wine that I realized that he had answered my spoken thought.

"I did not know that your mother was looking for a fly."

"Yes, she was. It has grown quite a lot, but I recognized it all right."

"Where did you see this fly, Henri, and... how did you recognize it?"

"This morning on your desk, Uncle Françoise. Its head is white instead of black, and it has a funny sort of leg."

Feeling more and more like Commissaire Charas, but trying to look unconcerned, I went on:

"And when did you see this fly for the first time?"

"The day that Papa went away. I had caught it, but *Maman* made me let it go. And then after, she wanted me to find it again. She changed her mind." And shrugging his shoulders just as my brother used to, he added, "You know what women are."

"I think that fly must have died long ago, and you must be mistaken, Henri," I said, getting up and walking to the door.

But as soon as I was out of the dining room, I ran up the stairs to my study. There was no fly anywhere to be seen.

I was bothered, far more than I cared to even think about. Henri had just proved that Charas was really closer to a clue than had seemed when he told me about his thoughts concerning Hélène's pastime.

For the first time I wondered if Charas did not really know much more than he let on. For the first time also, I wondered about Hélène. Was she really insane? A strange, horrid feeling was growing on me, and the more I thought about it, the more I felt that, somehow, Charas was right: Hélène was *getting away with it!*

What could possibly have been the reason for such a monstrous crime? What had led up to it? Just what had happened?

I thought of all the hundreds of questions that Charas had put to Hélène, sometimes gently like a nurse trying to soothe, sometimes stern and cold, sometimes barking them furiously. Hélène had answered very few, always in a calm quiet voice and never seeming to pay any attention to the way in which the question had been put. Though dazed, she had seemed perfectly sane then.

Refined, well-bred and well-read, Charas was more than just an intelligent police official. He was a keen psychologist and had an amazing way of smelling out a fib or an erroneous statement even before it was uttered. I knew that he had accepted as true the few answers she had given him. But then there had been all those questions which she had never answered: the most direct and important ones. From the very beginning, Hélène had adopted a very simple system. "I cannot answer that question," she would say in her low quiet voice. And that was that! The repetition of the same question never seemed to annoy her. In all the hours of questioning that she underwent, Hélène did not once point out to the Commissaire that he had already asked her this or that. She would simply say, "I cannot answer that question," as though it were the very first time that that particular question had been asked and the very first time she had made that answer.

This cliché had become the formidable barrier beyond which Commissaire Charas could not even get a glimpse, an idea of what Hélène might be thinking. She had very willingly answered all questions about her life with my brother—which seemed a happy and uneventful one—up to the time of his end. About his death, however, all that she would say was that she had killed him with the steam-hammer, but she refused to say why, what had led up to the drama and how she got my brother to put his head under it. She never actually refused outright; she would just go blank and, with no apparent emotion, would switch over to, "I cannot answer that question."

Hélène, as I have said, had shown the Commissaire that she knew how to set and operate the steam-hammer.

Charas could only find one single fact which did not coincide with Hélène's declarations, the fact that the hammer had been used twice. Charas was no longer willing to attribute this to insanity. That evident flaw in Hélène's stonewall defence seemed a crack which the Commissaire might possibly enlarge. But my sister-in-law finally cemented it by acknowledging:

"All right, I lied to you. I did use the hammer twice. But do not ask me why, because I cannot tell you."

"Is that your only... misstatement, Madame Delambre?" had asked the Commissaire, trying to follow up what looked at last like an advantage.

"It is... and you know it, Monsieur le Commissaire."

And, annoyed, Charas had seen that Hélène could read him like an open book.

I had thought of calling on the Commissaire, but the knowledge that he would inevitably start questioning Henri made me hesitate.

Another reason also made me hesitate, a vague sort of fear that he would look for and find the fly Henri had talked of. And that annoyed me a good deal because I would find no satisfactory explanation for that particular fear.

André was definitely not the absent-minded sort of professor who walks about in pouring rain with a rolled umbrella under his arm. He was human, had a keen sense of humour, loved children and animals and could not bear to see anyone suffer. I had often seen him drop his work to watch a parade of the local fire brigade, or see the *Tour de France* cyclists go by, or even follow a circus parade all around the village. He liked games of logic and precision, such as billiards and tennis, bridge and chess.

How was it then possible to explain his death? What could have made him put his head under that hammer? It could hardly have been the result of some stupid bet or a test of his courage. He hated betting and had no patience with those who indulged in it. Whenever he heard a bet proposed, he would invariably remind all present that, after all, a bet was but a contract between a fool and a swindler, even if it turned out to be a toss-up as to which was which.

It seemed there were only two possible explanations to André's death. Either he had gone mad, or else he had a reason for letting his wife kill him in such a strange and terrible way. And just what could have been his wife's role in all this? They surely could not have been both insane?

Having finally decided not to tell Charas about my nephew's innocent revelations, I thought I myself would question Hélène.

She seemed to have been expecting my visit for she came into the parlour almost as soon as I had made myself known to the matron and been allowed inside.

"I wanted to show you my garden," explained Hélène as I looked at the coat slung over her shoulders.

As one of the "reasonable" inmates, she was allowed to go into the garden during certain hours of the day. She had asked for and obtained the right to a little patch of ground where she could grow flowers, and I had sent her seeds and some rosebushes out of my garden.

She took me straight to a rustic wooden bench which had been made in the men's workshop and only just set up under a tree close to her little patch of ground.

Searching for the right way to broach the subject of André's death, I sat for a while tracing vague designs on the ground with the end of my umbrella.

"François, I want to ask you something," said Hélène after a while.

"Anything I can do for you, Hélène?"

"No, just something I want to know. Do flies live very long?"

Staring at her, I was about to say that her boy had asked the very same question a few hours earlier when I suddenly realized that here was the opening I had been searching for and perhaps even the possibility of striking a great blow, a blow perhaps powerful enough to shatter her stonewall defence, be it sane or insane.

Watching her carefully, I replied:

"I don't really know, Hélène; but the fly you were looking for was in my study this morning."

No doubt about it, I had struck a shattering blow. She swung her head round with such force that I heard the bones crack in her neck. She opened her mouth, but said not a word; only her eyes seemed to be screaming with fear.

Yes, it was evident that I had crashed through something, but what? Undoubtedly, the Commissaire would have known what to do with such an advantage; I did not. All I knew was that he would never have given her time to think, to recuperate, but all I could do, and even that was a strain, was to maintain my best poker-face, hoping against hope that Hélène's defences would go on crumbling.

She must have been quite a while without breathing, because she suddenly gasped and put both hands over her still open mouth.

"François... Did you kill it?" she whispered, her eyes no longer fixed, but searching every inch of my face.

"No."

"You have it then... You have it on you! Give it to me!" she almost shouted touching me with both her hands, and I knew that had she felt strong enough, she would have tried to search me.

"No, Hélène, I haven't got it."

"But you know now... You have guessed, haven't you?"

"No, Hélène. I only know one thing, and that is that you are not insane. But I mean to know all, Hélène, and, somehow, I am going to find out. You can choose: either you tell me everything and I'll see what is to be done, or..."

"Or what? Say it!"

"I was going to say it, Hélène... or I assure you that your friend the Commissaire will have that fly first thing tomorrow morning."

She remained quite still, looking down at the palms of her hands on her lap and, although it was getting chilly, her forehead and hands were moist.

Without even brushing aside a wisp of long brown hair blown across her mouth by the breeze, she murmured:

"If I tell you... will you promise to destroy that fly before doing anything else?"

"No, Hélène. I can make no such promise before knowing."

"But François, you must understand. I promised André that fly would be destroyed. That promise must be kept and I can say nothing until it is."

I could sense the deadlock ahead. I was not yet losing ground, but I was losing the initiative. I tried a shot in the dark.

"Hélène, of course you understand that as soon as the police examine that fly, they will know that you are not insane, and then..."

"François, no! For Henri's sake! Don't you see? I was expecting that fly; I was hoping it would find me here but it couldn't know what had become of me. What else could it do but go to others it loves, to Henri, to you... you who might know and understand what was to be done!"

Was she really mad, or was she simulating again? But mad or not, she was cornered. Wondering how to follow up and how to land the knockout blow without running the risk of seeing her slip away out of reach, I said very quietly:

"Tell me all, Hélène. I can then protect your boy."

"Protect my boy from what? Don't you understand that if I am here, it is merely so that Henri won't be the son of a woman who was guillotined for having murdered his father? Don't you understand that I would by far prefer the guillotine to the living death of this lunatic asylum?"

"I understand, Hélène, and I'll do my best for the boy whether you tell me or not. If you refuse to tell me, I'll still do the best I can to protect Henri, but you must understand that the game will be out of my hands, because Commissaire Charas will have the fly."

"But why must you know?" said, rather than asked, my sister-in-law, struggling to control her temper.

"Because I must and will know how and why my brother died, Hélène."

"All right. Take me back to the… house. I'll give you what your Commissaire would call my 'Confession.'"

"Do you mean to say that you have written it!"

"Yes. It was not really meant for you, but more likely for *your friend*, the Commissaire. I had foreseen that, sooner or later, he would get too close to the truth."

"You then have no objection to his reading it?"

"You will act as you think fit, François. Wait for me a minute."

Leaving me at the door of the parlour, Hélène ran upstairs to her room. In less than a minute she was back with a large brown envelope.

"Listen, François; you are not nearly as bright as was your poor brother, but you are not unintelligent. All I ask is that you read this alone. After that, you may do as you wish."

"That I promise you, Hélène," I said taking the precious envelope. "I'll read it tonight and although tomorrow is not a visiting day, I'll come down to see you."

"Just as you like," said my sister-in-law without even saying good-bye as she went back upstairs.

It was only on reaching home, as I walked from the garage to the house, that I read the inscription on the envelope:

TO WHOM IT MAY CONCERN
(Probably Commissaire Charas)

Having told the servants that I would have only a light supper to be served immediately in my study and that I was not to be disturbed after, I ran upstairs, threw Hélène's envelope on my desk and made another careful search of the room before closing the shutters and drawing the curtains. All I could find was a long since dead mosquito stuck to the wall near the ceiling.

Having motioned to the servant to put her tray down on a table by the fireplace, I poured myself a glass of wine and locked the door behind her. I then disconnected the telephone—I always did this now at night—and turned out all the lights but the lamp on my desk.

Slitting open Hélène's fat envelope, I extracted a thick wad of closely written pages. I read the following lines neatly centred in the middle of the top page:

> *This is not a confession because, although I killed my husband, I am not a*
> *murderess. I simply and very faithfully carried out his last wish by crushing*
> *his head and right arm under the steam-hammer of his brother's factory.*

Without even touching the glass of wine by my elbow, I turned the page and started reading.

*

For very nearly a year before his death (*the manuscript began*), my husband had told me of some of his experiments. He knew full well that his colleagues of the Air Ministry would have forbidden some of them as too dangerous, but he was keen on obtaining positive results before reporting his discovery.

Whereas only sound and pictures had been, so far, transmitted through space by radio and television, André claimed to have discovered a way of transmitting matter. Matter, any solid object, placed in his "transmitter" was instantly disintegrated and reintegrated in a special receiving set.

André considered his discovery as perhaps the most important since that of the wheel sawn off the end of a tree trunk. He reckoned that the transmission of matter by instantaneous "disintegration—reintegration" would completely change life as we had known it so far. It would mean the end of all means of transport, not only of goods including food, but also of human beings. André, the practical scientist who never allowed theories or daydreams to get the better of him, already foresaw the time when there would no longer be any airplanes, ships, trains or cars and, therefore, no longer any roads or railway lines, ports, airports or stations. All that would be replaced by matter-transmitting and receiving stations throughout the world. Travellers and goods would be placed in special cabins and, at a given signal, would simply disappear and reappear almost immediately at the chosen receiving station.

André's receiving set was only a few feet away from his transmitter, in an adjoining room of his laboratory, and he at first ran into all sorts of snags. His first successful experiment was carried out with an ash tray taken from his desk, a souvenir we had brought back from a trip to London.

That was the first time he told me about his experiments and I had no idea of what he was talking about the day he came dashing into the house and threw the ash tray in my lap.

"Hélène, look! For a fraction of a second, a bare ten-millionth of a second, that ash tray has been completely disintegrated. For one little moment it no longer existed! Gone! Nothing left, absolutely nothing! Only atoms travelling through space at the speed of light! And the moment after, the atoms were once more gathered together in the shape of an ash tray!"

"André, please... please! What on earth are you raving about?"

He started sketching all over a letter I had been writing. He laughed at my wry face, swept all my letters off the table and said:

"You don't understand? Right. Let's start all over again. Hélène, do you remember I once read you an article about the mysterious flying stones that seem to come from nowhere in particular, and which are said to occasionally fall in certain houses in India? They come flying in as though thrown from outside and that, in spite of closed doors and windows."

"Yes, I remember. I also remember that Professor Augier, your friend of the College de France, who had come down for a few days, remarked that if there was no trickery about it, the only possible explanation was that the stones had been disintegrated after having been thrown from outside, come through the walls, and then been reintegrated before hitting the floor or the opposite walls."

"That's right. And I added that there was, of course, one other possibility, namely the momentary and partial disintegration of the walls as the stone or stones came through."

"Yes, André. I remember all that, and I suppose you also remember that I failed to understand, and that you got quite annoyed. Well, I still do not understand why and how, even disintegrated, stones should be able to come through a wall or a closed door."

"But it is possible, Hélène, because the atoms that go to make up matter are not close together like the bricks of a wall. They are separated by relative immensities of space."

"Do you mean to say that you have disintegrated that ash tray, and then put it together again after pushing it through something?"

"Precisely, Hélène. I projected it through the wall that separates my transmitter from my receiving set."

"And would it be foolish to ask how humanity is to benefit from ash trays that can go through walls?"

André seemed quite offended, but he soon saw that I was only teasing and again waxing enthusiastic, he told me of some of the possibilities of his discovery.

"Isn't it wonderful, Hélène?" he finally gasped, out of breath.

"Yes, André. But I hope you won't ever transmit me; I'd be too much afraid of coming out at the other end like your ash tray."

"What do you mean?"

"Do you remember what was written under that ash tray?"

"Yes, of course: Made in Japan. That was the great joke of our typically British souvenir."

"The words are still there, André; but... look!"

He took the ash tray out of my hands, frowned, and walked over to the window. Then he went quite pale, and I knew that he had seen what had proved to me that he had indeed carried out a strange experiment.

The three words were still there, but reversed and reading:

Made in Japan

Without a word, having completely forgotten me, André rushed off to his laboratory. I only saw him the next morning, tired and unshaven after a whole night's work.

A few days later André had a new reverse which put him out of sorts and made him fussy and grumpy for several weeks. I stood it patiently enough for a while, but being myself bad tempered one evening, we had a silly row over some futile thing, and I reproached him for his moroseness.

"I'm sorry, chérie. I've been working my way through a maze of problems and have given you all a very rough time. You see, my very first experiment with a live animal proved a complete fiasco."

"André! You tried that experiment with Dandelo, didn't you?"

"Yes. How did you know?" he answered sheepishly. "He disintegrated perfectly, but he never reappeared in the receiving set."

"Oh, André! What became of him then?"

"Nothing… there is just no more Dandelo; only the dispersed atoms of a cat wandering, God knows where, in the universe."

Dandelo was a small white cat the cook had found one morning in the garden and which we had promptly adopted. Now I knew how it had disappeared and was quite angry about the whole thing, but my husband was so miserable over it all that I said nothing.

I saw little of my husband during the next few weeks. He had most of his meals sent down to the laboratory. I would often wake up in the morning and find his bed un-slept in. Sometimes, if he had come in very late, I would find that storm-swept appearance which only a man can give a bedroom by getting up very early and fumbling around in the dark.

One evening he came home to dinner all smiles, and I knew that his troubles were over. His face dropped, however, when he saw I was dressed for going out.

"Oh. Were you going out, Hélène?"

"Yes, the Drillons invited me for a game of bridge, but I can easily phone them and put it off."

"No, it's all right."

"It isn't all right. Out with it, dear!"

"Well, I've at last got everything perfect and I wanted you to be the first to see the miracle."

"*Magnifique*, André! Of course I'll be delighted."

Having telephoned our neighbours to say how sorry I was and so forth, I ran down to the kitchen and told the cook that she had exactly ten minutes in which to prepare a "celebration dinner."

"An excellent idea, Hélène," said my husband when the maid appeared with the champagne after our candlelight dinner. "We'll celebrate with reintegrated champagne!" and taking the tray from the maid's hands, he led the way down to the laboratory.

"Do you think it will be as good as before its disintegration?" I asked, holding the tray while he opened the door and switched on the lights.

"Have no fear. You'll see! Just bring it here, will you," he said, opening the door of a telephone call-box he had bought and which had been transformed into what he called a transmitter. "Put it down on that now," he added, putting a stool inside the box.

Having carefully closed the door, he took me to the other end of the room and handed me a pair of very dark sun glasses. He put on another pair and walked back to a switchboard by the transmitter.

"Ready, Hélène?" said my husband, turning out all the lights. "Don't remove your glasses till I give the word."

"I won't budge, André. Go on," I told him, my eyes fixed on the tray which I could just see in a greenish shimmering light through the glass panelled door of the telephone booth.

"Right," said André throwing a switch.

The whole room was brilliantly illuminated by an orange flash. Inside the booth I had seen a crackling ball of fire and felt its heat on my face, neck and hands. The whole thing lasted but the fraction of a second, and I found myself blinking at green-edged black holes like those one sees after having stared at the sun.

"*Et voilà!* You can take off your glasses, Hélène."

A little theatrically perhaps, my husband opened the door of the booth. Though André had told me what to expect, I was astonished to find that the champagne, glasses, tray and stool were no longer there.

André ceremoniously led me by the hand into the next room in a corner of which stood a second telephone booth. Opening the door wide, he triumphantly lifted the champagne tray off the stool.

Feeling somewhat like the good-natured kind-member-of-the-audience who has been dragged onto the music hall stage by the magician, I refrained from saying, "All done with mirrors," which I knew would have annoyed my husband.

"Sure it's not dangerous to drink?" I asked as the cork popped.

"Absolutely sure, Hélène," he said handing me a glass. "But that was nothing. Drink this off and I'll show you something much more astounding."

We went back into the other room.

"Oh, André! Remember poor Dandelo!"

"This is only a guinea pig, Hélène. But I'm positive it will go through all right."

He set the furry little beast down on the green enamelled floor of the booth and quickly closed the door. I again put on my dark glasses and saw and felt the vivid crackling flash.

Without waiting for André to open the door, I rushed into the next room where the lights were still on and looked into the receiving booth.

"Oh, André! *Chéri!* He's there all right!" I shouted excitedly, watching the little animal trotting round and round. "It's wonderful, André. It works! You've succeeded!"

"I hope so, but I must be patient. I'll know for sure in a few weeks' time."

"What do you mean? Look! He's as full of life as when you put him in the other booth."

"Yes, so he seems. But we'll have to see if all his organs are intact, and that will take some time. If that little beast is still full of life in a month's time, we then consider the experiment a success."

I begged André to let me take care of the guinea pig.

"All right, but don't kill it by overfeeding," he agreed with a grin for my enthusiasm.

Though not allowed to take Hop-la—the name I had given the

guinea pig—out of its box in the laboratory, I tied a pink ribbon round its neck and was allowed to feed it twice a day.

Hop-la soon got used to its pink ribbon and became quite a tame little pet, but that month of waiting seemed a year.

And then one day, André put Miquette, our cocker spaniel, into his "transmitter." He had not told me beforehand, knowing full well that I would never have agreed to such an experiment with our dog. But when he did tell me, Miquette had been successfully transmitted half a dozen times and seemed to be enjoying the operation thoroughly; no sooner was she let out of the "reintegrator" than she dashed madly into the next room, scratching at the "transmitter" door to have "another go," as André called it.

I now expected that my husband would invite some of his colleagues and Air Ministry specialists to come down. He usually did this when he had finished a research job and, before handing them long detailed reports which he always typed himself, he would carry out an experiment or two before them. But this time, he just went on working. Once morning I finally asked him when he intended throwing his usual "surprise party," as we called it.

"No, Hélène; not for a long while yet. This discovery is much too important. I have an awful lot of work to do on it still. Do you realize that there are some parts of the transmission proper which I do not yet myself fully understand? It works all right, but you see, I can't just say to all these eminent professors that I do this and that and, poof, it works! I must be able to explain how and why it works. And what is even more important, I must be ready and able to refute every destructive argument they will not fail to trot out, as they usually do when faced with anything really good."

I was occasionally invited down to the laboratory to witness some new experiment, but I never went unless André invited me,

and only talked about his work if he broached the subject first. Of
course it never occurred to me that he would, at that stage at least,
have tried an experiment with a human being; though, had I thought
about it—knowing André—it would have been obvious that he would
never have allowed anyone into the "transmitter" before he had been
through to test it first. It was only after the accident that I discovered
he had duplicated all his switches inside the disintegration booth, so
that he could try it out by himself.

The morning André tried this terrible experiment, he did not show
up for lunch. I sent the maid down with a tray, but she brought it
back with a note she had found pinned outside the laboratory door:
Do not disturb me, I am working.

He did occasionally pin such notes on his door and, though I
noticed it, I paid no particular attention to the unusually large hand-
writing of his note.

It was just after that, as I was drinking my coffee, that Henri came
bouncing into the room to say that he had caught a funny fly, and
would I like to see it. Refusing even to look at his closed fist, I ordered
him to release it immediately.

"But, *Maman*, it has such a funny white head!"

Marching the boy over to the open window, I told him to release
the fly immediately, which he did. I knew that Henri had caught the
fly merely because he thought it looked curious or different from
other flies, but I also knew that his father would never stand for any
form of cruelty to animals, and that there would be a fuss should he
discover that our son had put a fly in a box or a bottle.

At dinner time that evening, André had still not shown up and, a
little worried, I ran down to the laboratory and knocked at the door.

He did not answer my knock, but I heard him moving around and
a moment later he slipped a note under the door. It was typewritten:

HELENE, I AM HAVING TROUBLE. PUT THE BOY TO BED AND COME
BACK IN AN HOUR'S TIME. A.

Frightened, I knocked and called, but André did not seem to pay any
attention and, vaguely reassured by the familiar noise of his typewriter, I went back to the house.

Having put Henri to bed, I returned to the laboratory where I found
another note slipped under the door. My hand shook as I picked it up
because I knew by then that something must be radically wrong. I read:

HELENE, FIRST OF ALL I COUNT ON YOU NOT TO LOSE YOUR NERVE
OR DO ANYTHING RASH BECAUSE YOU ALONE CAN HELP ME. I
HAVE HAD A SERIOUS ACCIDENT. I AM NOT IN ANY PARTICULAR
DANGER FOR THE TIME BEING THOUGH IT IS A MATTER OF LIFE
AND DEATH. IT IS USELESS CALLING TO ME OR SAYING ANYTHING,
I CANNOT ANSWER, I CANNOT SPEAK. I WANT YOU TO DO EXACTLY
AND VERY CAREFULLY ALL THAT I ASK. AFTER HAVING KNOCKED
THREE TIMES TO SHOW THAT YOU UNDERSTAND AND AGREE, FETCH
ME A BOWL OF MILK LACED WITH RUM. I HAVE HAD NOTHING ALL
DAY AND CAN DO WITH IT.

Shaking with fear, not knowing what to think and repressing a furious
desire to call André and bang away until he opened, I knocked three
times as requested and ran all the way home to fetch what he wanted.

In less than five minutes I was back. Another note had been slipped
under the door:

HELENE, FOLLOW THESE INSTRUCTIONS CAREFULLY. WHEN YOU
KNOCK I'LL OPEN THE DOOR. YOU ARE TO WALK OVER TO MY DESK
AND PUT DOWN THE BOWL OF MILK. YOU WILL THEN GO INTO

THE OTHER ROOM WHERE THE RECEIVER IS. LOOK CAREFULLY
AND TRY TO FIND A FLY WHICH OUGHT TO BE THERE BUT WHICH
I AM UNABLE TO FIND. UNFORTUNATELY I CANNOT SEE SMALL
THINGS VERY EASILY.

BEFORE YOU COME IN YOU MUST PROMISE TO OBEY ME IMPLIC-
ITLY. DO NOT LOOK AT ME AND REMEMBER THAT TALKING IS QUITE
USELESS. I CANNOT ANSWER. KNOCK AGAIN THREE TIMES AND THAT
WILL MEAN I HAVE YOUR PROMISE. MY LIFE DEPENDS ENTIRELY
ON THE HELP YOU CAN GIVE ME.

I had to wait a while to pull myself together, and then I knocked
slowly three times.

I heard André shuffling behind the door, then his hand fumbling
with the lock, and the door opened.

Out of the corner of my eye, I saw that he was standing behind
the door, but without looking round, I carried the bowl of milk to
his desk. He was evidently watching me and I must at all costs appear
calm and collected.

"*Chéri*, you can count on me," I said gently, and putting the bowl
down under his desk lamp, the only one alight, I walked into the next
room where all the lights were blazing.

My first impression was that some sort of hurricane must have
blown out of the receiving booth. Papers were scattered in every
direction, a whole row of test tubes lay smashed in a corner, chairs
and stools were upset and one of the window curtains hung half
torn from its bent rod. In a large enamel basin on the floor a heap of
burned documents was still smouldering.

I knew that I would not find the fly André wanted me to look
for. Women know things that men only suppose by reasoning and
deduction; it is a form of knowledge very rarely accessible to them

and which they disparagingly call intuition. I already knew that the fly André wanted was the one which Henri had caught and which I had made him release.

I heard André shuffling around in the next room, and then a strange gurgling and sucking as though he had trouble in drinking his milk.

"André, there is no fly here. Can you give me any sort of indication that might help? If you can't speak, rap or something… you know: once for yes, twice for no."

I had tried to control my voice and speak as though perfectly calm, but I had to choke down a sob of desperation when he rapped twice for "no."

"May I come to you, André? I don't know what can have happened, but whatever it is, I'll be courageous, dear."

After a moment of silent hesitation, he tapped once on his desk.

At the door I stopped aghast at the sight of André standing with his head and shoulders covered by the brown velvet cloth he had taken from a table by his desk, the table on which he usually ate when he did not want to leave his work. Suppressing a laugh that might easily have turned to sobbing, I said:

"André, we'll search thoroughly tomorrow, by daylight. Why don't you go to bed? I'll lead you to the guest room if you like, and won't let anyone else see you."

His left hand tapped the desk twice.

"Do you need a doctor, André?"

"No," he rapped.

"Would you like me to call up Professor Augier? He might be of more help…"

Twice he rapped "no" sharply. I did not know what to do or say. And then I told him:

"Henri caught a fly this morning which he wanted to show me, but I made him release it. Could it have been the one you are looking for? I didn't see it, but the boy said its head was white."

André emitted a strange metallic sigh, and I just had time to bite my fingers fiercely in order not to scream. He had let his right arm drop, and instead of his long-fingered muscular hand, a grey stick with little buds on it like the branch of a tree, hung out of his sleeve almost down to his knee.

"André, *mon chéri*, tell me what happened. I might be of more help to you if I knew. André... oh, it's terrible!" I sobbed, unable to control myself.

Having rapped once for yes, he pointed to the door with his left hand.

I stepped out and sank down crying as he locked the door behind me. He was typing again and I waited. At last he shuffled to the door and slid a sheet of paper under it.

HELENE, COME BACK IN THE MORNING. I MUST THINK AND WILL HAVE TYPED OUT AN EXPLANATION FOR YOU. TAKE ONE OF MY SLEEPING TABLETS AND GO STRAIGHT TO BED. I NEED YOU FRESH AND STRONG TOMORROW, MA PAUVRE CHERIE. A.

"Do you want anything for the night, André?" I shouted through the door.

He knocked twice for no, and a little later I heard the typewriter again.

The sun full on my face woke me up with a start. I had set the alarm-clock for five but had not heard it, probably because of the sleeping tablets. I had indeed slept like a log, without a dream. Now I was back in my living nightmare and crying like a child I sprang out of bed. It was just on seven!

Rushing into the kitchen, without a word for the startled servants, I rapidly prepared a trayload of coffee, bread and butter with which I ran down to the laboratory.

André opened the door as soon as I knocked and closed it again as I carried the tray to his desk. His head was still covered, but I saw from his crumpled suit and his open camp-bed that he must have at least tried to rest.

On his desk lay a typewritten sheet for me which I picked up. André opened the other door, and taking this to mean that he wanted to be left alone, I walked into the next room. He pushed the door to and I heard him pouring out the coffee as I read:

DO YOU REMEMBER THE ASH TRAY EXPERIMENT? I HAVE HAD A SIMILAR ACCIDENT. I "TRANSMITTED" MYSELF SUCCESSFULLY THE NIGHT BEFORE LAST. DURING A SECOND EXPERIMENT YESTERDAY A FLY WHICH I DID NOT SEE MUST HAVE GOT INTO THE "DISINTEGRATOR." MY ONLY HOPE IS TO FIND THAT FLY AND GO THROUGH AGAIN WITH IT. PLEASE SEARCH FOR IT CAREFULLY SINCE, IF IT IS NOT FOUND, I SHALL HAVE TO FIND A WAY OF PUTTING AN END TO ALL THIS.

If only André had been more explicit! I shuddered at the thought that he must be terribly disfigured and then cried softly as I imagined his face inside-out, or perhaps his eyes in place of his ears, or his mouth at the back of his neck, or worse!

André must be saved! For that, the fly must be found!

Pulling myself together, I said:

"André, may I come in?"

He opened the door.

"André, don't despair, I am going to find that fly. It is no longer in the laboratory, but it cannot be very far. I suppose you're disfigured, perhaps terribly so, but there can be no question of putting an end to all this, as you say in your note; that I will never stand for. If necessary, if you do not wish to be seen, I'll make you a mask or a cowl so that you can go on with your work until you get well again. If you cannot work, I'll call Professor Augier, and he and all your other friends will save you, André."

Again I heard that curious metallic sigh as he rapped violently on his desk.

"André, don't be annoyed; please be calm. I won't do anything without first consulting you, but you must rely on me, have faith in me and let me help you as best I can. Are you terribly disfigured, dear? Can't you let me see your face? I won't be afraid... I am your wife you know."

But my husband again rapped a decisive "no" and pointed to the door.

"All right. I am going to search for the fly now, but promise me you won't do anything foolish; promise you won't do anything rash or dangerous without first letting me know all about it!"

He extended his left hand, and I knew I had his promise.

I will never forget that ceaseless day-long hunt for a fly. Back home, I turned the house inside-out and made all the servants join in the search. I told them that a fly had escaped from the Professor's laboratory and that it must be captured alive, but it was evident they already thought me crazy. They said so to the police later, and that day's hunt for a fly most probably saved me from the guillotine later.

I questioned Henri and as he failed to understand right away what I was talking about, I shook him and slapped him, and made him cry in front of the round-eyed maids. Realizing that I must not let myself go, I kissed and petted the poor boy and at last made him understand what I wanted of him. Yes, he remembered, he had found the fly just by the kitchen window; yes, he had released it immediately as told to.

Even in summer time we had very few flies because our house is on the top of a hill and the slightest breeze coming across the valley blows round it. In spite of that, I managed to catch dozens of flies that day. On all the window sills and all over the garden I had put saucers of milk, sugar, jam, meat—all the things likely to attract flies. Of all those we caught, and many others which we failed to catch but which I saw, none resembled the one Henri had caught the day before. One by one, with a magnifying glass, I examined every unusual fly, but none had anything like a white head.

At lunch time, I ran down to André with some milk and mashed potatoes. I also took some of the flies we had caught, but he gave me to understand that they could be of no possible use to him.

"If that fly has not been found tonight, André, we'll have to see what is to be done. And this is what I propose: I'll sit in the next room. When you can't answer by the yes-no method of rapping, you'll type out whatever you want to say and then slip it under the door. Agreed?"

"Yes," rapped André.

By nightfall we had still not found the fly. At dinner time, as I prepared André's tray, I broke down and sobbed in the kitchen in front of the silent servants. My maid thought that I had had a row with my husband, probably about the mislaid fly, but I learned later that the cook was already quite sure that I was out of my mind.

Without a word, I picked up the tray and then put it down again as I stopped by the telephone. That this was really a matter of life and death for André, I had no doubt. Neither did I doubt that he fully intended committing suicide, unless I could make him change his mind, or at least put off such a drastic decision. Would I be strong enough? He would never forgive me for not keeping a promise, but under the circumstances, did that really matter? To the devil with promises and honour! At all costs André must be saved! And having thus made up my mind, I looked up and dialled Professor Augier's number.

"The Professor is away and will not be back before the end of the week," said a polite neutral voice at the other end of the line.

That was that! I would have to fight alone and fight I would. I would save André come what may.

All my nervousness had disappeared as André let me in and, after putting the tray of food down on his desk, I went into the other room, as agreed.

"The first thing I want to know," I said as he closed the door behind me, "is what happened exactly. Can you please tell me, André?"

I waited patiently while he typed an answer which he pushed under the door a little later.

HELENE, I WOULD RATHER NOT TELL YOU. SINCE GO I MUST, I WOULD RATHER YOU REMEMBER ME AS I WAS BEFORE. I MUST DESTROY MYSELF IN SUCH A WAY THAT NONE CAN POSSIBLY KNOW WHAT HAS HAPPENED TO ME. I HAVE OF COURSE THOUGHT OF SIMPLY DISIN-TEGRATING MYSELF IN MY TRANSMITTER, BUT I HAD BETTER NOT BECAUSE, SOONER OR LATER, I MIGHT FIND MYSELF REINTEGRATED. SOME DAY, SOMEWHERE, SOME SCIENTIST IS SURE TO MAKE THE SAME DISCOVERY. I HAVE THEREFORE THOUGHT OF A WAY WHICH IS NEITHER SIMPLE NOR EASY, BUT YOU CAN AND WILL HELP ME.

For several minutes I wondered if André had not simply gone stark raving mad.

"André," I said at last, "whatever you may have chosen or thought of, I cannot and will never accept such a cowardly solution. No matter how awful the result of your experiment or accident, you are alive, you are a man, a brain... and you have a soul. You have no right to destroy yourself! You know that!"

The answer was soon typed and pushed under the door.

I AM ALIVE ALL RIGHT, BUT I AM ALREADY NO LONGER A MAN. AS TO MY BRAIN OR INTELLIGENCE, IT MAY DISAPPEAR AT ANY MOMENT. AS IT IS, IT IS NO LONGER INTACT, AND THERE CAN BE NO SOUL WITHOUT INTELLIGENCE... AND YOU KNOW THAT!

"Then you must tell the other scientists about your discovery. They will help you and save you, André!"

I staggered back frightened as he angrily thumped the door twice.

"André... why? Why do you refuse the aid you know they would give you with all their hearts?"

A dozen furious knocks shook the door and made me understand that my husband would never accept such a solution. I had to find other arguments.

For hours, it seemed, I talked to him about our boy, about me, about his family, about his duty to us and to the rest of humanity. He made no reply of any sort. At last I cried:

"André... do you hear me?"

"Yes," he knocked very gently.

"Well, listen then. I have another idea. You remember your first experiment with the ash tray?... Well, do you think that if you had put it through again a second time, it might possibly have come out with the letters turned back the right way?"

Before I had finished speaking, André was busily typing and a moment later I read his answer:

I HAVE ALREADY THOUGHT OF THAT. AND THAT WAS WHY I NEEDED
THE FLY. IT HAS TO GO THROUGH WITH ME. THERE IS NO HOPE
OTHERWISE.

"Try all the same, André. You never know!"

I HAVE TRIED SEVEN TIMES ALREADY, was the typewritten reply
I got to that.

"André! Try again, please!"

The answer this time gave me a flutter of hope, because no woman
has ever understood, or will ever understand, how a man about to
die can possibly consider anything funny.

I DEEPLY ADMIRE YOUR DELICIOUS FEMININE LOGIC. WE COULD
GO ON DOING THIS EXPERIMENT UNTIL DOOMSDAY. HOWEVER,
JUST TO GIVE YOU THAT PLEASURE, PROBABLY THE VERY LAST I
SHALL EVER BE ABLE TO GIVE YOU, I WILL TRY ONCE MORE. IF
YOU CANNOT FIND THE DARK GLASSES, TURN YOUR BACK TO THE
MACHINE AND PRESS YOUR HANDS OVER YOUR EYES. LET ME KNOW
WHEN YOU ARE READY.

"Ready, André!" I shouted, without even looking for the glasses and
following his instructions.

I heard him move around and then open and close the door of his
"disintegrator." After what seemed a very long wait, but probably was
not more than a minute or so, I heard a violent crackling noise and
perceived a bright flash through my eyelids and fingers.

I turned around as the booth door opened.

His head and shoulders still covered with the brown velvet cloth,
André was gingerly stepping out of it.

"How do you feel, André? Any difference?" I asked, touching his arm.

He tried to step away from me and caught his foot in one of the stools which I had not troubled to pick up. He made a violent effort to regain his balance, and the velvet cloth slowly slid off his shoulders and head as he fell heavily backward.

The horror was too much for me, too unexpected. As a matter of fact, I am sure that, even had I known, the horror-impact could hardly have been less powerful. Trying to push both hands into my mouth to stifle my screams and although my fingers were bleeding, I screamed again and again. I could not take my eyes off him, I could not even close them, and yet I knew that if I looked at the horror much longer, I would go on screaming for the rest of my life.

Slowly, the monster, the thing that had been my husband, covered its head, got up and groped its way to the door and passed it. Though still screaming, I was able to close my eyes.

I who had ever been a true Catholic, who believed in God and another, better life hereafter, have today but one hope: that when I die, I really die, and that there may be no after-life of any sort because, if there is, then I shall never forget! Day and night, awake or asleep, I see it, and I know that I am condemned to see it forever, even perhaps into oblivion!

Until I am totally extinct, nothing can, nothing will ever make me forget that dreadful white hairy head with its low flat skull and its two pointed ears. Pink and moist, the nose was also that of a cat, a huge cat. But the eyes! Or rather, where the eyes should have been were two brown bumps the size of saucers. Instead of a mouth, animal or human, was a long hairy vertical slit from which hung a black quivering trunk that widened at the end, trumpet-like, and from which saliva kept dripping.

I must have fainted, because I found myself flat on my stomach on the cold cement floor of the laboratory, staring at the closed door behind which I could hear the noise of André's typewriter.

Numb, numb and empty, I must have looked as people do immediately after a terrible accident, before they fully understand what
has happened. I could only think of a man I had once seen on the
platform of a railway station, quite conscious, and looking stupidly
at his leg still on the line where the train had just passed.

My throat was aching terribly, and that made me wonder if my
vocal cords had not perhaps been torn, and whether I would ever be
able to speak again.

The noise of the typewriter suddenly stopped and I felt I was
going to scream again as something touched the door and a sheet of
paper slid from under it.

Shivering with fear and disgust, I crawled over to where I could
read it without touching it:

NOW YOU UNDERSTAND. THAT LAST EXPERIMENT WAS A NEW DIS-
ASTER, MY POOR HELENE. I SUPPOSE YOU RECOGNIZED PART OF
DANDELO'S HEAD. WHEN I WENT INTO THE DISINTEGRATOR JUST
NOW, MY HEAD WAS ONLY THAT OF A FLY. I NOW ONLY HAVE EYES
AND MOUTH LEFT. THE REST HAS BEEN REPLACED BY PARTS OF
THE CAT'S HEAD. POOR DANDELO WHOSE ATOMS HAD NEVER COME
TOGETHER. YOU SEE NOW THAT THERE CAN ONLY BE ONE POSSIBLE
SOLUTION, DON'T YOU? I MUST DISAPPEAR. KNOCK ON THE DOOR
WHEN YOU ARE READY AND I SHALL EXPLAIN WHAT YOU HAVE TO DO.

Of course he was right, and it had been wrong and cruel of me
to insist on a new experiment. And I knew that there was now no
possible hope, that any further experiments could only bring about
worse results.

Getting up dazed, I went to the door and tried to speak, but no
sound came out of my throat... so I knocked once!

You can of course guess the rest. He explained his plan in short typewritten notes, and I agreed, I agreed to everything!

My head on fire, but shivering with cold, like an automaton, I followed him into the silent factory. In my hand was a full page of explanations: what I had to know about the steam-hammer.

Without stopping or looking back, he pointed to the switchboard that controlled the steam-hammer as he passed it. I went no farther and watched him come to a halt before the terrible instrument.

He knelt down, carefully wrapped the cloth round his head, and then stretched out flat on the ground.

It was not difficult. I was not killing my husband. André, poor André, had gone long ago, years ago it seemed. I was merely carrying out his last wish... and mine.

Without hesitating, my eyes on the long still body, I firmly pushed the "stroke" button right in. The great metallic mass seemed to drop slowly. It was not so much the resounding clang of the hammer that made me jump as the sharp cracking which I had distinctly heard at the same time. My hus... the thing's body shook a second and then lay still.

It was then I noticed that he had forgotten to put his right arm, his fly-leg, under the hammer. The police would never understand but the scientists would, and they must not! That had been André's last wish, also!

I had to do it and quickly, too; the night watchman must have heard the hammer and would be round any moment. I pushed the other button and the hammer slowly rose. Seeing but trying not to look, I ran up, leaned down, lifted and moved forward the right arm which seemed terribly light. Back at the switchboard, again I pushed the red button, and down came the hammer a second time. Then I ran all the way home.

You know the rest and can now do whatever you think right.

So ended Hélène's manuscript.

★

The following day I telephoned Commissaire Charas to invite him to dinner.

"With pleasure, Monsieur Delambre. Allow me, however, to ask: is it the Commissaire you are inviting, or just Monsieur Charas?"

"Have you any preference?"

"No, not at the present moment."

"Well, then, make it whichever you like. Will eight o'clock suit you?"

Although it was raining, the Commissaire arrived on foot that evening.

"Since you did not come tearing up to the door in your black Citroën, I take it you have opted for Monsieur Charas, off duty?"

"I left the car up a side-street," mumbled the Commissaire with a grin as the maid staggered under the weight of his raincoat.

"Merci," he said a minute later as I handed him a glass of Pernod into which he tipped a few drops of water, watching it turn the golden amber liquid to pale blue milk.

"You heard about my poor sister-in-law?"

"Yes, shortly after you telephoned me this morning. I am sorry, but perhaps it was all for the best. Being already in charge of your brother's case, the inquiry automatically comes to me."

"I suppose it was suicide."

"Without a doubt. Cyanide the doctors say quite rightly; I found a second tablet in the unstitched hem of her dress."

"Monsieur est servi," announced the maid.

"I would like to show you a very curious document afterward, Charas."

"Ah, yes. I heard that Madame Delambre had been writing a lot, but we could find nothing beyond the short note informing us that she was committing suicide."

During our tête-à-tête dinner, we talked politics, books and films, and the local football club of which the Commissaire was a keen supporter.

After dinner, I took him up to my study where a bright fire—a habit I had picked up in England during the war—was burning.

Without even asking him, I handed him his brandy and mixed myself what he called "crushed-bug juice in soda water"—his appreciation of whisky.

"I would like you to read this, Charas; first because it was partly intended for you and, secondly, because it will interest you. If you think Commissaire Charas has no objection, I would like to burn it after."

Without a word, he took the wad of sheets Hélène had given me the day before and settled down to read them.

"What do you think of it all?" I asked some twenty minutes later as he carefully folded Hélène's manuscript, slipped it into the brown envelope, and put it into the fire.

Charas watched the flames licking the envelope from which wisps of grey smoke were escaping, and it was only when it burst into flames that he said slowly raising his eyes to mine:

"I think it proves very definitely that Madame Delambre was quite insane."

For a long time we watched the fire eating up Hélène's "confession."

"A funny thing happened to me this morning, Charas. I went to the cemetery where my brother is buried. It was quite empty and I was alone."

"Not quite, Monsieur Delambre. I was there, but I did not want to disturb you."

"Then you saw me..."

"Yes. I saw you bury a matchbox."

"Do you know what was in it?"

"A fly, I suppose."

"Yes. I had found it early this morning, caught in a spider's web in the garden."

"Was it dead?"

"No, not quite. I... crushed it... between two stones. Its head was... white... all white."

British Library Tales of the Weird collects a thrilling array of uncanny storytelling, from the realms of gothic, supernatural and horror fiction. With stories ranging from the nineteenth century to the present day, this series revives long-lost material from the Library's vaults to thrill again alongside beloved classics of the weird fiction genre.

We welcome any suggestions, corrections or feedback you may have, and will aim to respond to all items addressed to the following:

The Editor (Tales of the Weird),
British Library Publishing
The British Library
96 Euston Road
London, NW1 2DB

We also welcome enquiries through our Twitter account, @BL_Publishing.